LADY & THE Pirate

A NOVEL of HISTORY and ROMANCE

Winner of the Royal Palm
Literary Award for Romance

JM Bolton

An IDBPI Book

Published by IDBPI
USA

The LADY & THE PIRATE ebook
is available through most popular
sources including Barnes & Noble, Amazon, &
Smashwords.

Send email to

jmbolton.author@gmail.com

ISBN 978-1-57550-129-1

Printed in the United States of America

Cover Art by Johanna M. Bolton
First Printing October 2011
Second Printing 2021
International Digital Book Publishing Industries

Some reviews for author JM Bolton

THE ALIEN WITHIN

"This is a novel full of the sort of adventure and the kind of characters that keep space opera entertaining." LOCUS

"Quite entertaining space opera with a suitably complex plot and above average characterization." s.f. Chronicle

"This new version is better than the original, and that's saying something because the original was very good to begin with!" LW

MISSION:TORI

"The characters are well developed, the writing is quite good, and the plot is straightforward as well." Mixed Media

THE CITY OF THREE MOONS

"I found this traditional hard science fiction novel enjoyable ... the exploration of ideas was entertaining and fresh." Sift.com

"If you like Linnea Sinclair, you'll like this book. It's space adventure at its best, with the added bonus of a satisfying romance. A must read." Subject: Adventure.

LADY & THE PIRATE
WINNER OF THE
2011 ROYAL PALM LITERARY AWARD

Romantic, Dashing Characters! *What else can I say about Lady and the Pirate except buy this book and you won't be disappointed! Morgan makes you wish were sailing the high sea, and sure wish Daniel was there with you.* LB of Stargait

TANGLED TALES

"Most enjoyable! Especially liked "Steampunk Society." It could be a novel, something like Gabaldon's Outlander *series."* DM

This book is dedicated to
Di & Don Kafrissen
*who lived on a sailboat and actually sailed the Caribbean.
I really wish I could have been there!*

Acknowledgements:

I would like to express my gratitude Ray Caughlin and Marlene Becker who listened and read and commented and corrected. Thank you for your patience!

And to Jill Svoboda, a wonderful writer who did such a thorough edit for me – I can't believe you found all those typos and misplaced commas!! Thank you!

Thanks also to Lynwood Wilson for being one of the first readers of this story. Thank you for your encouragement - love you.

Norma Noble, I wish you were still here to see this book finished. I will always be grateful for your hours of help with the research. This was before computers when we had to actually search through libraries and real books! What fun!!

Any mistakes, I will claim as my own. I know, I know, you told me so, but, of course I don't listen. To be fair though, everything's the characters' fault; they actually write the books, not I!

A word from the author:

When I started writing this book way back in 1960, I titled it *The Pirate's Lady*. It's kind of hard to rename a book after it's been around for so many years, but when I googled *The Pirate's Lady*, I came up with a lot of books with the same title. And so, a new title was in order -- *Lady and the Pirate*.

Whenever I tell people that I came up with this story when I was sixteen years old, they immediately assume it's a juvenile. Pl-ease! It's NOT a juvenile! I just had an idea for the plot when I was 16. Most of the book didn't get written until many years later. I actually carried this manuscript around almost 50 years, taking it out now and then, and adding a bit here and there. I did pick the name for my heroine when I was a teenager. The name Morgan is Welsh and means *of the sea*. I knew it was fitting for my heroine.

The clothing and hair styles are as authentic as I could make them. But, as writers will do, I embroidered some of the historical facts. For example, Daniel's ship, the *Kestrel*, is a brigantine, but I have stretched her a somewhat, making her larger than the actual vessel would be. I also wanted desperately to make the *Bright Folly* a schooner, but alas, schooners were still some years in the future.

However, the earthquake that destroyed Port Royal actually happened on that day. The city had been renown as the most sinful city in the world and people considered the devastation of earthquake and fire as God's retribution. Any mistakes … well, this is fiction. Just have fun with it.

Lady
& the
Pirate

Chapter 1

1672 – Moorhouse Plantation on Cayman Brac, Caribbean.

"Faith, but she's a wee one!" Robert Moorhouse murmured. He held out his hand and tentatively stroked the baby's rosy cheek. It felt so soft against the roughened skin of his finger that he wasn't even sure he'd touched her. He straightened up and looked at his beautiful wife lying in bed, propped up by big down pillows. Her long auburn hair was neatly confined in braids and decently covered by a cap of lace. The ribbons in her cap matched the bed jacket of rose satin trimmed in blond lace covering her shoulders. The tiny bundle that was their new daughter slept, tucked in the crook of her arm.

"We'll name her Morgan," Robert said, "in honor of the admiral. Maybe he'll come to the christening, if he gets back from England in time."

Anna Maria expected something like this. Henry Morgan was her husband's hero, but for all that, he was still a pirate and a marauder. Morgan was such an unsuitable name for a girl child! Rather than argue, however, she suggested a compromise.

"We'll call her Catherine Santiago as well," she said, her gentle voice hiding the strength with which she managed her husband. "With a name like Morgan to live up to, she will have need of heaven's blessings."

"Tempering the bad with the good, eh?" Robert commented with a grin, for he understood his wife. Managed he might be, but it was with his full knowledge and consent, for he truly loved the wonderful woman he had won for his own.

The baby, the object of all this discussion, slept on, her rose-pink lips slightly parted as she enjoyed the rest of the innocent, unaware of her mother's concern.

Anna Maria's life was difficult, for she was a highborn Spanish gentlewoman living in exile among English settlers in the West Indies. Not that she regretted her marriage to Robert; he was good to her and she loved him almost as much as he loved her. But England was still at war with Spain, and she knew how difficult life would be for a daughter coming from both of these worlds. Would little Morgan be able to find peace in either one? Anna Maria breathed a silent prayer to the Blessed Virgin, for, although she now went to church with her husband, the Church of England was a religion of men and she knew only another woman could understand and sympathize with her fears.

Anna Maria decided then and there that her beautiful little daughter would learn to live in either world. She would grow up speaking English and Spanish, as well as learning

2

the culture of both. With those thoughts in her mind, she closed her eyes and drifted off into sleep. Hana, her black maidservant, gently took the tiny baby back to her own little bed.

Thus she was named Morgan Catherine Santiago Moorhouse. However, her namesake, Lieutenant Governor Sir Henry Morgan, wasn't able to come to her christening. When he returned to the Caribbean from England, he was a vastly changed man. Not only had he been knighted by King Charles II, but he also took his new position as governor seriously and began to persecute the very men he once sailed with, the freebooters and privateers. Within a short period of time, Sir Henry Morgan swept Jamaica free of his fellow pirates and earned for himself the facetious title of "Knight of the Double Cross."

But these events didn't affect Robert or his family. On the day he brought his beautiful bride home he ceased being a privateer and settled into the life of a planter instead. The years passed peacefully and little Morgan grew up on the plantation on Cayman Brac, not knowing any other life, until the fateful year of 1690.

Chapter 2

1690, George Town, Grand Cayman Island.

A brilliant morning sun gleamed through the thick glossy
leaves of tropical plants that shaded the terrace and dappled
the paving stones with golden light. The light reflected
through billowing curtains and into the dining room where
Hilda Ramsey sat at her breakfast table, sipping chocolate
from a fragile porcelain cup. A matching saucer sat on a
heavy damask tablecloth beside a delicate silver spoon. Hilda was a round little woman, and despite her best efforts, her
delicate pink and white prettiness had been transformed by
time and six children into middle-aged plumpness. Worry
lines on her once smooth white face betrayed the fussy concern she brought to every detail of her life. Right now she
was in a quandary trying to decide where to put her house-
guests when they arrived.

The provincial governor, who just happened to be her

4

husband, had called a meeting of all the major landowners of the islands. Since the occasion made a perfect excuse for a social event, she extended the invitation to include their families. But now she had to decide where to put them all. Not precisely all, she amended. A number of families lived close to the capital and could sleep at home. Some could stay with friends, and others were fortunate enough to maintain their own townhouses. But that still left eight or nine who would have to be accommodated.

Hilda glanced across the table at her husband absently eating his breakfast with one hand, his attention focused on a pamphlet he held in the other. As she watched, he set his fork down and raised an earthenware tankard to his lips, taking a large swallow of ale. George belched and setting the tankard down, wiped his mouth on the back of his hand. Hilda frowned; no matter how hard she tried to introduce him to polite manners, George Ramsey would never be anything other than a simple country squire.

Trying to attract his attention, Hilda gave a loud sigh, twitching a fold in the skirt of her gown, making the fabric rustle loudly. The pink dress, a shade known as Maiden's Blush, was taffeta silk, lavishly trimmed with lace and ribbons, a costume more appropriate for a formal occasion. The dress had been extremely expensive, and she hesitated to wear it for a simple breakfast at home, but she selected this dress in particular, hoping it would attract her husband's attention.

Apparently, she'd failed. Again. For all the notice he paid her this morning, she decided, she might as well be wearing rags. Hilda pursed her lips and wrinkled her forehead with displeasure as she cleared her throat loudly. Deliberately, her husband set the pamphlet down and picked up a letter from the pile of papers beside his plate.

Defeated, Hilda turned her attention to other problems. She could put both Sally Farnsworth and Mrs. Bodden in the big bedroom at the end of the hall. Their husbands didn't need a place to sleep as they would be up all night with the rest of the men, playing at cards or something. Hilda sniffed, her lips thinned in disdain. There would be some very wild blood among the guests. What passed for gentry in the West Indies was not so much bred as bought, seeing how much of the land had been won or purchased with prize money ... money stolen by privateers.

Privateers! She had been told that they helped protect the colonies from the marauding Spanish, but she still couldn't believe they were any better than marauders themselves. Hilda shook her head and the long locks of hair called "heart-breakers" falling over her ears swayed as if in sympathy with her sentiments. Unfortunately there was nothing she could do about who was invited. All she could hope was that some rough behavior wouldn't disturb her more civilized guests overly much.

She opened her lips to voice her feelings when her husband let out a loud inarticulate sound and slammed his fist down on the table with a bang. Hilda and the dishes jumped. Chocolate splashed from her cup onto the skirt of her beautiful new gown.

"Oh! No, no, no! That was certainly too bad of you!" she exclaimed, setting the cup back into the saucer so she could dab at the silk with a napkin. "Look what you made me do!"

"Eh?" her spouse managed, glancing over at his wife at last. "What did you say?"

She clucked in irritation at his obtuseness as much as the mess of her skirt. "Well, what is it? What made you shout like that?" she demanded.

"Another delay," he explained. He frowned at the letter as he held it up in front of him rereading that part. "Haverton writes that the wench will have to remain with us another month! Another whole month," he articulated with disgust.

"You know you mustn't call her that," Hilda protested. "She is under our protection, and she is an orphan. We must be charitable, even if she does have some ... ah," she searched for an appropriate word, "unfortunate blood. She is still a gentlewoman."

"We've been charitable enough just by keeping her under our roof for the past seven months." He huffed and scowled. "I wouldn't mind if she was a properly brought up young woman, but she's none of that."

"Morgan Moorhouse is as well-bred as your own children," his helpmate reminded him. "It's too bad her mother was a Spaniard, but at least she was well born."

"As far as I'm concerned, Spanish blood is the least objectionable thing about Mistress Moorhouse," the governor said breathing harshly through his nose. "And if she were anywhere else, I wouldn't be concerned about her behavior. But when she gets your children into scrapes ..."

"*Our* children," Hilda interrupted, correcting him. "And if you're talking about the time that she persuaded Matthew to let her take one of your precious horses ..."

"That occasion was enough to show me what kind of a hoyden we'd taken into our home! And as you pointed out, my horses are precious. You know what it cost to bring good bloodstock to these islands."

To her disgust, his wife did. But really, she thought, he should show such concern for members of his own family! She remembered the care he lavished on the beasts during the Atlantic crossing. While she and her daughters languished in a tiny cabin, prey to seasickness and all kinds of discomfort, was he there? No! He remained with his precious bloodstock.

"Well," the governor was saying, "I'll not wait for Haverton any longer. Now that he's as near as Port Royal, I'll send the wench to him."

"And just how will you do that?"

"By the first ship that comes into this harbor."

"You can't mean it," Hilda protested taking him literally. "You have no idea what kind of riffraff might sail in!"

"I don't care. She has to go and go she will! God's bloody bones!" the governor exploded, slamming his fist on the table and setting the dishes jumping again. "What was her father thinking when he allowed her such unseemly freedom?"

"You forget yourself, sir," his wife said, bridling. "I'm not accustomed to hearing such language at my breakfast table."

"Damme if I can't express myself in my own house," the governor exclaimed, his cheeks flushed as he prepared to enter into battle with his spouse.

Perhaps it was for the best that their eldest son, Brian,

chose this moment to come into the room. He'd just been down to the harbor and had some interesting news.

"Time to get up, young ladies," Katie called. She bobbed up and down, trying to see around Hana whose majestic girth blocked the doorway. Hana walked in front, taking precedence, for she was a free servant and not a slave like the other blacks in the house. She held a tray supporting a pitcher of chocolate and two earthenware mugs. Katie had to use both hands to carry a big brass can of hot water. She made her way over to the wash stand and emptied the bowl there into the chamber pot before refilling it.

Hana set her burden down on a table beside Morgan. "What are you doing, sitting in the window wearing nothing but your chemise?" she demanded of her mistress.

Morgan rubbed her eyes and yawned. "Good morning, to you too" she replied, smiling at the woman who'd taken care of her since she was born. "It was too hot to sleep."

"And so you opened the window," Margaret Ramsey observed acidly as she sat up in bed. Shrugging into a long dressing gown, she came to the table and dropped into a chair. "You'll make us all sick if you're not careful," she told Morgan, watching as Hana poured chocolate. "Mother says night air is poisonous, especially here in the Indies. But," she continued thoughtfully, her eyes narrowed as she gazed at Morgan over the rim of her cup, "perhaps it won't affect you, seeing as how you were born here." Margaret sipped her

9

chocolate, unaware that she sounded very like her mother.

Morgan refrained from answering.

"His Honor wants to see you as soon as you're dressed," Hana announced.

"Do you know what he wants?" Morgan asked.

"No, I don't. You been getting into trouble again?" the maid wanted to know, eyeing her suspiciously.

"I don't think so."

"He's still mad because you took his horse last week," Margaret pointed out.

"He already yelled at me for that. Besides I really didn't do anything wrong. The horse needed exercise."

"Father doesn't think ladies should ride unattended. At least he never lets us do so."

"The rules were different where I grew up."

Margaret smirked. "Yes, but you're under my father's roof now. You should abide by his rules."

Morgan's eyes narrowed and she was about to reply when Hana intervened.

"Instead of arguing, you'd best get dressed. It won't do for you to keep the governor waiting."

Without another word Morgan went to the wash basin. She flipped the thick braid of her hair over her shoulder and began to wash her face and hands. Hana searched through the clothes press and brought out an indigo dyed dress made from native-grown cotton. The custom was for women to wear three skirts, but Morgan hated the heavy white cotton petticoats even though they were necessary to create a fashionable silhouette. The first skirt hung straight to her ankles in the front, and was deeply pleated around the hips and in back. Over this went another petticoat, this one of fine lawn. Hana held up the blue overdress so Morgan could slip it on, and then pulled the huge lace trimmed sleeves of her chemise down to hang beneath the blue. Ribbons dyed a shade darker then the dress marched down the long bodice, hiding hooks that held it closed. The blue skirt was cut short in front, allowing the pretty embroidered lawn petticoat to show. It was a simple costume, without corsets, rich fabrics, or extensive decoration, but Morgan was still young enough to prefer clothing that allowed her physical freedom and comfort instead of the fantastic gowns designed to enhance the allure of a woman's body.

However, nothing could detract from Morgan's fabulous head of hair. Released from the braid, it flowed, a glorious shade of red, in a riot of waves and curls. The hair reflected a heritage both from her father's Celtic ancestors and from the Germanic tribes that invaded Spain in the 10th century, leaving their genetic markers in her mother's people. Because of this, blondes and redheads were not unusual highborn Spaniards. But Morgan neither knew nor cared about the source of her red hair as she watched Hana in the looking glass. Her maid deftly coiled the copper mass into a neat bun high at the back of her head and fastened it in place with long bone pins. When this was finished she draped a white kerchief demurely around the girl's shoulders.

Margaret remained silent while all of this was going on. Even though Katie had brought a similar dress for her to wear, she ignored it. Instead she sipped her chocolate, lost in some plans of her own, until Morgan bent over to slip a pair of soft leather shoes on her feet. They had the flat soles she

11

preferred in the house to high heels.

"You're not wearing stockings," Margaret snipped.

"It's too hot," Morgan replied.

"Mother won't like it."

"But she won't know, now, will she," Morgan responded, a militant light in her eyes.

Margaret backed down before that look. She remembered one time when she crossed Morgan and was rewarded with a couple of angry geckos in her clothes chest. The lizards scared her out of her wits when they leaped on her, trying to escape. She sniffed and turned her attention back to her breakfast drink. Her mother warned her that red hair was often an indication of an unstable temperament. This was certainly true of her reluctant houseguest.

Morgan gave one last look in the silvered mirror hanging over the tiring table before she went to see what she had done wrong this time.

Chapter 3

"There's a ship in the harbor that will take you to Port Roy-al," Mark Preston announced. The governor's secretary, he stood beside his employer's desk, a thin, dusty-looking little man who had no life beyond his civil duty. It was he, rather than the governor, who was responsible for most of the decisions affecting the policies of the region. A capable administrator in his own right, the only things keeping him from holding the post of governor himself were his lack of birth and connections.

A small building attached to the front of his house served as the governor's office. Having a work place so close to home allowed him to be convenient to both his family and the residents of George Town. Ramsey sat behind his desk in the place of authority, but he was content to let Preston take care of most of the business, including this interview with Mistress Moorhouse.

"I thought my cousin Oliver was coming here," Morgan said as she stood before them.

"His ship suffered some small damage during the Atlantic crossing, and he has been detained. Therefore you will be sent to him."

Here it was at last, Morgan thought, time for her to leave the only home she'd ever known. Lady Ramsey had tried to give her some idea of what it would be like to live in England - visits to London perhaps, parties, shopping expeditions. Hilda described everything she herself missed most since coming to the colonies. She never stopped to think that these amusements might not be to Morgan's taste, and that the young woman considered her move to England as exile from everything she knew and loved. Morgan was even more daunted by Lady Ramsey's warnings about the conduct expected of a young lady. The governor's wife thought it necessary to suggest that her behavior, while it might be tolerated in the colonies, would be considered highly improper in England.

Morgan listened to Hilda's almost contradictory list of anticipated pleasures and strictures, and wondered if she wouldn't be better off staying in the Indies, even if it meant defying her family. Her mind was in turmoil. Although she was curious to see new places, she didn't want to put herself into the hands of people who seemed destined to make her life miserable. She wondered for the hundredth time what would happen if she refused to go.

She studied George Ramsey's face from under her lowered lashes. His nose and cheeks were red, colored by broken capillaries. His eyes were small, and they glared at Morgan with dislike. She knew he considered dealing with her a distasteful task, and imagined he would be very glad to see the last of her.

She considered defying him, but then realized if she did, the governor was perfectly capable of using the might of his office to force her to obey. A night in the stocks and a whipping was not to her taste.

"You and your servant will make ready to board Captain Harris' ship," Preston was saying. "He will take you to Port Royal."

"Harris?" Morgan looked up in surprise. "Captain Daniel Harris?"

Startled, Preston looked up from the papers in his hand. He glanced quickly at the governor who frowned at Morgan's words.

Ramsey was glad his daughters displayed more seemly reticence. "It isn't the ship I would have chosen," the governor said, mistaking Morgan's interest for criticism. "But it's all that's available at the moment."

"Despite a somewhat unsavory reputation, we're certain Captain Harris can be trusted," Preston added.

"Oh, yes, Captain Harris can be trusted, you may be assured of that," Morgan said, unconscious of their astonished stares. "He was one of my father's good friends. He was often at the house, and they were even partners in some sailing ventures."

"Indeed?" the governor replied dryly, glad that circumstances made it unnecessary for him to make inquiries into the precise nature of Robert Moorhouse's involvement with

Daniel Harris. "While I doubt many of those 'sailing ventures' would bear close examination, I am even more surprised that you would know anything of them."

Morgan dropped her eyes demurely, but her hands were clenched into angry fists behind her back. One of the things she missed about her parents was being treated as a rational human being. Governor Ramsey and Mr. Preston seemed to think that women lacked intelligence! Oh, how she would be glad to be gone from them!

The governor glared at her for a long uncomfortable moment before he relaxed back in his chair. "Humph," he intoned. "Perhaps your being known to the captain is a good thing. He will already be aware of the necessity of keeping you under a tight rein." He put his hand out for the papers his secretary held. "I suggest the most profitable use for your time now would be to pack your belongings and make yourself ready," he told her. It was dismissal, and his attention was already on the new documents before him.

Morgan sketched a brief curtsy and fled.

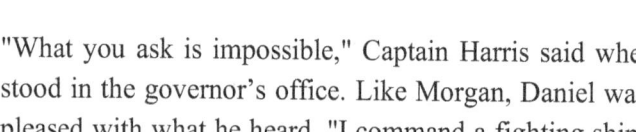

"What you ask is impossible," Captain Harris said when he stood in the governor's office. Like Morgan, Daniel was not pleased with what he heard. "I command a fighting ship," he explained. "I don't have room for passengers, and especially not for female passengers."

"Nonetheless, you will make room," the Governor Ramsey told him. "You will take Mistress Moorhouse to

Port Royal."

"That is your destination, is it not?" Preston added quickly.

Daniel didn't answer, and the governor looked at him with a certain amount of distaste. Not that there was anything about the captain's appearance that would disgust. He was tall and lean, and although his skin had been burned dark by constant exposure to the sun, he was generally considered by the ladies to be handsome in a rough sort of way. And he had changed his clothes and wore his best to answer the governor's summons. This included a long coat of dull gold brocade silk over black knee breeches and matching stockings. His shoes were the latest French style and had high red heels. The only way he differed from current fashion was in his refusal to wear a wig in the tropical heat, preferring his own hair pulled back and tied with a black ribbon.

Preston didn't meet the captain's eye as he continued, speaking softly. "You wouldn't be coming from the Carolinas, would you?" he asked.

One of the Harris's eyebrows went up in surprise. "Is there a reason I shouldn't come from the Carolinas? We're not at war with them."

Even the governor looked at Preston now, waiting to learn what was behind this question.

"Perhaps there is a good reason," the secretary said. "I've heard some ships have been running goods to ports there, which is contrary to the Navigation Act. These laws, if you weren't aware, prohibit the export of anything to the colonies unless they have first landed in England and are shipped on a vessel that was both built in England and flies

17

the English flag."

"I am familiar with the Acts," Daniel told him. "And, since running goods to the Carolinas is illegal, I would hardly be doing it, now would I?"

"You tell me," Preston challenged softly. "Perhaps we might question your crew?"

Daniel smiled, picturing the reception the governor's secretary would have among the lads he sailed with.

"Or check your bills of lading," Preston added, understanding the reason for Daniel's grin. "You do carry bills of lading, don't you?"

"Not being a merchant ship ..." Daniel began, only to be interrupted by Preston.

"Yes, yes," the secretary snapped, his irritation with the tall captain showing for the first time. "We are aware that the *Kestrel* is a fighting ship. However, I doubt if your recent, or perhaps if *any* of your activities would survive our investigation. And it is the duty of this office to keep close watch on all ships sailing these waters."

"However," Harris interjected smoothly, "you might be induced to overlook certain activities for a consideration, perhaps?" The captain was familiar with the direction this conversation was taking. "That sounds suspiciously like blackmail to me."

"Not at all! No, not at all," Preston was at haste to reassure him, his feelings hidden behind a polite mask once more. "The governor is only doing his duty."

"Heh?" The governor looked up again at these words, but wisely let Preston handle Harris.

"If you will be so good as to turn over your logs." Preston said, ignoring his superior.

Captain Harris knew when he had been backed into a corner. "That won't be necessary. I'll deliver Mistress Moor-house to Port Royal. But we sail on the morning tide and I'll not wait. See that she is onboard in time."

He picked up his tricorn hat from a chair by the door and, sweeping a low mocking bow to the governor and his secretary, turned on his heel and was gone.

Chapter 4

The weather had turned in the early hours of the morning when Morgan was awakened to begin her long journey to England. Stars hid behind dark clouds, and raindrops pattered on the trees and shrubs, washing dust from the leaves. Rain loaded the air with moisture, humidity that made plants thrive and humans gasp for breath.

Morgan and her maid boarded the ship in darkness broken only by yellow lantern light. Preston accompanied them down to the docks, not from any concern for their well-being, but because he wanted to be sure they were safely aboard and no longer his responsibility.

Morgan felt in complete sympathy with him, but only because she couldn't wait to get out of the governor's oppressive household. She followed a crewman below decks out of the drizzling rain and watched as Hana directed the sailors who hauled her boxes into the cabin. The four trunks had been made from native mahogany covered with rawhide by craftsmen on her father's plantation. They contained everything she owned in the world.

The cabin was neatly tucked into the stern of the *Kestrel*. It was Daniel Harris' cabin, hastily abandoned to make room for her. The bulkheads were lined with cabinets and closets, cunningly shaped to make use of limited space.

Rain beat against narrow panes of glass in the wide window above the captain's bunk. The window was thick glass and faintly green, the kind that the glassblowers made for ships built in the colonies. The view might be distorted, but the windows would allow sunlight into the cabin, Morgan decided. She yawned and dropped down in a chair before a small writing table.

Hana closed the door after the departing sailors and carefully set the latch before turning to her charge.

"Get that wet cloak off," she admonished. "You'll catch your death of cold sitting there! What are you thinking?"

Morgan laughed as she obeyed. She had an excellent constitution, and Hana knew that it would take a lot more than a simple wetting to make her ill.

"And while we're on this pirate ship ..."

"This isn't a pirate ship," Morgan quickly interjected.

"Huh," Hana grunted in disbelief as she spread the cloak over the back of a chair to dry, then draped her own across the edge of the table. "You can't tell me it ain't what my own eyes can see it is," she argued. "This here's a pirate ship, and Captain Harris is a pirate. Everyone knows that."

"Hana, Captain Harris was my father's good friend.

21

They were privateers. That's a lot different from being a pirate."

"Privateers. Buccaneers. Call 'em what you want. I know pirates when I see 'em!"

Hana opened one of the trunks as she spoke, searching among the contents. "And even your blessed Daddy, may the Good Lord rest his soul, had some friends that weren't fit for you and your sainted mother to meet."

Morgan laughed again. "Mother used to sail with father all the time. She knew all his friends, and I know she liked Daniel Harris."

Hana gave a loud disapproving sniff since she couldn't think of a suitable response. She pulled a clean dress out of the trunk and hunted for Morgan's hairbrushes and a linen towel. "Get out of those wet clothes. Let's get you dry."

She helped Morgan, untying the ribbons and unhooking the bodice. Morgan stood in her chemise and dried her arms and neck while Hana pulled the pins from her hair and let it tumble down her back, the thick silky strands brushing her hips. "I'm not that wet," she commented.

"How wet don't matter," Hana muttered.

"What about you? You were in the rain too."

"Me?" Hana laughed. "I ain't sugar! I won't melt in a little rain!"

"Well I'm not sugar either," Morgan responded with a mock pout.

"You're a sassy one," Hana told her. "You'd better watch yourself." She picked up the hairbrush, turned Morgan so that her back was to her, and started stroking the shining red strands. "Until we get to Port Royal, you and me are go-

22

ing to stay right here."

"In the cabin?" Morgan exclaimed pulling away and turning so she could face her maid, a look of dismay on her face.

"In the cabin," Hana repeated. "I have to keep you safe until your cousin can take care of us."

"We have always been able to take care of ourselves," Morgan protested. "Besides, there's no danger on this ship."

Hana pushed her back around and resumed work on her hair. She was well aware of the dangers threatening an innocent young woman alone in the world, and now that she was wound up, nothing would deter her from having her say. "This time you're gonna to listen to me," she muttered. Her words came in the same rhythm as the brush. "We're the only women on this ship. There's no one on deck but a lot of men, whisperin' and starin' and whatever. I know them," she grumbled. "And Captain Harris ain't no good either. I can tell you that for sure."

Morgan's eyes were half closed as she relaxed with the brush strokes. She could ignore the words, and Hana's voice was soothing.

"The captain's no good," the maid continued. "And I don't care if Governor Ramsey did pick this ship. He just took what he could find. I don't know why he couldn't wait and get a proper ship for us. Or send someone along to look after us. He should know what's due for a lady of your station."

"Who would he send? Preston?"

"Huh!" Hana intoned. "He wouldn't be no good for anything!"

"Everyone else is too busy getting ready for Patience's baby."

"You'd think no one ever had a baby before. An' she's as big as a cow ...."

"Hana!" Morgan chuckled. "How could you compare Patience to a cow?"

"I've heard you say worse of her, missy! Don't you go getting all huffy with me!" Her strong arm continued to stroke Morgan's shining hair. "He could have sent some of our own men folk along," she ventured after a couple of quiet seconds. "Billy or Tony ..." She was referring to two of the hands from the Moorhouse plantation on Cayman Brac.

Morgan knew Hana missed their old home as much as she did. "Are they related to you?" she asked, referring to the two men her maid had mentioned.

"Those boys?" Hana asked with surprise. "They're no kin of mine! Good boys most of the time, though," she amended.

Morgan's mind drifted. What, she wondered, would be a proper ship on the Caribbean in 1690? She couldn't think of one. As for Captain Harris ... well, she'd been in the courtyard, and just happened to be standing near an open window to the governor's office when she heard Captain Harris arguing with Preston about taking her to Port Royal. She wasn't sure why he would be reluctant. It wasn't unusual for a woman to be on board a ship, especially for a brief trip from one island to another.

Morgan looked around the cabin again. Although it was small, it was still larger then she would have expected on a ship such as the *Kestrel*. It was also surprisingly neat and clean. Since there hadn't been time to scrub it just for them, she decided that Captain Harris must be a naturally orderly person. The wood of the deck and bulkheads wore a satiny glow and the brass fittings shone in the light from the lamp suspended from a beam.

Morgan had seen Captain Harris now and then over the years when he visited her parent's house. Once -- when she was a lot younger -- she even fancied herself in love with him. She remembered the feeling of excitement when he was expected, and how she watched for his ship from the summer house on cliff above the beach. Another time she had spied on him from a window over the garden where he and her father sat talking late into the evening. But that was years ago. She was older now, too mature for childish infatuations. Still, Morgan realized suddenly, she really didn't know very much about Daniel Harris. She found herself wondering about him, the man whose cabin she had usurped.

A knock at the door interrupted Morgan's musing.

Hana's head snapped up, and a militant light came into her eyes. "Who's there?" she demanded. She glanced quickly around the cabin, and realizing Morgan was standing in nothing but her shift, grabbed a huge shawl from one of the trunks and swirled it around her change. Then, holding the hairbrush like a weapon, she went to the door and cracked it open it just enough to look out.

A small swarthy man with a magnificent mustache stood there, his eyes wide with surprise as he gazed up at the tall black woman in such an obviously militant pose.

He cleared his throat. "*Senorita*," he said, looking past the maid to her mistress. "Captain Harris sent me to tell you we are catching the tide. We are departing, *si*?"

Hana didn't relax even though the intruder spoke politely and appeared inoffensive.

The man grinned as he finished his message. "Also, my name is Juan. If you need anything, I will find it for you."

Morgan looked past her maid's broad shoulder and smiled. "Thank you, Juan. If we need anything, we'll certainly call you." She cast a quick sideways look at her nurse. "Please ask the captain when I can come up on deck."

"*Si, senorita*. I will. Until then, Captain Harris asks that you please remain below. The deck is very busy right now. You understand, *si*?"

"Humph," Hana intoned.

"Is there anything else I can do for you?"

"No!" Hana snapped.

"No, thank you," Morgan said at the same time, but in much friendlier tones.

Juan grinned, sketched a brief bow, and turned away.

Hana harrumphed again and closed the door. She latched it carefully and then turned the bulk of her back against the wood.

"Don't you be fooled," she said. "Pirates are born bad. He may look harmless and talk polite, but I know better!"

Morgan laughed, and Hana glared at her.

"And how come," the black maid continued her tirade. "How come, after what I told you, you're asking when you can go up on deck. I told you, you can't go up there!"

Morgan just smiled as she dropped the shawl on the bunk and started braiding her long hair.

The ship was moving now, the deck lifting and falling

beneath her feet. The early morning drizzle wore itself out as clouds dissipated in a cool breeze off the ocean.

Hana busied herself rearranging the damp clothing but kept a suspicious eye on her charge all the while. Unaccustomed to being closed in, Morgan wandered idly around the cabin, touching this and that. Too bad I never had a taste for needlework, she thought. There just weren't that many occupations permitted ladies, and especially not on a ship.

In order to reach the wide casement above it, Morgan climbed onto the bunk and knelt there crossing her arms on the window sill. Resting her chin, she watched the dark island fade away behind the ship. She could see the silhouettes of a couple of fishing boats as they set out for a day on the water. They followed the *Kestrel* for a while, but soon turned off, heading for the good fishing grounds in North Sound. It was still too dark for Morgan to pick out individual buildings back in George Town, but she amused herself trying until the town became an amorphous shape blending into the lush tropical vegetation. Even the bright strip of beach faded into shadow and the whole island became a long low silhouette against the horizon.

The Cayman Islands were the only home Morgan had ever known, but that part of her life was behind her now in more ways than one. Tears formed behind her eyelids and she blinked them away angrily. This was no time for weakness. There had to be some way she could stay in the Caribbean. She vowed to think of something before they arrived at Port Royal.

One by one the stars blinked out as morning came, flooding the sky with color -- purple, rose, and then gold –

becoming lighter and brighter, heralding the sun. As that nearest star sent its rays over the eastern horizon, the heavens took on a serene cerulean blue, and the vast gray sea changed to a lively blue-green, like glass reflecting back the sky. Foam marking the ship's passage glittered crystalline, tumbling in brilliant light. Unable to stand it another moment, Morgan threw the casement wide and breathed deeply of the fresh salty air. Closing her eyes, she rested her head on her folded arms, feeling the ship move her.

But her energy refused to allow her to be still for long. She sat back on her heels and looked around the tiny cabin. It felt as if hours had passed, and yet Juan still hadn't brought her permission to come up on deck. Obviously, Morgan decided, the captain intended to treat them like cargo, kept safely out of the way for the entire trip. "Well, we'll see about that!" she articulated, breaking the silence.

"Huh? What did you say?" Hana asked.

Morgan smiled innocently. "Nothing. Just thinking out loud."

Her maid narrowed her eyes. She knew when the girl was up to something.

Ever since her parents died, Morgan had been forced to live the restricted life of an unmarried woman, and she was tired of it. She was tired of being confined and doing someone else's bidding. No one thought she might have something to say about how she spent her time.

Her life had been a lot different at home. Ever since she was big enough to sit on her own horse, Morgan had spent long hours riding with her father. He talked to her as if she was a rational human being, not just a social pawn like other girl-children. As a result, she preferred to be out in the fresh air, spending her considerable energy in physical activity, not sitting demurely indoors. She remembered the wonderful times she spent sailing with her parents. Would she have similar opportunities when she got to England, she wondered?

She did not like to admit it, but she was frightened. England was an unknown country, and the customs there were quite different from what she was used to. If life in the governor's house was anything like what she could expect, she didn't want to go. Therefore, apprehensive about her coming exile and tired of being confined by convention and physical barriers, it might be understandable that Morgan rebelled. She wasn't going to spend two whole days confined to a tiny cabin when she wanted to be on deck in the fresh air!

Morgan climbed off the bunk and busied her fingers with the buckles fastening one of the trunks.

"What are you doing, missy?" Hana asked suspiciously.

"I want my brown dress."

"What for?"

Morgan looked Hana right in the eye as if daring her to argue. "I'm not going to stay locked away like a piece of cargo. I'm going up on deck," she said firmly.

"No, you are not!"

"Hana, if I don't get out of here I think I'll explode! I'll ... I'll faint or have a fit. Or something."

Morgan pushed the lid of the trunk back on its leather hinges and started rummaging through the contents. She pulled out two dresses, flinging them willy-nilly onto the bunk before she found what she wanted. When she looked up, Hana was standing like a colossus in the middle of the cabin, her arms crossed and a determined look on her face.

"Hana, let me go," Morgan begged. "If you don't, I'll be seasick."

"Seasick? You ain't never been seasick your whole life!"

"Well, I will be now," Morgan promised. She struggled and just managed to get the brown dress over her head. She didn't notice a fold of the skirt tucked into the back of the waistband. Morgan began tying the laces that fastened the bodice up the front, but the ruffles of her chemise were bunched in the sleeves making movement difficult. She made a small sound of annoyance and yanked angrily at them.

"You're no better than a baby," Hana scolded coming to help her before she ripped the lace. She untangled the skirt, and quickly had her charge properly dressed. "What's going on in your head, missy? If you go out there you'll get worse than seasick. I know you will!"

Morgan didn't answer. Skirts twitching with her impatient steps, she went to the door and flung it wide, her maid right behind her.

"First you go and get all wet in the rain," the woman grumbled. "Now you want to go out there with all them pirates. You're tempting fate for sure."

Chapter 5

Hana hard on her heels, Morgan started up the narrow wooden steps to the patch of sunlight outlined by the open hatch above them.

The sun had risen higher, its brightness reflecting off white sails spread to catch the Caribbean winds. Gulls followed the ship, their raucous voices loudly arguing and blending into the creak and strain of rigging. The air moved, alive with the light, and with the sounds and smells of the sea.

Morgan paused on the top step. She could feel the ocean beneath the ship, the lift of waves through the deck under her feet. She took a deep breath of air filled with the scent of salt and the ship. She loved sailing, and being on a ship again filled her with a kind of euphoria, as if she could just float away on the wind.

"If you're just gonna stand in this doorway all day," Hana complained, breaking into her reverie "maybe you best come back down to the cabin."

Morgan blinked and remembered her surroundings. She climbed the last step and walked to the rail, staring out over the water, enjoying the feel of the wind on her face. Hanna remained safely in the shelter of the superstructure. The solid feeling of wood at her back was more to her taste.

"Well, lass, I see you're bound and determined to disrupt my crew," said a voice. The men who stopped to gawk when Morgan appeared quickly returned to their work.

Daniel Harris had come up behind her on silent feet. He still wore his own brown hair clubbed at the back of his neck, but now he was dressed like an ordinary sailor in loose blue trousers and a coarse white cotton shirt. The ties of the shirt were open, exposing a swell of muscles and his tanned chest to the cool sea breeze. But even though Daniel dressed simply there was no mistaking him for anything but the captain. He carried himself with the air of assurance that distinguishes men accustomed to command.

Morgan raised her chin and looked up into his face. "I couldn't stay in the cabin any longer," she told him. "After all those months in the governor's house, I feel as if I've finally escaped from prison."

"Is that any excuse to disobey my orders?"

"Did you really intend for me to stay below like some kind of cargo?" she inquired with deceptive sweetness.

"Since I am required to deliver you to Port Royal, that's exactly what you are."

"Cargo? Me?" Her cheeks flushed with anger.

32

"Well, maybe not," he began, and she was mollified until he added, "cargo doesn't talk back and argue."

Morgan started to give a sharp retort until she saw his lips twitch as he fought back a smile, and realized he was teasing.

From the telltale creases around his eyes, she decided he was more accustomed to laughing than being angry. And so she smiled back at him.

Since she was obviously not going to remain below, Daniel knew when to give in. "Come onto the quarterdeck. It's out of the way," he told her, climbing a short flight of ladder-like steps to the stern.

Morgan followed with Hana close behind. Her maid clutched at the risers, expecting to be flung into water any second by the tossing ship. She didn't trust this man with her charge and so she hovered protectively, her face set with disapproval.

Morgan found Daniel's voice pleasant but noted a trace of an unfamiliar accent. "Even though I've known you all my life," she commented. "I really don't know very much about you. Where are you from, captain?"

"I was born in Wales. I lived there until I was fourteen years old," he replied, looking down at her hair.

Sunshine brought out gold lights in the flame red, while the breeze played with the soft tendrils escaping from her long braid, silken wisps caressing her face. He'd never seen hair this color except on Lady Maria and her daughter. It was so beautiful, like some exotic silk. He always wanted to touch it, to feel its warmth, and now here she was, standing right before him. He almost reached out, but then Hana stirred uneasily, her skirts rustling, and the sharp sound pulled his wandering thoughts back. "Don't you know you should never ask a sailor about his past? And especially not in the Indies," he added, pleased his chagrin wasn't apparent in his voice. Where had those feeling come from he wondered? This was his old friend's daughter, a lady, not some dockside strumpet he could fondle at will.

"Why is that?" she wanted to know.

"The Indies are part of the New World, a place where people come to reinvent themselves. There's an unwritten law that what's in the past stays in the past."

"Ah! Secrets." She considered this for a moment. "Well, that isn't fair. You know all about me."

He looked out to sea, taking a moment to control his conflicted feelings. "Your father was my friend. I was very sorry to hear of his death," he told her finally. "It must have been very difficult for you losing both your parents like that. Please accept my deepest sympathy."

She caught her breath on the little pang his words caused her, but his sincerity was soothing. "Thank you," she whispered. She missed them so much, and she knew by now that she always would -- something else she would have to live with.

She stood in silence, unaware he was looking at her again until she glanced up, meeting his steady gray eyes with her golden brown ones. Something about him made her feel she could trust him. Not that he appeared in the least soft. Quite the contrary, he radiated strength and purpose, and there was something in his eyes that told her he wouldn't be a man to cross. But she felt safe with him, despite Hana's warnings about his piratical reputation.

"You and my father sailed together," she began.

"We were partners in a number of ventures. We were involved in one of them when he died."

"Can you tell me about it?" she asked.

"That's what brought me to Charles Town," he admitted.

"My father? But... You mean you came to see me?"

"That I did. Your father and I were building a ship. It's a special design, shallow draught and slim, built for speed and maneuverability among the islands."

"Is that why you were in the Carolinas?" she asked, remembering part of the conversation in the governor's office. "Visiting ship builders?"

He looked at her suspiciously. "How did you know I'd been in the Carolinas?" he asked. "I didn't realize you were in the Governor's confidence."

Then she remembered she had been eavesdropping when she overheard this conversation. She flushed, but her chin went up. "I have my ways," she told him boldly.

"I bet you do," he replied, admiration and amusement in his voice.

"Please continue," she insisted, nettled by his knowing response. "Tell me more about the ship. Does it have a name?"

"*Bright Folly*." He glanced down at her, not sure how much she knew about her father's business.

As if she could read his mind, she answered. "*Folly* sounds about right for some of father's business dealings," she commented.

His eyebrow raised in amused surprise, but he still didn't comment.

"Mother and I always knew he was a smuggler," she told him disingenuously. "But he never called it that, of course."

"Of course," he repeated, not sure how to respond to this strangely well informed young woman. Usually one didn't discuss such topics openly.

"He explained it to us, about the unfair Navigation Act, and how it made it so hard for the colonies to get materials and supplies."

"That's true."

"So, are you a smuggler too?"

He had to laugh. "That's not something you should ask, or that I should answer."

She grinned back at him. "You don't have to be afraid. The only reason I told you father's secret is because I know you had a part in it. Else I wouldn't have said anything." He didn't look convinced, and she sighed. "Tell me more about the *Bright Folly*."

"You should know that, as your father's heir, you own half of her."

"I own half of a ship?" She looked interested.

"Half of what's built. It's not finished yet. We were paying for it slowly, you see, a bit here and a bit there. By rights you owe half the expenses too."

"I see." There was nothing of this in the will, but it was obvious why it would have been kept secret, nothing on paper. In such a venture, each man's honor would serve as a bond. She looked at Daniel Harris again, understanding just why her father had trusted him. Under the circumstances, he didn't have to reveal this to her at all. He could have kept the ship for himself and she would never have known.

"I came to Charles Town to bring you an offer," Daniel was saying. "I want to buy your half of the *Folly*. I can't pay you all at once, but I have a hundred guineas for you now, if you'll accept my offer."

"A hundred? How much is half of a ship worth?"

"This one? As well as the hundred, perhaps a grand. That's another thousand guineas."

"And how much of that will I eventually get?"

"Nine hundred more. But I won't have it for a while," he added quickly.

Morgan nodded, stunned by this unusual revelation. "Well, all right. I can't imagine what I would do with a ship. Especially not if I'm living in England."

Daniel smiled. "Then I will hand over a hundred guineas before you disembark. But," he hesitated, thinking of how much this child -- no, he amended, this young woman -- still had to face. "I suggest you keep it secret. At least until you're with someone you can trust. It might be a good thing to have money of your own."

"You're right," she agreed. The money would be invaluable, she thought. If she went to England, or even if she was able to stay in the Indies, the gold would give her independence. Yes, it would be a good thing.

"Thank you. I accept your offer," she told him, standing there on his deck, her red hair flaming in the sunlight, the picture burned in his memory.

Chapter 6

Although Daniel would have preferred that she remain below, out of the way for the rest of the voyage, Morgan was determined to remain on deck. She wanted to enjoy her freedom for as long as it lasted, as well as the wonderful feeling of being at sea. She unconsciously balanced herself on the swaying vessel, her dress unheeded as it was tugged this way and that by the wind.

Daniel kept himself busy and away from this woman who had been forced upon him. But still he watched her, hyper-aware of that slender figure. Something about her drew him, some feeling he didn't want to acknowledge and therefore found confusing. The attraction was more than just her beauty, more than the warm sensuality suggested by the curves of her figure, the barely confined wealth of her fascinating red hair, her generous mouth and the direct gaze of her golden-brown eyes. Her eyes could change, he noticed, reflecting her mood.

Daniel had known Morgan for years, but as his employer's daughter, just another member of the family that treated him kindly. She was beyond his touch then, and she is now, he reminded himself again. Not only is she a lady, but she's the daughter of an old friend.

Daniel frowned, annoyed with feelings he had so much trouble keeping under control. And then he realized he was staring at her, and she was looking back at him, an intent look on her face.

"I wonder," she began swaying over to where he stood. She ignored the way his eyebrows creased in suspicion, and continued, "since you've been there and all, when I get to England ..."

"Nay, lass," he interrupted hastily. "I can't tell you anything about England. I haven't been there since I was a lad." He looked beyond her to Hana. "Your maid was right when she warned you about the dangers aboard my ship."

"Danger? Here?" So he had heard Hana's scolding.

"That you could ask such a question proves your innocence." He frowned at her, trying to look stern.

"Where is this danger?" she demanded.

"All around you, lass. Though the *Kestrel* serves England's interests, she's still a fighting ship, manned by fighting men. Under the circumstances, we don't have a lot of experience with gently bred ladies. You need to know that you're safe only because I'm the captain and because I've given Governor Ramsey my word to deliver you unharmed to Port Royal."

39

"Only because of your word?"

"Only because of my word," he repeated. "As long as I command this ship." His gaze swept over the deck and back to Morgan. "These are not regular seamen. They're not conscripted, and they're not paid wages. They sail with me of their own free will, knowing it'll be worth their while in plunder. We search out the richest ships and towns, and we take what we will."

"Then Hana's right, you are pirates," she accused him, reacting to the antagonism he deliberately created between them.

"Privateers," he corrected. "I'm commissioned by William Sikes, the Governor of Port Royal. Still, everything that comes on board this ship belongs in shares to the men who sail her. Everything." He watched Morgan, curious to see her reaction.

"Do you mean by allowing me to be a passenger on your ship you're depriving your men of their rightful booty?"

A chuckle escaped before he could curb his mirth at her use of the term, and the smile lit his features. "Nay, lass. It's not that bad. We were on our way home to Port Royal when we stopped off at Charles Town. We've already made our profit this trip."

Was he laughing at her? Her chin went up and her back stiffened. "Are you telling me I'm sailing on a ship stuffed with plunder - gold and jewels and the like?"

He laughed. "Hardly. The ship we took sailed on ahead with a prize crew. Haven't you noticed how lightly manned we are?"

"Since this is the first time I've been allowed up on

deck, I scarcely could have had the opportunity to notice anything," she snapped.

"It would have been much better if you remained below," Daniel said unhappily, and she wasn't sure what he meant by this abrupt change of mood.

"So we're back to that, are we? I'm just part of the cargo?" she asked sweetly, a dangerous glint in her eye. "Out of sight. Out of the way?"

"I wouldn't have chosen quite those words. But I should perhaps point out that on a ship, it's customary to abide by the captain's wishes."

"Wishes? Don't you mean orders?" Her eyes flashed golden fire. "No, Captain Harris, I do not submit meekly to anyone's orders," she spat. "I am not a box full of goods that you can pack away and forget."

"Aye. You're none of that," he breathed, mostly to himself. He knew he would not forget this woman easily or soon.

Morgan bristled from his goading and he was sorry for the necessity of provoking her. But even more, he was angry at himself for getting into a position where he had to play nursemaid to a spoiled woman, even if she was breathtakingly beautiful. What he wanted, he told himself, was to use her as he did other women, to take her into his arms and kiss her breathless, and then ...

But this was no common dockside wench to be tumbled where he found her. Damn Ramsey anyway!

"Since you insist on having your way," he said, "I'd better make arrangements for your comfort. Excuse me." Abruptly he turned, taking the steps down to the ship's waist

41

two at a time.

Although he wouldn't have called them rules, Daniel still had some guidelines he tried to live by. One of them was to keep his world as uncomplicated as possible. He liked his life; he was a joyous individual even in the midst of the hazardous trade he followed. Robert Moorhouse used to laugh at him and say he was addicted to danger. Daniel always agreed this was true. Still, there was more to him than that, for he also valued the quiet moments on his ship, riding the lift and thrust of her beneath his feet as she cleaved through the waves, feeling the salt spray and the pull of the wind. He valued his freedom, and this precluded any permanent involvement with women, especially women of Morgan's class. They demanded stability, and as long as his resources were committed to the *Bright Folly*, and his energy to his life as a privateer, he had nothing left for them.

Still there was something about Morgan Moorhouse that haunted him. More than her beauty, he found himself liking the girl for herself. She had grown from an appealing child into a woman both spirited and apparently unaffected. Despite her obvious intelligence, she was also trusting of him in a way that made him feel protective toward her. Beyond the debt of friendship he owed her father, he would have wanted to help her just for herself. At the same time there was something about Morgan implying she might be able to take care of herself if the need arose. At least she would be a spirited fighter. And, on top of it all, she was the most beautiful woman he had ever seen.

No, he told himself firmly, leave her alone! He'd been forced to give her passage to Port Royal. From there her cousin would take her to a new life in England, a life in which there was no place for a buccaneer captain.

Morgan stood against the stern rail where Daniel left her. One minute he'd been laughing with her and the next he was gone. She didn't understand the sudden change in his mood. Unless she was mistaken he'd suddenly become angry with her. But why?

"What was that all about, missy?" Hana asked interrupting her thoughts.

"I'm not sure." Morgan admitted. "I think I've been warned not to inflame the crew to lustful thoughts."

"Such language! A young lady has no business thinking such things, much less talking about them. And with strange men, too! I told you to stay in the cabin," she grumbled. "But do you listen to me? No. You don't listen to old Hana. What do I know anyway? Huh."

Morgan brushed the loose wisps of hair from her eyes and moved forward to look down into the waist of the ship. She heard Hana's words, but she didn't really listen to them.

The captain was below her, staring up into the rigging where a couple of men were at work replacing a line. Suddenly their eyes met and Morgan glanced quickly away. When she looked again he was busy talking to Juan. She couldn't hear what they were saying, but it had to be about her. The Spaniard looked up once and smiled, before giving his attention back to the captain. Then Juan nodded, and when the captain moved away, called a couple of the crew to help him.

Morgan watched as they brought a piece of canvas from the sail locker, and rigged an awning over the hatch leading to the captain's cabin. Then they brought two chairs and placed them in the shade. This done, the seamen returned to their business while Juan swung up onto the quarter deck.

"*Senorita*," he said with a bow and a flourish. A huge grin was buried in his mustache, but visible by the twinkle in his eye. "You will perhaps remember me? I am Juan Smyth, quartermaster of the *Kestrel*, at your service once again."

Morgan nodded, while Hana glared and maintained a dignified silence.

"The captain has directed me to prepare a place where you can take the air without being troubled by the sun. May I escort you?"

"Thank you," Morgan replied, following him. Gallantly he gave her his hand as she descended the steps. He even offered this support to Hana. Although she pointedly refused to have anything to do with him, he didn't seem to mind.

It was pleasant in the shade under the awning where a breeze swept away the heat, and Morgan sank gratefully into one of the chairs.

"If there is any further service I can perform, I hope you will not hesitate to honor me," Juan told them, bowing again.

"Well," Morgan began, ignoring Hana's outraged stare. "I was wondering ... What is the custom aboard the *Kestrel* for serving dinner?"

"Ah, *senorita*, before you came, the captain, the first mate and I had dinner here on deck or in his cabin. But now I do not know. The first mate is gone, commanding the prize ship that sailed ahead of us. What the captain has planned, he has not seen fit to divulge to me." Juan grinned at her. "Shall I make inquiries?"

"Better than that," she began. "Since I would not upset the routine on the ship, perhaps you and the captain would join me here this evening for dinner." Morgan deliberately didn't look at Hana, even though she knew she would have to listen to recriminations as soon as Juan was out of earshot. "It would be pleasant to sit here at a table in the cool of the evening, don't you think?"

"Certainly, *senorita*. I will convey your very kind invitation to the captain."

He was barely out of sight when Hana opened her lips to speak.

"No, Hana, not now," Morgan said quickly, forestalling her. "I know what you're going to say."

"Then why did you invite those men to have dinner with you?"

"To be troublesome. To meet new people. To flirt with Captain Harris. Oh, Hana, I don't know! I just don't want to be stuck on this ship with no one to talk to and nothing to do. I had enough of that at the governor's house."

"Huh. You're never happy less you're making trouble. You're asking for it, missy!" she warned.

"Nothing's going to happen, Hana. You're going to be with me every second, and you heard the captain say that I had his protection."

"Some protection," Hana grumbled under her breath. "It's like putting a lion in the pen to guard the goats."

Chapter 7

Morgan prepared carefully for dinner that evening. She selected a dress of dull gold satin brocade over a petticoat of cream-colored silk. The under-skirt was trimmed with a wide band of gold embroidery around the hem, and the dress decorated with cream and rust colored ribbons in rosettes holding the skirt parted in front and pulled up to the waist in the back. It was a grand toilette, suitable for a ball, and Morgan looked magnificent. Hana dressed her hair in a fashion called hurluberlu, parted in the middle with masses of red curls cascading down her back except for one ringlet persuaded to fall across her shoulders in front. She talked Hana into giving her the necklace of pearls set in gold and matching earrings that had been locked away in the bottom of the smallest trunk. Holding a hand mirror she tried to see herself, but the glass was too small.

"Oh, Hana, how does it look? Is my hair right?" she asked turning from side to side, the mirror held out at arm's length.

Hana glowered at her. "What're you asking me for? You won't believe me. You don't listen to anything I say, 'cause if you did you wouldn't be doing this. You wouldn't be getting all dressed up so those pirates can see how much you're worth and maybe get ideas about holding you for ransom! Or worse!"

"Why, Hana, what could be worse?" Morgan teased, her eyes alight with mischief.

"Huh! Straighten your skirt." Hana gave the stiff material a tug that settled it in place. "There," she said, looking at her charge and hiding the pride she felt. Morgan was easily as beautiful as her mother. Maybe even more so.

"You'll do," she admitted. "But you'd best behave yourself. Remember your station!"

"How could I forget with you to remind me?" Morgan tamed her grin into a more suitable expression, although the haughty look was marred by the twinkle in her eyes as she led the way out the door.

She reached the deck in time to see the sun sliding down the western horizon, painting the sky with bands of rose and violet streaked with gold. The sea reflected the colors, and the ship sailed on purple waves edged in gilt.

Morgan forgot to maintain her pretense of hauteur, and gazed about with delight. Someone, probably Juan, she thought, had decided to honor their guests with the best the *Kestrel* had to offer. A table covered with a dampened cloth of costly damask held a set of fine china framed by eating

47

utensils of heavy silver. Precious crystal goblets were set by each place. Candles on the table, sheathed in thick glass columns, would give light after the sun set.

Juan and the captain had also dressed for their parts, Juan magnificent in ruby velvet, and Daniel cool in heavy black silk. Their linen was spotless, and their cravats and shirt cuffs trimmed with yards of costly lace. Both flashed jewels that any man would envy, although such extravagant signs of wealth were common in the Indies, and especially on the persons of buccaneers. Although the quartermaster completed his dress with a curled black wig, Daniel wore his own hair, neatly brushed back and tied with a black ribbon.

Daniel bowed to Morgan when she joined them, his face expressionless, although he appreciated her gorgeous dress and how it set off her unique coloring. Without a word he gave her his arm and escorted her to the table, holding the chair as she seated herself. He took his place opposite her. Hana settled behind her charge on a bench against the bulkhead. Juan bustled about the table, serving the wine. This done, he took his seat and from there served the courses as they were brought up by the cook.

Morgan accepted everything she was offered. She was amazed at how well it was prepared and said so.

"I stole the cook," Daniel informed her with a grin. "He was on his way to be tried by the Inquisition and, given a choice, decided that life as privateer was preferable."

"I don't blame him," she said fervently. "My mother told me stories of some of the injustices attributed to the Order. I certainly wouldn't want to fall into their hands."

"Nor I," Daniel agreed. "Juan was their guest once. He

would probably tell you all about it, but I don't recommend the story during meals. Or too close to bedtime."

"You're lucky to have escaped," she told Juan in Spanish.

"*Si, senorita*," he replied.

"You speak Spanish well," Captain Harris said to her, also speaking in that tongue.

"You knew my mother; she taught me," Morgan replied. "She always said that, even if I might never visit Spain, I should at least be aware of my heritage."

"All of it? The good and the bad?"

"Precisely."

"Your mother was Spanish?" Juan wanted to know. "How did she come to marry an Englishman?"

"It's a long story," she protested, but he smiled at her to continue. "My father was with Morgan at the sack of the City of Panama. My mother was there, visiting relatives. Then the pirates broke into the house where she was staying. Even though my father was one of them, he rescued her and kept her safe. She always said it was love at first sight for both of them. Because of her love for my father, she abandoned her old life and accompanied him back to Cayman Brac where they were married."

"It is a romance!" Juan exclaimed, delighted.

"It wasn't all happy. I know she loved my father and would never have left him, but her family were hidalgos and they disowned her. She was formally excommunicated and stricken from the family rolls. She never spoke of it, but I know it made her unhappy."

"But she became a good Englishwoman," Daniel added,

pouring more wine into his glass. "And your father would have done anything to make her happy."

"I know he did. He stopped being a privateer and became a planter because of her. But I also think it must have been uncomfortable for her to live in an English colony when they were at war with Spain."

The sun sank out of sight and Juan rose to light the lanterns. He then lit the candles on the table inside their thick glass columns.

"I think you are also half Spanish?" she commented when Juan resumed his seat.

"Yes, but my father bestowed no more than me and his name on my mother before he disappeared. How he met her, I'll never know."

"Where did this happen?" she asked.

"In a small Spanish settlement outside of Portobello." He grinned. "But we lived there peacefully with her family until the good Fathers came. Following the tradition that anything different had to be wrong, they decided my last name was a heresy and put me to the question."

Daniel leaned over and whispered, "That means torture. I wouldn't ask for details if I were you."

"I know that," she replied, slanting a look at him from under her eyelids. She smiled at Juan. "Continue your story," she invited, as the captain watched her and sipped his wine.

"There isn't much more," Juan told her. "They were zealous champions of the church and wanted to be certain the name was the only sin against me."

"But how did you escape?" she demanded.

"Ah," Juan laughed. "It wasn't very difficult, *senorita*.

As I said, it was a very small village. The jailer was my uncle and the guards were his two sons, my cousins. They helped me to the waterfront where I kept a little boat, and so I put to sea. Unfortunately there was a big storm that night. Fortunately I was picked up by Captain Harris and thus you see me here."

"Captain Harris just plucked you from the sea and put you to work on his ship?"

Juan shrugged. "He insisted. It was my name, you see. The captain liked it." Juan lowered his voice and gave a fair imitation of the captain. "'Half Spanish, half English,' he said to me. ' You walk in two worlds. I have need of such a man.' And so here I am. I have many talents and I have been very useful," Juan concluded without a shred of modesty.

"And one of your talents is a too ready tongue," Daniel interjected dryly. "Since you have claimed so many talents and I see you've finished your dinner, why don't you play for the *senorita*?"

"It will be my very great pleasure," he assured them, rising with a bow and a flourish. He disappeared into the depths of the ship and returned in minutes with a bulky object wrapped in canvas.

The captain swirled the wine in his glass watching as the candlelight reflected through the deep red liquid. "I think Juan's mother was more than a Spaniard," he said idly. "There may have been gypsy blood there. I've seen evidence of it on numerous occasions. But whatever she may have been, and despite his too ready tongue, Juan has been very useful. He has skills as a trader and has kept us well supplied from ports that would normally be closed to an English buccaneer. He is also an unusually fine musician as you will see."

Juan opened the package and carefully removed a guitar. He brushed his hands across the strings and then adjusted the tuning, before turning to Morgan. "For you, *senorita*, I will play the music of Spain as my uncle, Paco, taught it to me. Listen ..."

He started with a chord and then expanded it, playing a delicate melody over a traveling bass line. The music he played had delighted listeners for centuries and consisted of a unique texture woven of traditional sounds brought to Spain by the Moors from Africa, the Jews from their eastern homeland, and then added to the ancient folk melodies of the native Spaniard. It was complex music and difficult to play, but sound poured from Juan's fingers like liquid, dazzling, sensuous and breath-takingly beautiful. Morgan had never heard anything like it.

Daniel leaned back in his chair and watched her. His eyes caressed her as his hands longed to do. He imagined stroking the soft mane of her hair out of its confining style and draping it over her shoulders like a cloak. Her soft round breasts rose and fell with her breathing, the gold gleaming at her throat with each movement. The music and the beauty of the woman brought magic to his ship as it sailed into the black night.

Juan's fingers slowed and blended sound into a final chord. The music trembled and faded away.

Morgan sat motionless for another minute. The she drew a deep shuddering breath and let it out in a sigh.

"I have never heard anything so wonderful," she said,

smiling at the musician. "You are truly an artist, *senor*. I have no words to describe how your music makes me feel."

Juan beamed. "Your praise, *senorita*, is the greatest reward I could ever have. It is my pleasure to make you happy."

"Well you have certainly done that!"

"Shall I play something else?"

"Oh, please." Her mind worked quickly. "Would you play a saltarello?"

"Do you dance, *senorita*?" he asked with surprise.

"My mother taught me," she replied. She cast a quick glance at Hana who stiffened and scowled, but didn't move to stop her.

As she rose to her feet with the rustle of silk and a glisten of jewels. The captain's lips quirked into a smile as he watched and sipped his wine.

Juan grinned. He picked out a single line of melody in three four time, accenting the second beat. Then he began to embroider the melody, adding point and counterpoint.

Morgan lifted her skirts above the toes of her elegant satin slippers and danced.

Composed of movements of simple elegance, the saltarello is a gracious figure born in the countryside, something that an innocent girl might dance at a fiesta. Morgan danced it well, simply and with grace. When it was over Juan slid with only a small pause into a another piece, music for a dance that resembled a gagliarda, but instead of the movements described by a delicate lady's slipper, this one was danced by bare feet beside a Spanish gypsy's fire. It was faster than the first piece of music. The postures and head

53

movements were flirty. Morgan stepped into it without hesitation, her flaming hair flashing in the light as she moved in and out of the shadows cast by lanterns and candles.

"Brava!" Juan called when she was finished.

She wasn't even breathing hard, but the exertion had brought a flush to her cheeks and her eyes sparkled.

Daniel rose to his feet and held out his hand. "Come," he demanded quietly, his voice deep and soft, his gray eyes compelling. "Dance with me." And just those few words held enough power and promise that Morgan couldn't refuse.

Juan smiled to himself as her slender fingers laced with Daniel's hand. He couldn't help but be aware of the current between the two of them.

Juan played the opening notes to a saraband, a dance that had been outlawed by the church for despite the fact that it was very slow and the movements most formal, it was still a dance of languorous seduction. At the first chords, Daniel glanced at him, an eyebrow raised in amusement, before he turned all of his attention to the dance.

The captain advanced, his eyes locked with Morgan's. She swayed back, coquettish in retreat. They moved then, advancing and retreating, becoming one with the music, their bodies not touching, but barely a breath apart. She pirouetted out of his arms, but he caught her to him again, his touch gentle, but strength evident in the hard muscle of his arms surrounding her.

She felt him beside her, the heat of his body seeming to burn through her clothing, turning her bones to liquid. Her mouth parted and her eyelids lowered. She wanted to surrender, to be overpowered by the strength of him, and she knew he wanted her just as much. Even as she trembled for him to take her, she knew a strange savage pride in her ability to evoke such passion in him.

All too soon the music drew to a close. His breath brushed her cheek as he held her one last time, and all life seemed suspended in that single long moment. Then his hands were gone and the music faded into the sounds of a ship on the sea, the hiss and slap of waves against wood, the creak of the rigging. Morgan stood there, her head held high even though her eyelids seemed too heavy to hold open. As he bowed to her, she automatically curtsied.

"Thank you for the dance and for your company at dinner," he said, exercising admirable control over his voice. "It's late and, I think, time for you to retire. Your maid is waiting, and I still have much to do tonight."

Before she could reply he was gone into the darkness, leaving her standing there.

Juan wrapped his guitar. The candles on the table had burned down, and one of them was flickering in its holder, about to go out. Hana was on her feet, waiting for her to go below. Morgan's knees were trembling, but the movement of the ship gave her an excuse to clutch the railing as she descended to her -- no, to *his* cabin.

Sleep wouldn't come. Morgan lay awake in the darkness, her emotions stretched too tightly to allow her to rest. Her mind kept racing from thought to thought, from image to image. Her body felt as if it was filled with strange sensations, like bubbles humming through her veins. Juan's music echoed in her mind as she listened to the sounds of the ship over Hana's gentle snoring.

Because of his wealth and position in island society, none of the planters cared to snub Robert Moorhouse despite what they considered his unfortunate marriage. In truth, he was a pleasant enough a gentleman, open-handed and generous in entertaining his neighbors, and they enjoyed his company. Still, although their friendship for him and his beautiful Spanish wife was sincere, they didn't want such blood in their own families. Because Robert had a beautiful daughter, there was consternation among the parents of eligible young bachelors. And so, although several of the young men did come courting her, it was fortunate that Morgan would have none of them. She was dismayed by their stiff manners and their inability to carry on what she considered a rational conversation. She was accustomed to the company of her parents, who spoke to her as a sensible individual.

Morgan had never been in love except one time. The focus of this youthful infatuation had actually been Daniel, a romantically mysterious, handsome young man who occasionally sailed in to visit her father. Anything beyond a frustrated attraction, however, was thwarted by Daniel's oblivion. All he saw was the daughter of his partner, a bashful child who sometimes stared at him with big brown eyes.

As she grew older, her parents protected her from the more exuberant attentions that might have been directed toward her, and so her experience with men was limited. That never bothered her -- until now. She didn't understand the emotions raging through her, and not just emotions, the physical sensations that kept her tossing and turning late into the night. She wished she knew what to do about those feelings.

She lay there in the darkness, listening to the beating of her heart as it fueled the heat lingering from Daniel's touch. Morgan wondered what it would be like to have him there with her, touching her, his skin against her skin. She shivered as if in a sudden chill, or was it desire flooding through her?

The captain didn't get much rest either. He told himself it was because he was trying to sleep in a strange bed.

Chapter 8

Morning found Morgan dreamy eyed, her mind distant from the reality of life around her. Hana had to ask her twice what she would wear that day. The maid took a hard look at her charge and recognized the symptoms. Whether she realized it or not, the girl displayed all the signs of being in love, and with a pirate, too, of all the unsuitable people! Hana had promised her mistress she would always take care of Morgan, and she took her promises seriously. But what could she do about it while they were on this ship? Obviously locking Morgan in the cabin wasn't an option! She took a deep breath and prepared herself for a hard battle.

Finally dressed in a gown of soft green with primrose ribbons, and her hair neatly braided for once, Morgan escaped her maid's fussing and went up on deck. Squinting against the bright sunshine, she leaned over the railing, inhaling the fresh morning breeze.

Hana watched her efforts to dress Morgan undone in minutes as the wind blew her clothing and worked strands of hair loose from the tidy braids. The maid tightened her lips to a thin line and gave a sigh. That girl would never grow up, she decided.

After some time spent watching the movement of the waves and antics of the gulls that followed the ship, Morgan brushed a strand of hair from her eyes and glanced sideways. She saw the captain standing above her on the quarter deck beside the helmsman. Of course Daniel had seen her, but apparently he was avoiding her this morning. Piqued that he would be so distant after last night, after the way he danced with her, she took it as a challenge. But what should she do?

Morgan turned and under the pretense of adjusting her sleeve, looked back toward the wheel again. Daniel had to have noticed her. Instead he gazed up at the sails as if memorizing the rigging. When he looked down again, his face turned to listen to something the helmsman was saying.

Suddenly, to Morgan's surprise, he broke away and walked toward her. With a rustle of petticoats, Hana stirred on her seat under the awning, looking at her charge with a combination of warning and appeal.

"Morning, lassie," Daniel said softly. "Did you sleep well?"

"Good morning, Captain Harris," she replied sweetly. "I slept very well. And you?" She looked up into his eyes, a smile on her lips.

Hana groaned softly and forgot about the mending in her lap.

"Well, as always," the captain lied. And why, he asked himself angrily, am I standing here talking to her? I can't keep away, even when I know it's the thing to do.

"Captain Harris," Morgan began, hesitant. "I'm curious about something. I don't want to pry, but ..."

"Then perhaps you should endeavor to forget about whatever it is," Daniel suggested.

"I can't. Please." she placed her hand lightly on his arm and he stood as if turned to stone. "Have I done something to offend you?" she asked softly.

He looked down into her eyes, the brown depths lit with flecks of gold.

"I know you didn't want to take me to Port Royal," she told him. "I heard you arguing with Mr. Preston."

"Did you now? I didn't see you there."

"I ... I was walking in the garden. And the window was open."

His mouth fought to hold back a grin and lost. "Walking in the garden? How convenient for eavesdropping. Nay," he added quickly as she scowled at him. "I can't blame you, lass. If it was my future being discussed, I'd listen too."

"Well," she said, staring hard at his chest since she couldn't quite meet his eye. "It really was an accident. But I know it's true. You didn't want to take me on board. At first. But then yesterday, when we were talking, and then you let me come up here on deck, I thought you'd changed your mind."

"Especially after I danced with you last night," Daniel added sympathetically. He sighed. "Lass, you did nothing yourself to deserve it, but you're in a bad position. A woman on a ship usually means trouble."

"Because of the pirates' ... excuse me, I meant to say, the privateer's shares?"

Daniel laughed. "Ah, so you remembered that?"

Exasperated at his teasing, she scowled. "That's what you told me. Shouldn't I remember it?"

"Oh, indeed you should," he said, mirth vanishing. His voice was soft. "Young and beautiful," he murmured. "Such women could find themselves in terrible danger, especially when unchaperoned."

The sun was hot on Morgan's head as she watched him speak, her lips parted, her eyes on the strong column of his throat where it rose from the collar of his loose shirt. "I have Hana," she began in a small voice. She felt strange, as if she was floating somewhere, warm and relaxed. She was much too aware of his body so close to hers.

"Yes, you may have your maid with you, but that isn't the same as if you were traveling with your family -- brothers, father, someone like that," Daniel said, his voice quiet, smooth as the air that surrounded them, binding them together.

"I don't have any," she reminded him, her mind strangely detached from the words. The sun caressed her, turning her bones to water. She had a sudden urge to reach out and touch him, to put her mouth on him and taste the beads of sweat on his skin.

"I know," he responded. "It isn't just my crew I worry about. Pretty women are my weakness too." His hand came up and with a finger he slowly and carefully lifted a strand of hair that had fallen across her cheek. For an endless moment

61

they gazed into each other's eyes, every emotion poised on the edge of becoming, important words on the verge of being said, in a silence more meaningful than sound.

Daniel broke the spell by taking a step back from her.

Morgan drew a deep shuddering breath. "Do you mean that you might take advantage of me?" she asked, her voice sounding very small. She wished very much he would do just that.

One side of Daniel's mouth curved up in a lopsided grin. "Nay, lass. You're gentlefolk and I'm naught but a buccaneer captain."

Morgan noticed his accent could come and go. Right now it was particularly strong, but there were other times when she had heard him speak with the precision of an educated man. There were so many mysteries to this buccaneer captain!

"This is a fighting ship," he was saying. "'Tis not the merchantman that should be transportin' the likes o' you."

"Yer' fergettin'," she replied, deliberately matching his lilting brogue. "That yer speakin' to someone brought up on these isles. Not a pale, sheltered lady from London town."

He kept his smile under control. "I have at least enough breeding to know you're not a lass for me to dally with."

"But you wouldn't," Morgan reminded. "The governor wouldn't have sent me on this ship if he didn't think you were trustworthy."

Daniel had to laugh. "He didn't have a choice. Mine was the only ship going to Port Royal. Your cousin must be a pretty important man, or at least he has the governor thinking so. Seems it wouldn't do to keep him waiting for you."

"Huh," Morgan said in the same tone Hana used when she was skeptical. "If my cousin Oliver was in such a hurry, he could have come himself. No, the governor was just anxious to get rid of me. He considered me ," she paused remembering all the times she'd incurred his wrath. "Well, he thought I was a problem, you see."

"I would never have guessed." Daniel replied, keeping a straight face.

"Well, I am. Even Hana thinks I'm spoiled. But still, Cousin Oliver could have come. After the long trip from England, what's two days more to Charles Town?"

"Governor Ramsey mentioned his ship had been damaged," Daniel supplied. "It can't leave Port Royal until repairs are made."

Morgan tilted her head as she considered this. "And so you were his only choice?"

"I have said so." Daniel's eyes sparkled as he returned her regard. Then he sobered. "It was a mistake what I did last night," he admitted in a softer voice. "I should never have danced with you."

"Why?" she asked bewildered. "I don't understand why you think that. It didn't hurt anything. Besides," she smiled up at him, "you dance very well."

"You know why," Daniel insisted. "And it is you, not I who dance well."

Morgan laughed. "You should have seen my mother. I wish I could dance the way she did. She said she was taught by an old gypsy woman. She tried, to teach me, but ..." her voice trailed off. "Do they dance like that in London, I wonder?" she added.

63

"That's something I cannot tell you." The captain glanced at the sky, at the low thin clouds that had appeared on the horizon. "The wind is changing. I have to attend to my ship."

Chapter 9

Morgan waited on deck for evening when she might be able to talk to Daniel again. She braved a bank of angry gray clouds building in the west until a squall with violently gusting winds sent her and Hana running for the shelter of the cabin. Drenched by heavy rain, she stood dripping in the doorway, frustrated that she had to be sequestered even for a little while. After Hana argued her into dry clothing, she sat on the bunk, pouting at the storm through rain streaked glass. Her displeasure didn't seem to impress the storm, for the rain still whipped against the ship when Juan rapped on the door, bringing their dinner. Morgan and Hana ate in silence. After she finished, Morgan curled up against the pillows, day-dreaming.

Pictures of the captain drifted through her mind, especially Daniel up on deck in the sunlight, the wind ruffling his hair. Why did she keep thinking about him she wanted to know? What was so special about Daniel Harris other then the fact that every time she was near him, she wanted to throw herself into his arms. She shuddered deliciously. What would it feel like, she wondered? What would it taste like? She licked her lips. This afternoon she could barely restrain herself. Even now all she could think of was how it would be to have his arms around her, his body touching her own.

She had some experience with men. Well, they were really just boys, she decided, the sons of planters, very careful to observe the proprieties. And to be honest, her experience with them didn't extend to more than holding hands. Oh, once Charles Langdon put his arm around her, and once she had kissed Brian Douglas, but Morgan hadn't been impressed with the results of these experiments. And none of those boys made her feel the way Daniel Harris did. She considered the comparison for a moment. Daniel was certainly different physically from the others, taller, bigger, his form defined by hard muscle. He radiated strength and decision, which for some strange reason made her body feel heavy and weak.

And there was more to Daniel Harris than just her feelings. She was curious as to why one minute he seemed attracted to her and then the next acted as if he didn't like her at all. Did he worry he might compromise her if he was to become too familiar or allow her liberties? Or was he afraid of becoming entangled? She frowned as she pondered.

"I don't like what you're thinking," Hana grumbled, breaking into her thoughts.

"You don't know what I'm thinking."

"Oh, yes I do. And even if I didn't, just the look on your face is enough to scare my hair white. You're gonna make trouble."

Morgan laughed. "I don't see what trouble I can get into now. We'll be in Port Royal in the morning. And because of the rain, you and I are stuck in this cabin for the rest of the night. What do you imagine I can do here?"

"I don't know. But I know you, and I can tell when you're up to something."

Morgan got to her feet and started undressing. "The only thing I'm going to get into is bed," she said. "Would you help me with these hooks? Please?"

Hana helped Morgan out of her dress and petticoats and then started brushing her hair. "I watched you this afternoon, flirting with that pirate captain. I don't know what you were saying, but I know when you're asking for trouble, and I know trouble when I see it." She put the brush aside. "And that he is. Trouble." She started braiding, but Morgan took it away.

"I'll do that," she said, wishing Hana wasn't so concerned with her welfare. She pulled the heavy red hair over her shoulders so she could reach it, remembering how Daniel had lifted the lock of it, so gently. Morgan buried her face in her hair, imagining she could catch a whiff of sea air along with the sandalwood and camphor Hana packed in her trunks to keep her clothes safe from moths and mildew.

After winding her long hair into a thick braid, Morgan crawled into the bunk, curling up on her side, trying to fall asleep. Hana busied herself putting clothes away and tidying the cabin before she blew out the lamp and sought her own bed.

Morgan lay in the dark listening to the creak of the ship, feeling it rock more slowly, more gently as the squall blew itself out. The sound of rain grew dim and faded away. She decided Daniel Harris wasn't going to be easily or soon banished from her mind. She turned over and looked up at the sky through the thick glass. With the storm over, the moon shone behind a scattering of clouds, painting their edges with silver light.

Morgan told herself she was too warm to sleep. She knelt on the bunk and worked the latch that held the casement shut. It swung open with a muted groan letting a cool breeze into the cabin. The breeze also brought the sound of voices. As she listened, Morgan realized she was hearing the helmsman speaking almost directly above her head.

"Looks like it'll be calm for the rest of the night," came down to her. She didn't recognize this speaker, but the next voice made her heart stutter.

"Dennis will relieve you at midnight. Tell him I'll be up just before dawn," Daniel said.

"Aye, captain," the helmsman replied.

Then there was nothing but the slap of the waves against the stern, until Morgan's quick ears caught the sound of a footstep in the passageway outside the cabin door. She froze for a second until she heard another door close. She hadn't thought about it, but she supposed there were other cabins, and that's where Daniel Harris would be sleeping.

Morgan knelt in the darkness as an idea so audacious, so frightening came to her. Did she dare? Her mind darted over the possibilities. She took a deep breath, determined to try. All he could say was no. She swung her legs over the edge of the bunk and tiptoed slowly across the floor. Lifting the latch, she slipped outside and carefully closed the door behind her, making certain it didn't lock her out. She would need to get back in if her plan didn't work. Morgan caught her lower lip between her teeth. It won't do to think that way, she told herself firmly. Of course it will work. There's no reason to think otherwise.

The passage was dark, the only illumination from faint stars through the hatch left open to the night sky. As Morgan's eyes adjusted she could see the faint outline of two doors, side by side, across from her. After a moment's hesitation, she tried one of them. It was locked. She let go of the latch and her held breath with a feeling she realized was relief. She looked at the other door. What if …?

No! Stop that, she told herself. She reached for the other latch and eased that door open. As she stepped forward, the door swung closed behind her, leaving her in complete darkness. Suddenly strong arms grabbed her from behind... and as quickly let her go.

"Morgan?" Daniel whispered in the darkness. "What in hell's name are you doing here?"

She swallowed. "I'm looking for you."

"Why? Is something wrong?"

"No, I ..." Even though she couldn't see, she could smell the warm musky scent of him.

He drew a deep breath as his hand found her bare arm. The girl was in nothing but her shift, he realized with dismay. "I think you'd better go back to your cabin," he told her.

"No." She stepped into him, so close she could feel the heat of his body through her chemise.

"What do you want here," he asked, his breath warm against her face.

"I want to talk to you. There's something I have to tell you." Morgan put her hands up and found his chest. It was bare, the hard muscles covered by a sprinkling of delightfully soft hair. Unconsciously she moved even closer to him, her hands sliding up to trace his shoulders. He drew back, willing his rebellious body under tight control, but as she raised her face to him and he felt her warm breath he gave a low groan.

Defeated, Daniel's arms went around her, crushing her against him as his mouth came down, his lips opening hers, not at all gently. She went limp, her body pliant, molding to his as she responding to these completely new sensations. She felt drunk with wanting him and whatever he chose to do.

Morgan spread her hands against his back, pulling herself even closer, feeling the muscles move and contract as he breathed. Lightly she ran her fingers along the little knobs of his spine and down to his slender waist, down to the tight muscles of his buttocks.

Good heavens! He was completely nude. As she pressed herself against him, she could feel his erection against her belly. She had seen animals mating, but this was her first experience with a human male and she was curious. His male parts seemed rather larger than she thought they would be, and she wanted to touch them.

Daniel moaned, his mouth against hers, his eyes closed

as he fought to regain control. He wrenched back, holding her away from him. He had his limits and she strained them badly. He didn't know if she did it on purpose or in innocence. Either way, it didn't matter. He was within inches of breaking. This was too much!

"Do you see now?" he demanded, his voice harsh with passion. "Do you see how you can rouse a man? This is no game for you to play with me. It's not safe."

"Don't. Please..." she murmured, swaying toward him, her eyes closed as she tried to hold onto the delicious feeling of his body against hers. "I want ..."

"You have no idea what you want," he growled, his chest rising and falling as he tried to control his breathing. "Go back to your cabin," he ordered harshly.

"But you haven't heard why I came."

"Whatever it is can wait until morning when we're in better control of ourselves."

"Daniel... No." She cast herself back into his arms and they folded around her once again.

"You don't know what you are asking," he said, his mouth against her cheek. He kissed her eyelids slowly, then allowed his lips to glide across her eyebrow. "What is it that brought you here?"

"I need your help. I have an idea." But she was hesitant to divulge it, to break the wonderful spell. Oh, but he felt so good!

Daniel abruptly released Morgan and moved away. She heard the rustle of cloth as he regained his seaman's loose trousers. Then there came a scratch, and a light spread from the lamp suspended from the ceiling. Daniel lowered the chimney over flame before turning to a chest on the deck against the bulkhead. Rummaging inside he found a long wool cape the served as an outer garment to his dress clothes. He flipped it around Morgan, wrapping her in the heavy folds.

"Now, what is this idea?" he asked stepping back from her. He kept his voice calm although he was still breathing much too fast. Blood raced through his veins, pooling some-place most inappropriate under the circumstances. God preserve him from passionate virgins, he thought!

Morgan clasped the cloak around her, breathing in his scent. "I don't want to go to England. My home is here in the Indies."

Daniel shook his head. "I know England is different from the islands, but you'll find a home there."

Morgan shook her head vehemently. "Everyone keeps telling me that, but I know I won't! You just don't understand."

"But I do," Daniel responded. "You're afraid of such a major change in your life. It's perfectly natural to feel that way."

"Why? Why do I have to go?" she demanded, her voice rising.

"Hush," he warned. "You don't want anyone to know you're here."

"I don't care who knows I am here!" Morgan exclaimed.

Daniel's chin went up and his lips thinned. "If you don't care about your reputation, I do. I'm not about to compromise a virgin of your standing."

"How do you know I'm a virgin?"

"Because I knew your parents, remember? They were good people, and I know they raised you to be a lady."

"Lady be damned," Morgan spat. "Why won't you help me?"

"Short of marrying you, I don't see what I can do," Daniel admitted.

"But that's exactly what I had in mind. You don't have to ..."

"No," he interrupted firmly. "No! That's the worst possible solution to your problem. And it isn't even a problem!" Daniel glared down at the beautiful oval face surrounded by her long red hair. He wanted to reach out and touch it, but reminded himself that to do so would be to invite trouble. "What would you have me do, lass?" he complained. "You're not the sort of woman I'm used to. You're no woman for me."

"Why not? Are you already married?" she asked with perfect candor.

Daniel grinned and shook his head. "Nay, lass. Not to a woman if that's what you mean. But you might say that I'm wed to the sea, and to my ship."

"That's what every seaman says," Morgan argued. "And cold comfort it must be."

"Nonetheless, it's true. Don't play with me, lass. I like you very well. And I'll always remember you. And my friend, your father. But there's nothing to be gained by starting something that will make both of us unhappy. We'll be in Port Royal tomorrow. Then you'll be off with your cousin to a new life. And that's the last you'll think of this old seadog. And the Indies."

"Do you really think that?" Morgan was stung by his accusation. "I don't know what waits for me in England, but from what I have been told, I don't think it's anything I'll like very much." She looked back up at Daniel. "I was born on these islands. I had hoped to marry and spend my whole life here."

Daniel held himself in check. These were dangerous waters and he had to be very careful. "Why haven't you married then?" he asked. "You're of age."

"I never met anyone I could stand living with," she admitted. "My parents taught me to think and be active. The men I met all tried to treat me as if I was a porcelain doll, something that would break if it moved, and worse, something incapable of intelligent thought or speech."

"Why do you think I would be any different from these men?"

"Because you would be," she replied with a complete lack of logic. "And you do want me. I know you do."

"Whether I want you or not isn't the issue."

"But you do," she insisted.

"No," Daniel lied. "I would bed you, sure. Any man would. But that's all it would be."

"Don't you care about me?"

"You're my old friend's daughter. Certainly I care about you. But that's all it is. And I'll not betray his memory by bedding his only daughter."

"So you won't help me?" she asked, her voice small against his iron will.

"I can't help you, lass. Not the way you want. No."

Morgan shook her head and turned her face away from

him, tears pricking behind her eyelids.

"When you reach England, you will be part of a larger society," Daniel continued. "Surely you'll meet someone who will see you as a person and not as a doll."

"Perhaps." She whispered, but she wasn't listening to him anymore. One thought had hold of her, the thought that he wouldn't help her, that he didn't want her. She swallowed and fought to hold her tears back.

"I'm sorry for this intrusion," she managed, only the tiniest quaver in her voice. "Thank you for being so frank with me." She forced a sad smile. "But you have made a mistake."

"Oh?"

"Yes. Because I will remember you when I am in England. I will remember you and my islands. Forever."

She turned and reached for the door latch, moving quickly, determined not to show how abandoned she felt. How lost and how terribly alone.

Chapter 10

Morgan woke in a pool of sunlight streaming through the stern windows. She lay curled in the bunk, covered by Daniel's cloak, her fists wrapped in the cloth. She buried her face in the soft wool and closed her eyes, trying to return to the oblivion of sleep. Then the memory of the night before came flooding back to her. She felt a warm flush as she recalled the strength of Daniel's arms around her, and his lips soft against hers. It took her breath away.

She stretched her body and rolled over onto her back, aching for him to touch her again. But then the wonderful feelings faded as she remembered how Daniel had made it very clear he didn't want her. How could she have been so foolish as to imagine he would help her?

Resentment coiled inside of her. She offered him everything and yet it would seem it was not sufficient payment, not even for a favor to an old friend's daughter. She wondered what it would take to bring this haughty captain over to her side. Did he want gold? Perhaps that was it, she thought. Maybe she should have tried to impress him with her wealth. But then she realized, as her father's close friend he probably had a good idea what she was worth. Could it be he didn't find her attractive? Well he certainly didn't act as if he found her repulsive. Morgan sighed. It was so confusing. All she knew for certain was that she still faced the necessity of going to England with her cousin. No, she decided, curling her fingers into tight, determined little fists, she wouldn't give up. She would find another way out of her dilemma. She just needed time.

Morgan turned onto her side and peered out from under her lowered lashes. Hana sat at the table working on a piece of mending. Her nurse's face was as serene as ever, and Morgan fervently hoped she was unaware of her truancy last night.

Morgan gave a huge yawn and sat up. "Good morning, Hana," she said sweetly.

"Good morning yourself," the maid replied with some asperity. She was staring rather pointedly at the cloak.

Morgan looked down at the material as if she had never seen it before. How was she going to explain? "The cloak?" she began. "You're looking at this cloak?"

"Where'd it come from is what I'd like to know."

"I found it."

"Found it? Where'd you find something like that?"

"It w-a-s ..." Morgan thought fast. "In the cabinet. Over there." She waved her hand toward the bulkhead.

"That's a gentleman's cloak," Hana insisted, not fully

satisfied. She didn't believe Morgan but she also didn't want to think of an alternative explanation.

"I know." Morgan lifted the cloak and put it away from her, as if it accused her by its very presence.

"So how'd it get there, I want to know?"

"I don't know how it got into the cabinet," Morgan told her, regaining her presence of mind. "Quite probably it belongs to Captain Harris. All I know for sure is that I was cold last night, and I remembered it was there and went and got it."

"Huh." Hana eyed her charge askance but let the matter drop.

There was a shout from the deck and the sound of the loud footsteps overhead.

Hana's head turned to the casement and sniffed. "The Lord be praised! I can smell land," she commented. "We must be comin' into port. Now we can get off this pirate ship."

She looked at Morgan who was lost in her own thoughts. "You'd better get dressed, missy. You can't go anywhere in your shift."

Morgan got to her feet and quickly washed her face and hands. Hana searched through the boxes, looking for something suitable for Morgan to wear to meet her cousin.

"I wonder what he's like," Morgan said as she seated herself before the table, her head back so Hana could work on her hair.

"I don't know, but you'd better mind your manners around him. He's a proper English gentleman. Not what you're used to."

"My father was a proper English gentleman," Morgan insisted.

"Your daddy, God rest his soul, was a gentleman of a different sort." Hana frowned at the tangled locks. "Your hair's a mess, missy. I thought you braided it."

"What do you mean father was 'a different sort?'"

"Huh." Hana attacked a particularly bad snarl with the comb. "Your daddy was a gentleman, that's for sure, but that means something else in the Indies."

Morgan scowled at her maid's reflection in the hand mirror she picked up. "Different? You mean he won his own land and fortune."

Hana concentrated all of her attention on another knot in the silky red hair.

"That is what you mean, isn't it," the girl insisted.

Hana looked up with a scowl. "You sure are making a mighty lot of fuss about this. How come you all of a sudden so worried about whether your daddy's a gentleman?"

"I'm not worried about it. I know he was a gentleman. You're the one who said there was a difference!"

"Huh." Hana stroked the glossy hair finally free of snarls. She was saved from answering by the sound of knocking at the cabin door. Hana jerked to attention and looked quickly around. "Here," she said getting to her feet and handing Morgan the discarded cloak. "Put this around you."

Morgan, once again wrapped in the soft wool, watched as the maid crossed the cabin to stand behind the locked door.

"Who's there," she demanded. "What do you want?"

"Captain Harris."

Hana looked at her charge, indecision plain on her face.

"Let him in, Hana."

She turned to Morgan, a protest on her lips.

"If you don't, I will," Morgan warned forestalling an argument.

Hana scowled and unlatched the door, opening it a crack to see if it really was the captain.

He pushed the door open the rest of the way and strode in, instantly filling the space with his presence. Morgan glared at him, even though she suddenly found it hard to breathe. She clutched the cloak with both hands, armor against the feelings that raged through her. Her legs shook and something she couldn't name coiled in her belly. But one thing she couldn't hide was the telltale flush that brightened her cheeks.

Daniel was formally dressed this morning, in dazzling white stockings below breeches of dark blue. Over it all he wore a long coat of golden brown. It was an elegant outfit, quite different from what he usually wore at sea.

Daniel sketched a bow. "Good morning, Mistress Moorhouse. I trust your night was ... serene?" he asked with a straight face.

She cleared her throat, not sure how to answer him, until he raised a mocking eyebrow. She wanted nothing more than to slap his face. Instead she lifted her chin, her eyes narrowed to angry slits.

"Well enough. Thank you for asking," she told him, her bearing as formal as she could make it under the circumstances. She pulled the cloak more tightly around her, wishing there had been time to dress. In the dim light her brown eyes were dark pools where golden flecks shone like sparks of fire. "What brings you here?" she demanded. "It's much too early for a social call. I haven't had time to finish dressing."

He bowed again and, removing a heavy leather bag from the pocket of his coat placed it on the table. It was lumpy and clinked when it hit the wood. "This is only half of what I owe you," he said. "The *Bright Folly* takes most of my prize money now that I'm the only one paying for her. But I'll make arrangements to have the balance sent to you in England."

Morgan looked at the bag, her mind suddenly awhirl with possibilities. "But what if I wanted to remain part owner of the ship?" she asked. "Leaving you in complete control, of course," she added quickly.

He frowned. "I don't think that's a very good idea."

"Why not?"

"Have you thought what your cousin would have to say? And once you're in England you will marry. Then your husband will become owner of all your property. Unless he is an exceptional individual, he'll want some control of the use I make of the *Bright Folly*." Daniel shook his head. "I can't imagine such an arrangement working with anyone except your father."

"We could keep our arrangement a secret," she suggested.

"No. That's not possible. I think 'tis best I buy your father's share back from you. At least this way you will have some money of your own." He paused. "You may need it."

This was the second time that Daniel made this suggestion, but Morgan was too preoccupied with her own problems to think anything of it.

He bowed again. "Ladies," he said, and turning on his heel, was gone.

When the door closed, she reached for the leather sack, dragging it cross the table toward her. It was tightly filled and very heavy. As she untied the top, a thick gold coin rolled out.

Hana watched as more coins followed, gleaming in the lamplight.

"They're doubloons," Morgan said with awe. "New minted, Spanish doubloons."

"He said it was prize money," Hana added. "This here's pirate loot. Tainted money. Huh!"

Morgan grinned. "There were plenty of these coins at home, if I remember. My father wasn't above taking advantage of careless Spanish seamen. And neither will I."

She began counting, stacking the coins on the table in front of her. There were twenty stacks of five coins each, exactly one hundred, the amount Daniel told her the day before. But these were doubloons, not English guineas. Their weight was greater, and she estimated their value at half again the figure he named.

"We have to hide these," Morgan told her maid, looking around at her trunks. "We'll put some of them in with my clothes and sew some into each of our petticoats. That should be safe enough."

"Just hope we don't fall overboard," Hana snorted. But she still reached for her needle and thread.

Chapter 11

Morgan came up on deck with Hana protectively at her heels. She watched curiously as Port Royal came into sight. The city sat at the end of the Palisadoes spit at the mouth of Kingston Harbor, its red brick buildings bright in the sun. She had never seen a city this big. In the New World, only Boston was larger. Port Royal covered 50 acres, a home for more than six thousand people of all professions including the pirates and prostitutes. Her namesake, Sir Henry Morgan, who died three years before her father, was even buried here. The spire of Christ's Church rose above the buildings providing a note of sobriety to a place called "the most wicked and sinful city in the world." Port Royal hosted as many if not more gambling and drinking dens and brothels as places of worship. Still, all faiths were welcome and the town hosted a diverse religious population including Roman Catholics,

Presbyterians, Baptists, Quakers, and Jews.

If the value of the city could be measured in how well it was protected, Port Royal was rich indeed. No less than six forts guarded Kingston Harbor. The *Kestrel* had already passed three of them while in the narrow sea-channel. Around the point of Port Royal, they would come up against with Forts Walker and James, and inside the harbor itself the guns of Fort Carlisle stood guard. The harbor was immense stretching ten miles long and two miles wide. Across the water rose the fabled Blue Mountains of Jamaica, their sides a green tangle of jungle.

Brilliant sunlight bathed the air, fresh with a breeze blowing inland from the sea. The same wind sent the *Kestrel* westward to the island. One of the crew hung over the bow keeping watch for coral, but he was just insurance; the passage here was well known to the helmsman.

Through the passage, the enormous harbor was alive with all kinds of craft from large ocean going vessels to small ships owned by local traders and fishermen. Several stout merchantmen were moored at the wharf for unloading, the busy workmen a mixture of natives, blacks, and Europeans.

She watched the men work for a moment until a shout drew her attention to a three-master where carpenters were stepping a new mainmast. Perhaps this was her cousin's ship. Governor Ramsey had said it suffered damage during the ocean crossing. If so, it was the ship that would take her back to England. Morgan looked at it closely, not liking it at all. The name *Jordan's Bounty* embellished the stern in black and gilt letters.

As the *Kestrel* neared her berth, a command from the captain sent the crew into action, taking in the last of the sails. Swiftly and with no wasted motion the canvas was secured and, as the wind no longer had anything to work against, the ship slowed. The brigantine swung her stern in at a touch of the helmsman's hand and slid neatly alongside the brick and stone wharf. Half a dozen crew members jumped ashore with lines and quickly had her fast. It was a sharp maneuver and Morgan had to be impressed, especially if this was indeed a vagabond crew of mercenary seaman as Daniel had said.

"Port Royal." Daniel's voice was solemn as he gazed at the town before them, the slopes steep in the background.

Morgan hadn't heard him come up behind her. She resisted the urge to turn around, peeved at what had passed between them the night before. Still, she could feel the warmth of his body, and had an urge to lean back and let his strength support her. But it couldn't be. He made that perfectly plain the night before. Frustrated, she took a deep breath and let it out slowly.

"There aren't many inns in town suitable for gentry," he continued. "I would guess your cousin is staying at the governor's house. Perhaps you and your maid should wait here while I send someone to fetch a carriage for you."

"Why can't we use that one," Morgan asked pointing at the vehicle standing in the shade of a warehouse. It was a short wagon drawn by a pair of Moorish ponies. The driver leaned against the wheel, watching traffic pass along the wharf while his ponies dozed, hind hooves cocked, tails flicking flies.

"I'll see."

Captain Harris stepped onto the rail and leapt lightly to the wharf. He picked his way between stacks of freight and around fishermen's nets stretched to dry in the sun. The driver got to his feet as the captain approached. They spoke for a moment, but there was so much going on between them that Morgan couldn't hear what was said. At first the driver shook his head no, but then Daniel waved in their direction. The man peered toward the ship, and, at Daniel's further urging, and possibly swayed by the glint of a coin in his hand, finally nodded yes. Daniel left him and headed back to the ship.

"What did he say?" Morgan demanded as he swung over the rail.

"He's waiting for a shipment of wine that's supposed to be unloaded this morning. But as that hasn't happened yet, I convinced him to take you to the governor's house. It's not far."

"Is my cousin there?"

"Yes. He probably doesn't expect you so soon, but that's just as well. They're still working on his ship, although," Daniel glanced over at the *Bounty*, "it looks as if they're well along. I'd say they'll be finished tomorrow at the latest."

Morgan didn't care if the ship was ever repaired. "If we could have some help with my trunks?"

"I'll have someone see to them."

She nodded, staring at the town, not looking at him. How could he act as if nothing had happened between them last night? She sighed. "Then I'll say goodbye," she said finally. "Thank you for bringing us here." She turned her head and peered up at him. He was looking down at her, but she couldn't decide what he was thinking. He looked, if anything, sad. But how could that be? He had refused her. What cause did he have for regret?

"God speed you on your journey," he said quietly. "And I hope England provides a far better future than you anticipate. It's a land of many beauties, and I think you'll be surprised at what you find there."

"Thank you," Morgan repeated, her voice small and defeated.

Daniel stood beside her a moment more, and then turned to instruct a seaman to fetch her luggage. "With your permission," he said as he gathered Morgan in his arms. She gave a gasp of surprise and then relaxed against him, her eyes closed. But all he did was lift her as he climbed over the rail again. He set her on her feet and looked back at Hana.

"Oh, no, you don't!" the maid exclaimed in horror. "I'll walk off this ship all by myself!"

Juan heard her. He opened the railing and shoved a strong plank out to span the gap between ship and wharf. He offered Hana his hand, but she ignored him, lifting her skirts and stepping daintily across. Juan grinned and followed after her.

"Juan," Daniel said. "Please escort Mistress Moorhouse to the governor's mansion."

"Certainly," Juan agreed. "And when the governor asks for you?"

"Tell him I'm busy."

Morgan was curious. She looked at Daniel, a question in her eyes.

He jerked his chin to where a handsome brig was moored out in the harbor. No other vessels were near her, and a sailor with a musket was visible on deck. A guard, Morgan decided. But why? Then she understood.

"Your prize ship?" she asked.

"Yes."

She studied it, noting battle scars. The foremast was jury-rigged, and some of lines hung, sadly tangled, over the side. "Congratulations," she said, just a little sarcasm showing in her voice. She wanted to hurt him, but in her despair, couldn't find the energy.

"Thank you." Daniel gazed at her a moment more, than drew in a deep breath. "Once again," he said softly, "God speed." With that he turned and went back on board the *Kestrel*.

"*Senorita*," Juan said with a bow and a flourish. He guided them to the wagon where seamen were already helping the driver stack Morgan's trunks.

Morgan clambered onto the wagon and looked back one last time, memorizing the sight of the *Kestrel*, her black spars raking the sky. She could see Daniel directing his crew. She watched the ship until the vehicle rounded a corner and she could see it no more.

Cousin Oliver sat sweating in the governor's mansion. He felt as if he was suffocating in the heat, despite the floor to ceiling windows, shutters flung wide, inviting every stray breeze. A slave stood behind him, waving a huge fan, and on a table beside him stood a glass of native rum, its harshness diluted by the addition of freshly squeezed fruit juice, but none of this made him happy. His pale face was marred by a scowl and his gray eyes were narrowed with anger.

Once a handsome man, years and dissipation had left their mark, good food and drink bloating his body. He slouched, his head seeming to grow out of his shoulders, his stomach resting on fat thighs. His clothing was of good quality, but cut in a style that had been in fashion several years before. He'd discarded his wig in deference to the heat, and his cropped head was covered by a thin cotton turban.

"So," he said to the servant who stood before him. "My little cousin has finally arrived?"

"Yes, sir," the man intoned. He was lean and tall, an ascetic in appearance as well as mind. Jonny Samuels had served his master since they were both young men in the army. Although Oliver had willingly returned to a more luxurious life style, Samuels continued to cling to the beliefs of his hero, the other Oliver, Cromwell. "She arrived minutes ago and awaits your pleasure."

Oliver grunted. "Well, send her in. And then go find out when that damned ship will be ready so we can get out of this accursed hell hole."

"As you wish." Samuels nodded his head in an almost bow and hastened to do his bidding.

Even Hana was subdued as she followed Morgan and the stern-faced manservant. She started having feelings of foreboding as soon as they entered the governor's house. Something was about to happen and Hana didn't like it. She touched the charm hanging on a cord around her neck, hidden inside her dress, and muttered a prayer under her breath. She silently invoked the goddess *Lala Dahomida*, asking for protection for both herself and her mistress. Hana stayed very close to Morgan as they entered the shadowed room.

"Well," Oliver said in a pleasant voice, much different from the one he used earlier. "You are my cousin, Robert's daughter! Forgive me if I don't get up, but the crossing was very hard on me."

"Pray, remain seated," Morgan said politely. "I'm sorry if you have been unwell."

"Yes. Thank you." He gave a thin smile as he realized she was a beauty. That would certainly please his son, Giles. "The governor has very kindly placed his house at our disposal, but I hope we will be able to leave Port Royal for England before the week ends."

Morgan was startled at the swiftness of it. "But I thought you intended to visit the plantation first."

Oliver waved his hand in dismissal. "I have already sent an overseer to take the plantation in charge. There's no reason to delay our departure."

"I see," Morgan said.

"They promised me repairs to the ship could be swiftly completed. I've been away too long already," he told her. "And the voyage means another four weeks."

Morgan didn't know what to think of her cousin. She'd been prepared to dislike him, but instead she had a feeling of revulsion so strong it frightened her.

"Rooms await you," Oliver said. "I will see if someone in the house can wait on you until we leave. You'll have to attend to yourself during the voyage, I'm afraid."

"What do you mean?" Morgan asked. "Hana will take care of me. She always has."

"No. That won't be possible" Oliver shook his head. "And as it's too much trouble to ship her back to the plantation, I'll make arrangement to have her sold before we leave."

Morgan felt Hana stiffen beside her, and laid a hand on her arm.

"Hana is a free woman," she said firmly. "She cannot be sold."

Oliver looked at first surprised, then displeased at the news. "Nevertheless she cannot come to England," he insisted.

"And why not?"

Oliver's lips narrowed at Morgan's impertinence, but he controlled his temper. "Africans do not do well in the English climate. It is much too cold for them there." But Morgan still looked stubborn. "You will have to be reasonable about this," he continued. "And please understand, I am not accustomed to having my wishes thwarted. Also I am far better qualified than you to make this decision. You will dismiss your maid immediately."

Morgan wanted nothing more than to dismiss herself as well. She decided it would be best to appear to comply. "Very well. But please, may she continue to attend me until we sail?"

"Partings are easier if they are swiftly made," Oliver said. He looked at Hana. I will speak to the governor's steward on your behalf. Perhaps there is a place for you in his

91

household."

"Don't trouble yourself," Hana told him. "I have friends in Port Royal. I have a place to go." She turned to face the young woman who had been her charge from the time she was born. "Missy, you take care of yourself. You hear?"

"Yes." Morgan felt as if she was being wrenched in two. How could this be happening! First her home, and now Hana?

"You need anything, you find old Hana. I'll be staying here in Port Royal. You remember that."

"Yes. But, Hana ..."

"I'm goin' to find your things now so I can change my petticoat before I go," she said pointedly. "I'm wearing one of yours, remember?"

Petticoat! Morgan remembered the coins that were sewn into the hem. There had to be at least thirty guineas, enough to give Hana security. "No" she said quickly. "You can keep it. Cousin Oliver is right. Swift partings are best."

"But what about... "

"Please," Morgan interrupted. "Just go."

"You sure?"

"Yes. I'm sure."

Blinking rapidly, the maid turned to leave.

"Hana. Who are these people, the ones who will help you? In case I have to find you?"

"I have a good friend, Maximillian DePaul. He has a shop here," Hana told her. "He's a trader. You've seen him."

"I think so. He used to bring goods out to the plantation ..."

"Mistress Moorhouse doesn't need to be bothered with

all these details," Oliver interrupted peevishly. He realized the women were communicating something more, and it angered him, making him even more spiteful. "I'm sure you have been a good and faithful servant," he told Hana with a sneer. "But the time has come to sever the ties with your mistress. You should leave now."

"You'll have to pay her,' Morgan pointed out. " She gets a salary and I don't have enough money with me."

"My man servant will take care of it." He raised an imperious finger and brought Samuels to him. "Pay this woman off and see her to the street," he directed.

"Oh, Hana …" Morgan began, but her maid thinned her lips and shook her head.

"Lala Dahomida and the Blessed Virgin Mother guard you," she whispered.

Morgan threw her arms around Hana's neck and hugged her as tears filled her eyes and threatened to spill down her cheeks.

"Now don' go doing that," Hana said, removing Morgan's arms. She held the girl's hands tightly as she looked over at Oliver, her black face stern. "You take good care of her."

She released Morgan and, closely followed by Samuels, left the parlor. Her head held high, she strode out of the house, through the gates, and into the sun warmed street. She stopped there and stood a moment, looking down at the pitiful few pennies Samuels considered suitable wages for a lifetime of service. Then she turned her hand over and dropped the coins in the dust before striding away.

"If I didn't know better, I'd think that was a threat," Oliver observed when Hana had gone. "I don't see how you put up with such a servant. You're better off without her."

Morgan could barely contain her tears and didn't reply.

Daniel walked to the *Kestrel's* rail and watched the wagon as it drove out of sight. The act of watching was supposed to put a period to the part of his life touched by Morgan Moorhouse, but after she was gone he found himself thinking about her. He wondered what would have happened if he'd given in to her demands last night. He vividly recalled the feel of her in his arms, the silky velvet of her skin, the intoxicating scent of her hair, the softness of her lips under his mouth. She was obviously inexperienced at love, but a naturally passionate nature made up for it. He had wanted her very much, and only the most rigid self control prevented him from taking advantage of what she offered in such innocence.

That chance had passed. It was too late now to have regrets or to let the memory cloud his future. But oh, she had been so sweet in his arms!

There was a hail from the other side of the ship and Daniel turned away from the rail. Little Billy, his first mate, was climbing on board from a longboat bumping against the *Kestrel's* side. "Little" was a misnomer, for William Curran stood six feet five in his stocking feet. Today more than usual he was a startling sight, for he had dressed for this occasion in his best, a vivid scarlet brocade coat he had taken from some unfortunate Spaniard, worn over black jackboots that came up to his thighs and a dazzling white shirt with tiers of the finest Holland lace cascading down his front. This gorgeous dress was further embellished by a heavy gold chain that spanned his broad chest, gold hoop earrings and, Billy's pride, the long black mustaches that matched his thick curly black hair. Just in case Billy's size wasn't enough to intimidate troublemakers, a wide black leather belt encircled his waist supporting a cutlass, a dagger and a brace of pistols.

Little Billy had been in charge of the prize ship as it sailed home from Puerto Rico. The rest of the day, he and Daniel would oversee the division of spoils. Word had already spread that Captain Harris had brought in a rich prize, and buyers were waiting to bid on the merchandise.

Daniel greeted his old friend and mate, and prepared to descend to the longboat with him. Before he dropped out of sight, however, he looked back one last time to the road leading away from wharf. By now even the dust had settled. Morgan was gone.

The captain was away from the *Kestrel*, inspecting the prize ship and getting ready to bring her into the wharf when Juan returned from the governor's house. He brought a letter that had come all the way from England. The letter told how Daniel's older brother had died suddenly, leaving neither wife nor child. It was addressed to The Right Honorable Daniel Harris Thomas Rivington, the only surviving heir to the estate of the Baron of Rivington.

The letter was placed on the desk in the captain's cabin, but Daniel didn't return there until late the next day. The new baron spent the night drinking with his crew, trying to escape from the memory of gold flecked brown eyes and the warm scent of blazing red hair. Rum didn't dim the memory, but it did provide oblivion of a sort. Daniel slept that night under the table at an inn called the Devil's Trident.

Chapter 12

February 1692, London, England.

Morgan shivered, hugging the soft wool shawl tighter around her shoulders as she looked out the window at a gray sky and a seemingly endless cold drizzle. In the little park across from the townhouse, ice-covered hedges and tree branches swayed and broke under the assault of more rain and sleet.

So this was London, she thought with a sigh as she remembered the riot of tropical flowers in the garden surrounding the house on Cayman Brac. Flowers bloomed there even in the winter, shining in the sunlight and tossed by fresh breezes blowing in from the ocean. As she suspected, England was very different from her home. For one thing she couldn't seem to get warm. She couldn't imagine how anyone could live in such horribly cold damp weather.

Morgan glanced over at her cousin's wife, Amalia, dozing on a chaise by the fire, scarves and lap robes draped over her recumbent form and trailing onto the floor. She was a small woman with fine graceful bones. Rather than coarsening her features, age had gifted her face with additional refinement and skin that always looked as if it had a dusting of fine powder blurring any wrinkle or flaw.

Amalia liked to think of herself as frail, possibly as a defense against the men who inhabited her world. Her husband was an especially large, noisy creature who tracked mud and worse into her drawing room, and when he was drunk made incredible demands on her person. After the birth of her son, however, Amalia put a stop to this last indignity by developing a series of mysterious infirmities of a female nature. She even found a doctor sympathetic enough to reinforce her hypochondria, treating her with innocuous philters and potions.

Oliver was not at all dismayed when he found himself banned from her bedroom. His wife had done her duty by giving him a son, and so he could be finished with her. Besides, the idea of remaining faithful to one woman was completely alien to his hedonistic character. He sought his sexual pleasure anywhere he happened to be, not caring if his partner was a countess, a milkmaid or a comely stable boy.

Of the members of her cousin's family, Morgan found Amalia the easiest to deal with. Oliver still frightened her although she couldn't explain why. She was relieved when he left her in his wife's care, although she noted he made sure to oversee all their activities. He arranged it so she was never alone outside of the house. She couldn't even go for a walk in the garden unless she was accompanied by one of the maids. When she went into town, both a maid and Samuels went along.

She sighed. There was so much to remember, so many restrictions to being an English lady. And the clothes … she looked down at the brocade afternoon gown that she wore over three petticoats. Lace poured like a snowy froth from her sleeves and fell in graceful folds at her throat. Soon it would be time to change for dinner. Since they would be going to Lady Ashford's drum later that evening, she would have to choose a dress suitable for both occasions.

"What is the time?" Amalia asked suddenly in her thin tired voice.

Morgan looked at the timepiece on the cabinet beside the window. "A bit after five." She set the book she had been reading aside and rose to her feet. "I think I'll go to my room and dress for dinner. Can I do anything for you before I go?"

"No, dear. How kind of you to trouble yourself with me. Just ring for Jane."

Morgan dutiful pulled the bell cord. Within minutes the sour-faced maid, a fitting wife for dour Samuels, arrived to tend her mistress. Morgan escaped to her room.

Bridy, the little Irish maid who had been hired to attend her, was laying out the gown she would wear to the drum. She helped Morgan undress and shook out the brocade day gown before putting it away in the clothes press. Morgan washed her face and hands in the basin on the wash stand in the corner and shivered.

"You don't have to wait up for me again tonight," she told Bridy. "I don't know how late we're going to be, and I'm used to putting myself to bed."

"It's no trouble for sure, miss. And Mr. Samuels would have me hide if I don't wait up."

"You're my maid," Morgan told her. "Samuels has nothing to say as long as I'm satisfied."

"Yes, miss." But Bridy didn't seem convinced.

"Has he been giving you trouble below stairs?" Morgan demanded.

"Oh, no, miss. He's a very righteous man Mr. Samuels is he." Her green eyes sparkled as she spoke, her freckled nose wrinkled. "The Grace of God is verra near and dear to him, and he's as good as a parson when it comes to quotin' the scriptures, if ye catch my drift, miss."

"Yes, I've heard some of Samuels' impromptu sermons," Morgan said dryly. She sat at her tiring table, looking in the mirror. The hairdresser, Monsieur Lescaux, had come earlier in the day and dressed her hair in a new style called *en serpenteaux*. He had pulled the heavy masses back and secured them in a bun at the nape of her neck, leaving five or six long strands free on either side of her face. He had then wet the strands, coated them with a scented mixture that he claimed was his own very secret invention. Morgan didn't know what to think about it, but it seemed to work. Monsieur Lescaux curled the strands tightly against Morgan's head and let them dry. When they were unpinned they waved around her shoulders like glossy red snakes. Morgan touched the waves, not sure if she liked them or not.

"Ye look very pretty," Bridy offered. She stood back admiring the hairdresser's handwork, her head tilted to one side. "Still, it's a strange name for callin' a lady's hair if ye be askin' me," she added. "I mean, snakes, Lord love ye! Makes a body fairly shiver now it does and that's for sure."

Morgan laughed and searched in her jewelry box. "Have you seen my diamond earrings?" she asked.

"No miss. Not since Mr. Samuels himself came to take them to be fixed."

"To be fixed?" Morgan knew there wasn't anything wrong with the jewels. "When did this happen?"

"One, no maybe two weeks ago, I think. T'was the mornin' after ye wore them to the playhouse. I remember now. I finished brushin' off that grand golden dress ye wore and puttin' it away. That bein' done I went down to the kitchen to empty the slop bucket and t'fetch hot water, and he was up here himsel' when I came back. Said ye had most cartainly asked him to take the earrings for ye." Her brow wrinkled with concern. "I didn't do wrong, did I, miss?"

"No, you didn't do wrong," Morgan said soothingly. She wasn't going to admit it to her maid, but she knew she never made such a request. She would talk to Samuels about it later.

This wasn't the first time Morgan missed some pieces of her jewelry. At first she thought that Bridy might have taken them, but there was something too transparently honest about the young woman, and Morgan dismissed the suspicion. Now she knew she had been right in doing so. Obviously Samuels was behind the disappearances. Still, she couldn't imagine that such a staunch puritan would tempt the Lord's wrath by stealing. Right now it was nothing more than a nuisance, for the most valuable pieces were safe. Oliver had them locked away in his strong box.

She stood up and Bridy helped her into her gown. Unlike the old style, this skirt was not divided up the front, and consisted of no less than four rows of wide ruffles, terminating in a huge mass high in the back. The bodice was cut much lower than Morgan had ever worn before, displaying a great deal of cleavage behind a row of smaller ruffles. The dress was a deep bronze and set off Morgan's coloring admirably.

When the heavy skirts were settled over the petticoats and the back laced up, Morgan put on a pair of gold and pearl earrings. A matching broach decorated the lace and ribbon headdress that she wore. Then Bridy helped her wind a long strand of magnificent pearls twice around her neck where they shone like drops of some luminous liquid against her skin.

Bridy stood back, clapped her hands and beamed.

"Oh, miss," she intoned. "Ye be looking as beautiful as the blessed saints in heaven, ye are!"

Morgan smiled. "Thank you. Would you please have my cloak downstairs after dinner?"

"Certainly, miss."

Oliver insisted on ceremony. He had hired a large house in the best part of town for the season, since, as he said, his own townhouse was undergoing some renovations. This house had more sitting rooms and bedrooms than three people would possibly need. That evening Morgan sat down to dinner at a table big enough for a banquet. It was much too large for a quiet family supper.

In Morgan's opinion Oliver used money badly, keeping his estate outside of Bristol in very poor repair and then spending lavishly on housing the family in London. He even insisted on new, modish wardrobes for everyone, as well as new livery for the upper servants. He left the household staff, with the exception of a few personal servants, at the Bristol estate, hiring entirely new people in London. The expense of it all must have been tremendous. Morgan sometimes wondered if he might have come into a great deal of money recently.

Morgan sat straight and properly in her chair, toying with the portion on her plate. She knew it was some kind of meat, but it was smothered in a heavily spiced sauce and any flavor was disguised. She sipped from her wine glass and listened with half a mind to Amalia chattering to her husband about a proposed purchase.

"Sir," the footman came into the room and stood at attention just inside of the doorway. There was the sound of voices and a bustle of some sort from the hall behind him. "Someone's here, sir. He says his name is Giles Haverton," he began, only to be thrust out of the way by a tall young man who strode impetuously into the room.

Amalia dropped her fork with a clatter and rose to her feet with a glad cry. "Giles! My son!"

He embraced her very briefly, his face reflecting his distaste. Morgan was surprised, but thought this might be due to his mother's display of affection in front of a stranger. She watched as he turned to greet his father more formally. Giles was still in traveling clothes, but they were extremely modish and expensive. Morgan took the opportunity to study him. She thought him handsome, but there was something about his eyes she didn't like. Then she realized that father and son both shared the same small pale eyes and an expression of bored disdain.

"Morgan, my dear" Oliver was saying. "May I present my son, Giles Haverton?"

Morgan came to her feet and curtseyed politely.

"Giles," Oliver continued with a strange smile. "This is my ward and your cousin, Morgan Moorhouse."

"I am delighted," Giles said softly, as he bowed. He possessed himself of her hand and kissed the fingertips. He continued to hold her hand after he straightened up and gazed down at her face, liking what he saw. "Had I known I had such a beautiful cousin, I would have come home sooner."

"Ahem." Oliver cleared his throat and scowled at Giles, who released Morgan and held her chair as she reseated herself.

"Well now that you're here," his father told him, "you might as well accompany us to Lady Ashford's drum."

"But I've only just returned ..."

"Oh, do come," Amalia put in. "You can't possibly be that tired. Besides, your friends will all be there. They'll be glad to see you again."

"All my friends?" Giles asked with a raised eyebrow. He smiled. "Then perhaps I should come. It might be amusing."

"But no more trouble," Oliver growled at him. "You should have learned to behave yourself by now."

"Oh, yes," Giles assured him. "I've learned." He smiled at the ladies. "If you will excuse me, I will change my dress." With a short bow in their direction he left them to finish their dinner.

Chapter 13

Giles was Morgan's constant companion during the days that followed. At first she was unconcerned by his attention. His clever tongue kept her amused and, to be honest, just a little scandalized with revelations about many of the people they saw at the routs, balls, and other entertainments. Apparently, she told him one evening, he had an intimate knowledge of everyone in their society.

"No," he corrected her, "not everyone. Just anyone who matters."

Morgan laughed then, but she started to sense malice behind his wit, and his frivolous chatter began to bore her. His attentions too, were such that she felt stifled, for he was always at her side, insinuating himself into every conversation. When she dropped a hint that she found this displeasing, he only smiled and changed the subject.

From Giles' behavior, Morgan might have thought he was attracted to her, but his flattery was so blatantly false that only a very silly female could be fooled by it. It was also obvious that he could never care for anyone nearly as much as he cared for himself.

She tried to discourage him a number of times, but her efforts failed. She tried to think of someone she could ask for help. She considered Amalia, but the woman so obviously doted on her son that Morgan doubted she would even understand the complaint, much less bring herself to do anything about it. Then one day Morgan overheard part of a conversation and realized things were worse that she thought. Because of his constant attention to her, people thought she and Giles were betrothed. Nothing could have been further from the truth!

Morgan mulled over her problem as she came slowly down the stairs, holding the rust-colored overskirt of her new silk gown carefully out of the way of her high-heeled slippers of gilded leather. The lower hall was silent, although she could hear the servants moving about in the dining room as they finished preparations for dinner. Rather than disturb their work she made her way to one of the smaller sitting rooms. Oliver was there ahead of her, a glass of dark wine in his hand. He stood warming himself before a fire that danced in the grate.

"Good evening, Cousin Oliver," she said politely.

He turned to face her, his expression making Morgan feel, and not for the first time, as if she was intruding. Even though he was family, she had to admit she didn't like him. By now Morgan knew Oliver considered women little more than a decorative auxiliary, necessary for procreation or perhaps recreation, but other than that, to be dealt with briefly or ignored.

Although Oliver forced a smile to his lips, it did nothing to alleviate the chill of his gray eyes. "Good evening," he muttered.

Morgan felt a little shiver in his presence, but her voice was firm. "I'm glad to find you alone, Cousin." He raised a surprised eyebrow, as she tried to decide the best way to begin. "My Cousin Giles ..."

"I have noticed he is often in your company," Oliver interrupted. "People have commented on it."

"Yes," she assured him. "That's my problem."

"Problem? You should be flattered. How could his attention be a problem?"

"I would be pleased with less of his attention."

"Any young woman would be happy to have such a handsome young buck dancing attendance on her."

"Perhaps, but I am not one of them," Morgan said, an edge to her voice betraying her feelings.

Oliver's chin went up and his eyes narrowed. "Oh? Has he behaved badly?"

"No, but ..."

"Then I do not see what problem you could have." He turned away and stared at the fire.

"People have suggested we're betrothed," Morgan said quickly. "Since this is untrue, I thought you should know of it. And perhaps you can put a stop to it. Such unfounded rumors can only prove to be an embarrassment."

Oliver looked at her again, glaring from under half lowered lids. "I think it would be an excellent idea for you to be betrothed to Giles. You are past the age when you should have a husband. And as I cannot imagine what objection you could have to him, I will see to it." He turned away again.

"Never!" Morgan exclaimed, her loathing plain in her voice. "I will never marry Giles." She realized the insult of her hasty words and tried to mitigate them. "Why ... why he's my cousin! It wouldn't be right."

Oliver tried to temper his anger at her vehemence. "There is no reason why cousins even more closely related than you and Giles should not marry," he announced. He looked at her flushed cheeks and realized her agitation. The bitch wanted taming, he thought, but they would have to go carefully. "I had no idea you found Giles so repulsive."

"I don't find him repulsive," she said, still trying to correct the earlier impression she might have made on Oliver. "I ... I just don't want to marry yet."

"Yet?" His eyebrow went up again. "As I said, you are past the age when most women wed."

"Perhaps, but I thought -- that is, my parents promised to allow me to have some say in the choice of my husband."

"Then they made a serious mistake," Oliver told her. "A young woman such as yourself is not equipped to make such an important decision. You must allow yourself to be guided by your elders. Since your father is gone now, I am the one who stands in his place. And now that the thought has occurred to me, I believe Giles would make an admirable husband for you. Consider it, I beg of you," he drawled, "for it is done."

Morgan was aghast! Marry Giles? She'd rather die a

spinster! But Oliver had obviously finished with that conversation.

"There's another thing," she began tentatively.

"Eh?" Oliver couldn't have been more amazed. This woman was certainly trying his patience! He would have to tell Giles to school her better. But not until after they were married.

"Several pieces of my jewelry are missing," she said.

"Now that is a serious matter," Oliver replied. "Are you certain you haven't lost them? Or perhaps that maid of yours misplaced them, and is afraid to own up to it. Yes, that's it. She will be dismissed. I never thought she was suitable."

"No! It's not Bridy," Morgan replied. "Samuels took them."

"Samuels? How do you know? Did you see him?"

"No, I didn't. But Bridy ..."

"Ah. So she accuses him to cover up her own carelessness? Or perhaps guilt?"

Morgan could see exactly where this conversation was going. She felt as if her Irish maid was the only person in the household she felt comfortable with and could maybe even trust. "No. I don't think so, she said quickly, reluctant to put Bridy in jeopardy. "Maybe I should look again. Maybe I did misplace the pieces."

"Yes," Oliver told her. "I thought perhaps you had."

Giles chose that moment to come into the room dressed in a new suit cut in the latest fashion. Extremely high heels on his red shoes set off stockings embroidered in gold thread, and matched the red garters with knots of ribbons holding his pantaloons just below the knee. The rest of his small clothes were hidden by a purple velvet coat with a very full skirt, the sleeves of which were turned back to the elbow to show off the scarlet silk lining. A very long golden brocade waistcoat, covered most of his shirt, and yards of precious lace trimmed his cravat and sleeves.

From the toes of his shoes to his outrageous blond wig, Giles was a perfect picture of someone prepared for an evening on the town. Morgan decided she hated him. Before she could comment, however, a servant came to the door and with a low bow announced dinner.

Giles smiled at Morgan, and choosing to ignore the frosty look in her eyes, offered his arm. "May I be your escort?"

Oliver glared at her until she placed her fingers lightly on the proffered arm, and the three of them left the room together.

"So you were born in the Indies," a young matron commented to Morgan later that evening. "How fascinating, I'm sure."

Five women sat in a little alcove beyond the ballroom, their huge skirts surrounding them like the bright petals of some giant, exotic flowers. Giles had slipped away for an hour or two with his cronies in the card room leaving Morgan safely, he thought, in this strictly feminine company. All of the women seated here were near her age, but they were all married. Two of them were even with child, although their condition was decently draped by scarves and shawls.

"I was born on an island called Cayman Brac," Morgan responded. She watched the company in the ballroom as she spoke, her attention caught by one young man who seemed interested in her presence. "Who is that," she asked her companions.

"Who?" Lady Mary Watson asked, leaning forward to see better.

"The one in the pink coat."

"Oh that's James Challoner," Elizabeth Parkington supplied. "Poor thing."

"Poor thing? Why?" Morgan wanted to know. Elizabeth – everyone called her Betsy – was an excellent source of gossip.

"He's received, of course," Betsy said. "Even though his family was ruined during the Commonwealth." She leaned over and whispered under the cover of her hand. "He hasn't a penny. But then you should be familiar with that story."

"I?" Morgan blinked in surprise.

"Betsy, hush," Lady Watson warned.

"No, let her tell me," Morgan begged. "Please."

"It's really nothing," Betsy said, throwing a triumphant glance at Mary. "Poverty is no stranger to your family. The Havertons suffered the same fate during the revolution. But they seem to have made a miraculous recovery since you came here from the Indies."

Lady Mary Watson sat back in her chair, her mouth pursed in a moue of distaste. She was one of the pregnant ones and adjusted the concealing shawl over her bulging stomach. "It's warm in here," she commented, pointedly changing the subject. "Where are the servants with refreshments when you want them?"

"I'll find someone for you," Morgan offered rising, suddenly needing to get away from the gossiping women. She had to think about this new revelation about Oliver's family matters. She made her way gracefully through the crowd, searching for one of the liveried footmen.

"I can only hope you're looking for me," a voice said at her elbow. It was the man Betsy identified as James Challoner.

"No," Morgan told him with a smile. "I wasn't, but ..."

"But you have found me," James said quickly. "How can I be of service?"

"Have we been introduced, sir?" she wanted to know.

"Yes. If you remember, Lady Welsley presented me to you at her ball last week."

"Then it's all right," she remarked, relieved that she wouldn't be committing a social error just by talking to him. "If you must know, I am looking for a footman."

"Done." James offered his arm. "This way, please."

His manner was saved from being impertinent by his impish smile, and Morgan allowed him to lead her into the dining room where the servants were gathered. She gave instructions for refreshments to be taken to the ladies in the alcove.

"Now may I get something for you?" James asked. "Some supper perhaps?"

"Thank you. I would like that." Morgan was intrigued by the novelty offered by a new companion. She knew Giles would take her away as soon as he decided to come looking for her again, but until then she could take advantage of his absence.

It was a pleasing change, and although James was a more staid companion compared to Giles, she found him much more to her taste. They talked of many things and compared notes on their experiences in London.

"You are betrothed to Giles Haverton," James said later when they were seated at one of the small tables, picking over the plates of food provided by a servant.

"What? Giles? Oh, no!" Morgan said quickly.

James looked confused. "But I thought … I mean everyone says ..."

Morgan laughed. "I know. He acts that way, and my Cousin Oliver would like me to marry him, but I don't want to."

"Will you be allowed to refuse him?" James inquired.

Morgan's chin came up a fraction. "It's my choice who I marry."

James grinned ruefully. "I wish I could afford to be so free."

"Few people can," Giles said, breaking into the conversation.

He had found them, Morgan thought with dismay, watching as James came to his feet, facing the older man. Giles ignored him and took hold of the back of Morgan's chair.

"My mother has been looking for you," he said. "Allow me to escort you to her."

Morgan reluctantly rose and took Gile's arm "Thank you for a very pleasant supper," she told James.

"It was my pleasure," he replied with a bow.

"I hope I will see you again," Morgan tossed over her shoulder smiling. James might have to look for a wealthy wife, but she thought his manners particularly nice, and he was a definite change from her family. There was something about him that reminded her of someone, but for a moment she couldn't think who it was. Then it came to her - Daniel Harris. Their coloring was similar. And their height. Although, now that she thought of it, the staid James had nothing like the vitality of the buccaneer captain. She wondered what Daniel was doing, and wished, not for the first time, that she was back on board the *Kestrel*.

"You are a minx, my dear," Giles said softly. "Are you trying to make me jealous?"

"I don't know what you're talking about," Morgan protested.

Giles frowned at her, but quickly remembered where they were. Aware of at least a dozen pairs of eyes on them, he changed his expression into a smile. "I was speaking of your little tryst with Mr. Challoner. He's as poor as a church mouse, you know."

"I don't see how his financial situation could interest me," Morgan said stiffly. "All we did was have some supper, and talk about London."

"But that was enough. There will be tongues wagging about it all over town before another night is over."

"And so what if they do? People will always find something to talk about. You are making too much of it."

"Anyone with any sensibility would be mortified to be the subject of so much speculation."

Morgan's eyes flashed with anger. "If it doesn't bother

me, I don't see what business it is of yours. You have no right to criticize anything I choose to do. And," she added as a clincher, "I would rather not find you in my company so often." She detached her hand from his arm and walked ahead of him to the doorway.

Giles stood a moment, furiously glaring after her before following with hasty strides. He grabbed her arm, yanking her around to face him.

"Let me go!" she raged. She pulled back, tearing her lace in her haste to be free of him. Her bosom heaving, she met his eyes for a long moment, and then turned and walked quickly away. She left him standing alone in the hall, humiliated by her rejection.

Giles looked around, but no one was there to see the incident except a couple bored footmen. Hopefully they would find something more interesting to talk about before the evening was over. As for Morgan ... well, he would take care of her later.

Chapter 14

When Morgan finally arrived home, she left Amalia in the hands of her maidservant before she went to her own room. The hour was late, and she was glad the evening was finally over. She dropped her cloak on a chair and untied the row of ribbons fastening her bodice. When the heavy skirt and underskirt were off, she opened the hooks of her corset and let it drop with a sigh. Shrugging into a soft woolen dressing gown, she sat at her dressing table, elbows resting on the top and her hands under her chin as she stared at herself in the mirror.

The ball that evening had been especially interesting, she decided, because James Challoner was such a relief from Giles. She thought over the brief time she spent with James and hoped he would remember she rode every morning in the park. She would like to see him again and that might happen if he met her there.

She slowly removed her gold earrings and, wrapping them in a handkerchief, shoved them deep into a vase under the stems of a dried flower arrangement. She had carefully hidden all of her jewelry after Bridy told her Samuels was taking it. Morgan still didn't understand why he wanted it, or whether or not her cousin knew it was happening. She wouldn't put it past Oliver to order his servant to steal her jewelry. She never considered where he found the money to finance their London season until Betsy commented on Oliver's changed fortune. She wasn't sure how he had accomplished this, but began to suspect her inheritance might be the source.

Where was Bridy, Morgan wondered suddenly? She usually insisted on waiting up, so it was strange for her to be absent. Then she remembered the maid had asked permission to spend part of the evening with some of the other servants at a fair. She was probably having fun and forgot the time. Morgan envied them. How comfortable it must be to just go and enjoy one's self and not to have to consider the proprieties every minute.

Morgan unpinned the rosettes of gauzy ribbon holding the curls over her shoulders. Then she drew the pins from the chignon at the back of her head and let the rest of her long hair fall free. She reached for her brush when she realized someone was standing in the doorway watching her. A man.

Morgan came to her feet her back rigid with outrage. "What do you want here?" she asked.

Giles stepped into the candle light. "Since your maid's out for the night, I thought you might need some help getting to bed."

Morgan's eyes blazed with anger. "I'm perfectly capable of helping myself," she snapped. Her hand was clenched on the handle of the brush. "Please leave my room."

Giles smiled. "I don't think so, little cousin." He came toward her and lifted a strand of her hair, curling it around his finger and tugging gently. "Since we are to be wed, I thought I'd come and sample some of the delights awaiting me."

The smell of liquor on his breath and the wild glitter in his eyes told her Giles was intoxicated. "Despite your drunken fantasies, we will never be married," Morgan told him. "And if you don't leave immediately, I'll scream."

Giles laughed and pulled her into his arms. Grabbing a handful of her hair he pulled her head back so he could cover her mouth with his. He parted her lips ruthlessly and thrust inside with his tongue. While one hand pinned her arms behind her, his other hand tore at the ribbons holding her nightgown.

Morgan felt as if she was suffocating. Giles held her so tightly, and his breath stank of brandy. She struggled, wrenching her hands free and flailing at him with her fists. The hairbrush she still held hit his head with a resounding thump, but he grabbed it from her and sent it spinning across the room. Other than that he seemed oblivious to her efforts to free herself. Morgan had never been violently handled by a man, and was close to panic, for he proved to be much too strong for her. In less time than she would have thought possible he had her nightgown open and her breasts exposed. His fingers squeezed, pinching her cruelly. Releasing her mouth he dropped his head and viciously bit the tender flesh.

Morgan screamed then, and he pulled away, raising his arm to hit her.

"Miss!" Bridy called as she came into the room, ready to enter into battle. "Lord love ye, what's been happen' here!"

"Giles?" Oliver's voice came from the doorway. "What are you doing?"

Giles released her and stepped back. Bridy ran to her mistress' side, covering her with the cloak she snatched up from the chair as she came. Morgan gratefully wrapped herself in the velvet folds and sank down on a chair, trembling and trying to catch her breath. Bridy put her hand on Morgan's shoulder and stood protectively over her.

"I will speak to you," Oliver told Giles as he surveyed the scene. "In my room. Now." He looked at the two women with distaste and turned away.

With one angry look at Morgan, Giles followed.

Daniel Harris stood on a hillside looking down at the ruins of the house where he had been born. The building, its immediate grounds and a small wood were all that was left of a large estate. All around it now spread good sized farms. The acres under cultivation belonged to men who bought them from the old baron and his eldest son, Daniel's father, as they struggled to survive during the black years when Cromwell and his puritan followers ruled England. Any royalists left in England after Charles had been beheaded were punished with ruinous taxes, and the Rivingtons were no exception. Everything they had -- money, land, family treasures -- went to pay the outrageous taxes until there was hardly anything left to live on.

Daniel remembered helping chop the legs off the chairs during the first winter when they burned furniture to keep warm. These extreme measures were all because his father wouldn't let them cut down any of the trees in the home wood. He and his brother had already cleared the grounds of all the dead branches and, other than live trees and the furniture in the house, there was nothing left to burn. He remembered how his mother wept to see the beautiful rooms stripped of all the family heirlooms. Too soon the house echoed, haunted by memories. Those were the days when there was barely enough to eat. He wasn't sure how they managed to survive.

During the second winter Daniel's little sister died of an inflammation of the lungs. With her death, his grandfather began to realize that only the most drastic measures would save their home and his sons' inheritance. Even though he did everything he could think of, all of his efforts failed. The tax was inescapable. It broke him in the end when he had to sell the outlying farms. The rest of the estate followed, acres subtracted one by one, each loss another heavy blow.

By the time the old baron died, gone like his precious land, Daniel had already been sent to uncle who was a sea captain. Just fourteen years old, he learned to be a sailor on short runs to the ports of Europe. It was a hard way for a young man to grow up, but Daniel soon realized he had a liking for the sea. He rose to the position of boson's mate on his uncle's ship, and served faithfully until the lure of adventure and Spanish gold took him to the West Indies. Here his audacity and skill won him his first ship and a captaincy.

But all of that was long ago. Now his older brother was dead and Captain Daniel Harris had returned to England, a new baron come to Rivington.

As the sun sank beyond the distant wood, Daniel watched a thin stream of smoke rising from the kitchen, realizing the old caretaker, Webster, was probably cooking dinner for him. The house had been partly restored by Daniel's brother and kept up by the caretaker and his family. There was a small income from the home farm, and from another family estate in Gloucester, the only piece of property returned to the family when the Stuarts came back into power. Although the combined income wouldn't make Daniel rich, it would still provide a generous living if he chose to give up the sea. Whether he would do that or not depended on one thing. Daniel made inquiries and learned that the Havertons -- and Morgan -- were fixed in London for the season.

Morgan! She sang in his heart! Morgan of the sweet scented coppery hair, the gold flecked brown eyes, and the warm sweet shape that his hands and body remembered so well. She disturbed his sleep at night, and by day he was unable to stop thinking about her. The picture of her driving away on the wagon at Port Royal had burned into his mind, taunting him with thoughts of what might have been.

The letter telling him he inherited his brother's estate had come just as she left, probably on the same ship bringing her cousin to the Indies. As soon as he finished his business in Port Royal he followed her. Everything changed with that piece of paper. Now he had something to offer, a name and a home. Whether it was enough was yet to be seen. Only one thought troubled him; perhaps she was already beyond his reach.

The sun had set, and the moon and one bright star hung in a sky painted a dark, translucent blue. Daniel shivered as the temperature dropped, and started down the hill to the house. He would spend just one more night at Rivington, and in the morning depart for London.

"What do you mean by this behavior?" Oliver demanded.

Giles stood by the fire in his father's room, warming his hands. "She needs someone to teach her humility," he said sulkily.

"I couldn't agree more!" Oliver exclaimed. "But couldn't you wait until after you're married?"

Giles whirled around to face him. "If we're not careful I will never be married to her."

"What are you talking about?" his father demanded.

"She was with another man tonight. I found them in the dining room. Alone."

"Another man? And where were you, pray tell?"

"I had stepped out."

"I thought I told you never to let her out of your sight!" Oliver thundered.

Giles met his glare with eyes equally as frosty. "I cannot dance attendance on her every second. Besides I left her with a bunch of married hens. She should have been safe enough with them."

"Obviously you were wrong. Who is the man she had supper with?"

"His name is Challoner. A nobody. The family lost everything during the rebellion."

"Hummm." Oliver scowled. "Then he may be doubly dangerous. If he's after a fortune, Morgan will interest him. I suggest you hint him away."

"Hint? Why don't I just call him out," Giles suggested, his eyes burning with fervor.

"And have to leave England again for brawling? Don't be stupid."

"I don't see how it could be worse. I'm practically a prisoner here since I have to shepherd that spoiled bitch. A lesson in manners would do her the world of good."

"Perhaps, but you're not to administer it. At least not yet."

"She's ripe for a man. I can feel it."

"Yes, well you can have her all you want once you're wed. But not before. Do you hear me?"

Giles looked sulky.

"Perhaps you should remember who makes it possible for you to live in the lavish style you enjoy," Oliver said. "Without Morgan's money we will be reduced to poverty again."

"She's been allowed too many liberties," Giles complained. "Anyone else and I would have her eating out of my hand."

"Mishandling her the way you did tonight won't remedy

123

that."

"Then we should be married soon. I don't know if I can control myself much longer."

"All right," Oliver agreed. "I'll see what I can do. And should the idea of marriage continue to displease our fine cousin, I have another way to persuade her."

"What way is this?" Giles asked.

"It's perhaps best you do not know. But Mistress Moorhouse will find it hard to resist, I promise you."

Chapter 15

Morgan sat in bed the next morning, sipping a cup of hot chocolate. It was a little after dawn, much too early for anyone to be up, especially after a ball, but Morgan was determined to leave the house early before anyone was awake to stop her.

Bridy yawned as she wiped dust from Morgan's boots. She shook the wrinkles from a riding dress of dark blue wool, and retrieved a lace jabot to finish off the ensemble.

Morgan made a grimace of distaste as she set her cup down. "This chocolate tastes different. It's much too strong," she commented, throwing the covers aside and climbing out of bed. She started to pour hot water into the wash basin, but then set down the pitcher.

"Probably because Mr. Samuels himself made it," Bridy was telling her. "Sure and I've never met a man yet who wasn't all thumbs when it came to cookin'." She yawned again. "Cept, of course, the Frenchy Lord Delamer has over at his house. Faith, I've heard tell he's good a cook as any woman." She sniffed. "Though an' why they seem to think it makes food tastes better when some foreigner messes it up with fancy sauces and the like, I'll never know." She placed a pair of tasseled gauntlets on the dressing table. As she went to give Morgan a fresh towel, she realized something was wrong. "Miss, are you all right?"

Morgan was holding onto the edge of the wash stand, her face pale, beads of sweat on her forehead and upper lip.

"Here," Bridy said taking her arm. "Let me help you."

"No, I ..."

Morgan retched and threw up into the basin.

"There, there, Miss," Bridy soothed as she wrung a cloth in the water pitcher and wiped Morgan's face. She steadied Morgan back to the bed. "You lay back down and you'll be feelin' better again' in no time a'tall."

Morgan she collapsed against the pillows. "Thank you," she managed weakly as her maid tucked the covers back around her. "I don't know what happened. All of a sudden the room just started spinning."

Bridy nodded her head sagely. "Aye. Me mother felt the same way with her last three, but 'tis nothin' to worry about. She delivered fourteen fine wee ones just the same."

"You think I'm ...?" Morgan protested, "No, that's impossible. I've never -- I mean, how can I be?"

"Ye haven't been with a man, then?" Bridy asked, her eyes wide.

"Never," Morgan assured her with a faint smile. "And

126

don't count on miracles either. I'm not the type."

"Then 'tis probably something ye ate. Something from that fancy party last night."

"That's probably it," Morgan agreed.

Bridy emptied the basin into the slop jar. "I'll clean this up and be right back," she said. "Ye rest a bit and I'll bring ye a hot bottle for your feet and cup'a tisane me mother used when we had upsets. I've got the herbs in my room." She didn't wait for a reply, but backed through the door with her burden.

Morgan slid down in the bed and closed her eyes. She was so rarely ill and found the experience unsettling. Now that whatever she had eaten was out of her system, she soon felt better, but still she lay there, her eyes closed. She was almost afraid to get up lest the room start spinning again. But she did want to go riding in the park. James might be there. She sat up gingerly and drew in deep breath. When nothing awful happened, she flung the covers back.

"Here, now," Bridy protested as she came back into the room carrying a tray. "An' what might ye be doing there?" She pushed the cup of chocolate out of her way as she put her burden on the small table beside the bed.

"I feel better. I'm getting up," Morgan told her.

"An' are ye now?"

"And I'm going out," Morgan added firmly. There were times when Bridy sounded just like Hana. The thought of her old nurse brought a wave of homesickness, and she wished she was still in the Caribbean. She wondered what Hana was doing and if she was well. And Daniel Harris. No, she didn't want to think about him. Morgan looked at the hated walls

127

around her and thought of James. Maybe he could help her escape. He had to. He was the only one she knew outside of the family.

"Ye can't go out ridin'," Bridy protested. "What if ye get sick again?"

Morgan picked up the pitcher and sniffed the aromatic steam. "What's in this?" she asked.

"'Tis mint, chamomile and Solomon's seal. An' a couple other things -- for good luck, me mother says."

Morgan poured some into a fresh cup and took a sip. It felt good against her throat so she drank the cupful.

"Your mother is a wonderful woman," she told Bridy. "I'm cured."

"An' sure she is," the maid agreed. "Me family's been knowin' that for years. And all the neighbors come to her when there's sickness. But even so, I'm not so sure just one cup of her tisane is enough to cure ye. Least ways not so quickly!"

"But it has," Morgan assured her. "I feel perfectly well. And I am going riding."

Bridy shook her head in disbelief, but wisely held her tongue. She helped her mistress into the riding dress. After the hooks were all fastened, held up the long black coat so Morgan could slip her arms into the sleeves.

Morgan bundled her braided hair into a snood before putting on the high crowned hat. She checked in the mirror to be sure that it was settled at the right angle before she picked up her gauntlets and riding whip. She looked around the room one last time incase she'd forgotten anything. Her eyes lingered for a second on the half-finished cup of chocolate, then passed on.

Bridy caught up a heavy cloak of black wool lined and trimmed with warm fur, and followed Morgan into the hall. The house remained silent, everyone still abed. They took the back stairs to a door giving onto the cobbled yard separating the house from the stables. Here was a scene of bustling activity as horses were groomed and stalls mucked out.

The head groom came forward immediately when they appeared. "Mornin', Miss," he said, inclining his head. He glanced at Bridy out of the corner of his eye, but immediately turned his attention back to Morgan as she spoke.

"Good morning, Richards. Please have my mare saddled."

"Yes, miss." The head groom stepped back into the barn and they could hear him as he sent the grooms to do her bidding. On other days, word went down to the stable ahead of time and she would find the mare ready and waiting for her. This morning, however, she wanted to get away without alerting anyone to her plans or giving them a chance to intervene.

Richards seemed young to have such an important position as head groom, but Morgan knew Oliver had only just hired him, like the other servants, when they arrived in London. She realized something else, too, when she saw Bridy standing, staring after the tall young man with a bemused look on her face. Apparently Bridy found the head groom to her liking. And why not, she thought? He wasn't bad looking. He had well formed broad shoulders and straight, long legs. Clear blue eyes twinkled from under a shock of dark brown hair. Yes, he was definitely attractive.

"Bridy," Morgan called softly.

"Eh?" was all the usually loquacious maid said. "Oh!" She handed Morgan the heavy cloak and helped fasten it around her shoulders.

In minutes Richards brought a pretty little dappled gray mare from the stable. She was fresh and skittish, tossing her dark muzzle and flicking her ears while her black mane fell over her eyes and her long tail lashed about her hocks. She knew a ride was in order and exercise was just what she wanted. Bridy held the mare's head as Morgan stepped into Richards' cupped hands and was lifted onto the sidesaddle. She settled quickly, organizing reins and crop as well as her skirt while the mare danced on the cobbles.

A groom came forward with a long-legged sorrel gelding, and Richards swung into that saddle, preparing to accompany Morgan. Another groom, hastily summoned, mounted a sturdy cob and stood ready, his saddle, like Richards', flanked by holsters, the pistols therein loaded. Morgan led the way leaving Bridy watching as they left the yard in a clatter of iron shod hooves.

While much of the city of London was cramped with buildings, the land outside was green, consisting of forests, heaths and farmland. Unlike later years when the only places for an equestrienne to take exercise were the bridle paths in the parks, Morgan had her choice of miles of open land. But she remembered telling James her favorite ride was down Knightsbridge Road to Hyde Park, and so she turned her mare's head in that direction.

The horses were fresh, their breath steaming in the crisp air as they made their way carefully through the early morning traffic of carts and loaded wagons heading for market. There were beggars and vagrants, waking in the alleys as they passed. Many a covetous glance was cast after Morgan with her rich clothes and expensive thoroughbred mare, but the presence of an armed escort gave any would-be attackers pause.

The sky gleamed a clear blue this frosty winter morning, and although Morgan was warm enough in her woolen riding clothes and the long fur-lined cloak, she still longed for the more clement weather of her home. If she were there, she told herself, she could be galloping along a white sand beach, racing the waves, dressed in no more than a linen habit. She looked down at her hands, warm in heavy gauntlets. Beyond them the mare's silver-haired shoulders flexed and moved beneath her.

The buildings soon thinned out, and she could see the trees in the park just ahead. Her mare snorted and pulled at the bit, impatient for a gallop. Morgan held her tightly as they threaded their way through the last of the traffic and left the cobblestone streets for turf. Forgetting for the moment the possibility of meeting James, Morgan eased up on the reins and, leaning forward, touched the eager mare with her heel and whip. The gray needed no more encouragement and launched into a gallop. Richards and her escort followed as best they could.

After a short time Morgan pulled the mare down to a canter as she searched the park. Apparently no one else braved the crisp morning to take exercise on horseback. Then she saw a lone figure in the distance. As he came closer she recognized James Challoner, and her heart gave a leap of gladness. He remembered!

"God give a good morning to you" he said, sweeping off his hat as he bowed from the saddle. "We are well met."

"Well met, indeed," she answered as she reined her mount in beside his. Her escort turned to follow at a discrete distance. "I wasn't sure you would remember that I rode here."

"But I did," he responded. "Where is your cousin today?"

"Home and abed," she said harshly.

His brows drew together in a frown. "You do not seem fond of that gentleman."

"I loathe him," she admitted. She bit her lip as she pondered the best way to approach her problem. She liked James well enough, but also realized he had a very strong sense of propriety. "Did you mean what you said last night, that you would be happy to help me if the occasion arose?"

"If I said so then I mean it," James responded slowly, curious as to why she would ask him this.

"I think …" Morgan began carefully, "I think we may be in a position to help each other," she informed him."

"And how is that?"

"You told me you wanted more than anything to restore your estate to what it had been before the Commonwealth," Morgan said.

"Yes, that's true."

"Well, I know how you can do it."

"Nay," he protested. "What scheme are you brewing? Whatever it is, I'll not do anything to bring dishonor to my family."

132

"It isn't dishonorable," she assured him. "And you would be doing me the greatest service at the same time."

James wondered if his interest in this beautiful young woman has been a mistake. "What is it then? Please explain yourself."

Morgan took a deep breath. She turned in the saddle and leaned over to place her hand on his arm. "I'm an heiress. I have property in the colonies as well as in England. I am very wealthy, but you can have it all."

James frowned at her. "How can this be?"

"Marry me," she told him.

Chapter 16

"How can you say such a thing to me?" James protested, trying not to show how shocked he was. "It's unseemly, unmaidenly."

"I'm only doing it because I'm desperate," Morgan assured him.

Their horses walked slowly side by side down the wide path beneath ancient oaks whose branches were bare beneath a gray winter sky. The landscape was all black, white and gray, and as cold as the air.

"Desperate to wed? You haven't ..." James looked at her askance. "You're not with child, are you?"

She scowled, affronted by his question even though she could appreciate the reason for it. "Most certainly not, sir!"

"Forgive me, but you said ...," he began.

"There are other reasons why one may be desperate,"

Morgan assured him.

"If you're not with child, then I do not see any reason for your desperation."

Morgan sighed, beginning to wonder if James wasn't just too concerned with the proprieties to be of any use to her. "I'm an heiress, but while my cousin is my guardian, he has control of my fortune."

"And that is as it should be," James assured her. "Surely this is no reason for concern."

"What if I told you my cousin is taking unfair advantage of his responsibilities."

"What do you mean? He's a member of your family. Surely he has nothing but your best interests at heart."

"He does not. He means to wed me to his son so they can share my wealth."

"He means Giles to be your husband?" James pondered on this. "Perhaps your suspicions in this matter are bred from your dislike of Giles. I must own, his treatment of you last evening was not what one would expect from a gentleman."

"It is even worse than you know," Morgan assured him, anxious to arouse more of this chivalrous feeling in James' breast. "My maid has to sleep with me for fear he will take advantage."

"I did hear something," James said musingly. "Something about the reason for Giles' long absence on the continent."

"Whatever it is, no matter how terrible, it's probably true," Morgan was at haste to assure him.

"I don't know ..."

"Oh, why do you hesitate?" Morgan asked in despair.

135

"My fortune, my virtue, and probably my life are in danger!"

"Then I will speak with your guardian," James said. "I will request his permission to wed you."

"He will never agree," she told him flatly. "Oliver is determined that I marry Giles."

"Then I don't see what I can do."

"I have heard of a place in Scotland where marriages can be quickly arranged. A place called Gretna Green?"

"You cannot be serious! For us to go there would be a scandal!"

"Then you refuse to help me?" Despair filled Morgan's voice and she let a single tear slip out from under her lid and roll down her cheek.

"Here, now! I didn't say anything of the sort," James assured her, more alarmed by the tear than the thought of creating a scandal.

"But if you won't run away with me, I don't see what you can do." Morgan's head drooped and another tear escaped.

"I will think on it, and tell you what I decide."

"When will you know?"

"I ..."

"This evening. Please! We are going to a dinner party, and then there is to be gaming at Betty Jackson's. I'm told everyone is coming. Will you be there?"

"I had planned to attend."

"Good. You can give me your answer tonight."

"But what if I don't have an answer? 'Tis too little time!"

"You must. You will," Morgan told him.

"Perhaps..."

"You will," she repeated firmly. Morgan gathered the reins and turned the gray mare around. "Until this evening," she said smiling sweetly at her cavalier, tears forgotten. The mare cavorted, eager to move faster than a walk. Her ears pricked and her nostrils flared as she stepped lightly onto the frosty grass. Morgan loosened the reins and, followed by her retinue of grooms, cantered away.

Daniel Harris arrived in London just as the sun was setting. He rode a big Roman-nosed bay gelding that covered miles with a fast, smooth gait. A servant followed, and a groom who led a fourth horse loaded with baggage.

Not sure where Morgan would be found, Daniel took rooms in an inn called the Parson's Spoon. Here, refreshed by a good supper, he sent a servant out to make inquires. The man returned with an address.

The next morning Daniel set out guided by a kitchen boy who fell eagerly to the task when promised a shilling. They quickly found the residence of Oliver Haverton, and the lad was on his way home, the coin clutched in his fist.

The house Oliver rented was a large building constructed in the old style with timbers and plaster. For security, the only windows in wall facing the street were high in the second story. The only way into the building from the street was a through a big double gate leading to a cobbled yard. The yard was bordered by the stables and some other outbuildings across from the house.

At the gate stood a porter who asked Daniel his business, although politely, since this caller was obviously a gentleman.

"Tell Oliver Haverton that the Baron of Rivington wishes to speak with him." He still wasn't comfortable with the title, but a peerage would gain him entrance where a simple Captain Harris would not.

These words had the desired effect, and Daniel was admitted without further ado. As he rode beneath the archway, a groom came to take his horse. Daniel dismounted and looked around. The courtyard was a scene of activity as servants went about their daily tasks. The yard itself was well cared for and overall, prosperous looking. Oliver Haverton was obviously a man of some means.

As Daniel's horse was led away he stepped onto the wide porch and raised his hand to the gleaming brass knocker hanging there. Before he could ply it, however, the door was opened by Jonny Samuels. On Daniel's request to see his master, Samuels bowed and wordlessly led him up a flight of stairs to a parlor where he was left to wait Oliver's pleasure. Daniel paced back and forth across a bright Turkish carpet, pausing now and again to gaze out into the street through the mullioned window. Fortunately, his wait was not long.

"Good day," his host greeted as he entered the room. "What brings you out so early, sir?"

"My name is Anderson, Daniel Harris Anderson. I was a friend of Robert Moorhouse."

"Anderson? Yes, the name is familiar," Oliver drawled.

Daniel's eyes narrowed at this slight. Haverton knew his

name perfectly well. Rivington was just across the channel from Bristol, and the two families had a number of acquaintances in common.

"I also know," Oliver added smoothly, "that you were captain of the ship conveying my cousin to Port Royal. We never met, but I remember the governor mentioning your name."

Daniel acknowledged this with a slight inclination of his head.

"And," Oliver continued, "you are also Lord Anderson's younger son."

His manner was insolent, and Daniel couldn't understand the reason behind it.

"I did hear that the old baron died," Oliver said. "And your older brother as well. Please accept my condolences, my lord."

Daniel nodded his head again, not trusting himself to speak just yet. He had come to see Morgan, and this slug of a man had the power to keep her from him.

"What brings you to London?" Oliver inquired.

"Business. While I am in Town, I thought I would pay my respects to Mistress Moorhouse."

"Ah, yes, my little cousin. She is well. She's engaged to be married, you know."

Daniel felt as if someone kicked him in the stomach. He couldn't breathe. "I didn't know that." Too late! He was been afraid something like this might happen, but still held a kernel of hope. "Who is the lucky gentleman?"

"My son, Giles," Oliver said with obvious relish. "They seem quite taken with each other."

"I would like to see her, if possible, to offer my best wishes," he managed.

"Unfortunately she is not in. She's in the habit of riding out in the morning and has yet to return."

"Then I will trouble you no longer." Daniel bowed and went to the door, desperate to get away. He didn't remember descending the staircase or that Samuels opened the door for him.

Nothing had gone well since he returned to England. Rivington was still mostly in ruins and would take a great deal of work to set it right again. And now Morgan was promised to marry another man. In that instant Daniel knew it was time for him to return to his life in the Indies. There was nothing for him here.

His horse brought around, Daniel swung into the saddle. He turned the bay's head, ducking as the horse carried him beneath the archway and into the street. He paused there for a moment looking up at the house.

Perhaps he wasn't meant to settle down with one woman. Daniel sighed and urged the horse into motion, trotting off toward the Parson's Spoon.

Mounted on her lively gray mare, Morgan entered the other end of the street at almost the same instant. She saw a horseman silhouetted against the bright sun as he looked up at the house and then moved away. With her thoughts in such turmoil, however, she didn't even wonder who it might be.

James Challoner pondered what Morgan told him. He also recalled all the unsavory things people said about Giles Haverton, especially the scandalous rumors about why he had to go abroad. He remembered Morgan's beauty, even though her coloring was a bit overly bold for his taste. She looked nothing like a proper English gentlewoman, who should be refined and demure. Still much could be overlooked in the face of her wealth.

He sympathized with her obvious distress, but then she was only a woman. He knew they were prone to fantasies and easily upset over trifles. And so he decided to ignore her warning and visit her guardian. Surely the man would approve of his suit. His name was an old one, and his estate, however impoverished, extensive. All it needed was good husbandry, and money of course, to bring it to rights again. He would be, he decided, an excellent match for Mistress Morgan.

James dressed carefully and showed himself at the Haverton door at a seemly hour for visiting. He asked to see Oliver but was surprised to be shown instead to a small office in the back of the house. Here Jonny Samuels sat behind a worktable littered with papers and account books. Setting his pen aside, Samuels asked his business as if he were some tradesman or worse, a beggar!

Nettled to be brought before a servant and questioned, James once again demanded the master.

"And your business?" Samuels asked a second time.

James fidgeted, uncomfortably. "I don't see that it has anything to do with you," he finally said.

"I am delegated to act for my master," he was told. "If I

141

deem it pertinent, I will convey your wishes to Mr. Haverton."

"This is most irregular," James muttered. "If you must know," he finally admitted, "my business is of a sensitive nature."

Samuels smiled, or did something with his lips that might have been a smile. They thinned and stretched while his eyes glittered. He knew perfectly well why James had come, and he delighted in the power he held over the man. "Unless I am mistaken, you have come to ask for the hand of Miss Haverton, my master's cousin."

"And what does that have to do with you?" James demanded.

"As I have said, I am privy to my master's business. And the answer is no. You are to leave Miss Haverton alone. You are not to meet with her, ride with her, or even speak to her should you chance to meet at some social affair."

Offended pride won over James's good sense. "I do not take orders from servants," he insisted. "I will speak to Mr. Haverton."

"Not today, you won't," Samuels assured him. He rose and went to the door, calling to the footmen waiting in the hallway. "Mr. Challoner is leaving. Please remove him."

On either side, the footmen grasped James by the arms. Despite his angry words and struggles, they dragged him bodily from the house and threw him into the filth in the street. The gates snapped firmly shut behind him.

The indignity of this treatment stayed with him as he limped, soiled and furious all the way back to his lodgings. His anger simmered, feeding his need for retaliation. But after considerable thought, only one thing occurred that would salve his wounded pride. James called his valet and chose his best dress for that evening.

Morgan kept to herself for the rest of the day. She plotted and paced in her bedchamber until it was time to dress for dinner.

"You remember what I told you," she said to Bridy as she checked her hair in the mirror.

"And it's to be sure I do," the Irish lass replied. "But are you certain 'tis the only thing to do?"

"Yes. When I see James tonight, we'll set up the exact time and place. You're sure Richards can get a carriage?"

"It'll be no problem, miss. But ye don't want him to be drivin' you himself?"

"No. That won't be necessary. James will be there to keep me safe. But be sure you're packed and out of here at the same time. I don't want Oliver and Giles to blame you."

"You can be sure I'll be up and gone from here when they find out!"

"How do you know Richards will help you?"

Bridy laughed. "We've been plannin' to move anyways," she said. "The only problem was I didn't want to be leaving ye. But now that you're goin' too, everything's all right."

"Isn't Richards happy here?"

"He's not happy in Lunnon. He said it himself, many

143

times, 'twas a mistake to come to work in the city. He says it ain't no place for horses nor men, by his ken. He likes it better in the country. And that's where we be goin', to Robert's uncle in Epson. He's head groom for Lord Eastwick there."

"Then you'll be alright."

"Oh, aye. But before we go we're going to be married," she smiled. "That much I insisted on!"

"Married? That's wonderful! Well you should have these." Morgan gave Bridy two golden coins and the maid held them gaping. "You won't be able to collect your wages before you go, but this will make up for it. It will be enough to help you and Richards get started in your new home."

"Oh, aye, I'd say so, miss!" Bridy said in awe. She had never seen gold coins before, much less had one for her own. And now here were two of them!

"Put them somewhere safe," Morgan warned. "Remember how Samuels comes snooping. I wouldn't put it past him to search my rooms when we're not here."

"Yes, miss. And I'll remember you in my prayers this evening and forever. Thank you, sure an' God love ye!"

Morgan laughed and got to her feet. She was wearing a gown with green and gold stripes, her neck and arms surrounded by yards of gold lace. With her bright red hair and golden eyes the effect was stunning.

"After what happened last night, I'll sure to be here when ye come in," Bridy told her. She followed into the hallway, carrying the heavy fur-lined cloak and muff.

Oliver met Morgan at the foot of the stairs. "A moment of your time," he said.

It would have been churlish of her to refuse and so she

144

following him into the parlor. Giles was there and rose to his feet when she entered, an anxious look on his face.

"Morgan, I …" he stammered.

"I have nothing to say to you, sir," she told him and turned away.

"Give him a moment," Oliver said. "Please."

Morgan paused and then turned back.

"Forgive my behavior last night," Giles said, moving toward her. She took a step backward and he stopped, his hands raised. "I won't touch you," he assured her. "But we still live in the same house. I would have peace between us."

"Your behavior, sir, was inexcusable," she told him in a voice filled with ice. "If this is your custom, I want nothing more to do with you."

Morgan left the room, her head held high. Oliver followed, leaving Giles in a rage.

"Distressing news has come to my ears," Oliver told Morgan as they left the house. He took her arm, holding her back as she was about to enter the coach.

"I can't imagine what it would be," she replied, readjusting the heavy fur cloak around her shoulders.

"Giles says you were seen on two occasions with a young man. Challoner, I believe is his name."

"And what of it?"

"He's a fortune hunter," her cousin told her. "You are to stay away from him."

"And if I choose not to?" Morgan asked, anger underlying her words. She didn't wait for him to respond but stepped into the coach and settled herself comfortably.

Oliver watched her with narrowed eyes and then gave a

short laugh. Without another word he climbed in after her. The footman shut the door and folded up the steps.

As the heavy vehicle lumbered out of the yard, armed horsemen carrying lanterns fell in around it. Two rode ahead to light the way, while others followed close behind, ready to protect the occupants as the coach drove through London town.

Chapter 17

Morgan had a horrible time that evening. Because of her indiscretion, something as minor as just sitting and talking with James the night before, she wasn't allowed to be alone at Betty Jackson's. Either Giles or Oliver was constantly at her side. She'd been dismayed to learn that Oliver knew of her meeting with James in the park that morning. She couldn't imagine how he knew unless one of the grooms told him. She should have suspected something like that.

The situation was extremely frustrating, but there was nothing she could do about it. With all the people around them at the party, she had to accept Giles' hated presence with the appearance of complacency.

Morgan saw James several times, but warned him away with a frown and a shake of her head. It was almost midnight before she managed to exchange a few words with him.

Giles disappeared into the refreshment room on an errand of his own and Morgan turned around to find James at her elbow. She quickly drew him through a doorway and into a side room.

"Do you see how I'm put upon?" she whispered.

"I can understand their caution if they suspect me of being on the lookout for a rich wife, but I must say this does seem a trifle extreme," he responded, sliding one finger under his huge peruke to scratch his head. "Are you still determined to go on with your desperate plan?"

"Yes," she told him.

"Well, I've managed to investigate your claims ..."

"What claims?" she demanded. She deliberately kept her voice calm.

"Claims about your wealth. You did know I would do so, didn't you? With so much at stake, I must be careful."

"I hope the results were up to your expectations?" Morgan's voice dripped sarcasm, but James didn't seem to notice.

"Oh, yes. You are everything you say you are."

"Good. Then you will marry me?"

The memory of that morning's indignities was still fresh. "Yes, I will. I'll have to make some arrangements of course. We'll need a carriage ..."

"You need arrange nothing," she told him firmly. "I have secured a carriage, and we will leave in the morning."

"In the morning?" His voice reflected his astonishment. "But I don't know if I can go so soon."

"In the morning," she repeated. "We have to go then."

"But why such haste?"

"Because I don't think I'll have my freedom much longer. One of the grooms saw fit to inform my cousin that you and I had a meeting in the park this morning."

"Surely they couldn't have seen anything amiss! Why, we never left the backs of our horses!"

"We met and we talked. That was enough. I have no time to argue the whole thing over again. Giles will return any second and wonder what has become of me."

"You're set on the morning?"

"Yes. It is tomorrow morning or never."

James' already thin lips tightened into a determined line. Yes, as distasteful as it might be, it would be an excellent way to avenge his humiliation, as well as solving all his financial problems. "Then I am yours to command," he said with a small bow.

Morgan was almost ready to scream with frustration. Men could be so dense! But these were the words she'd waited to hear. "Good. We will meet at seven of the clock at Billingsgate Market. As I already said, I have secured a coach and outriders for the journey."

"At seven of the clock," he repeated.

Morgan smiled and was quickly gone, terrified that her meeting with James had been noticed. Giles was in the main gaming room, looking around him, a black scowl on his face.

He saw Morgan and came over to her.

"Where did you take yourself?" he growled.

"I felt nature call," she dissembled. "I was gone but a moment."

He looked as if he didn't believe her, but said no more about the matter.

Bridy had already packed her own belongings and taken them down to the stables. It was still dark when Morgan quickly assembled a few things of her own. After they were stowed in a small box, there was nothing more to keep her. All she took was the precious hoard of gold coins still sewn in her petticoat, all of the jewelry she had left, and a few articles of clothing. She wore her riding dress, thinking it would appear as if she was going for her regular exercise should anyone wonder why she was out so early.

Morgan looked around the low-ceilinged room one more time. It had been a haven of a sort, even if it had been successfully invaded that one time by Giles. Surely she wouldn't miss it and there was nothing more that she needed to take with her. A mug of chocolate sat on the table where Bridy had left it, steam rising in the cool air. For a second she thought to drink it, but then turned away. There was no time to waste. She slung the fur-lined cloak around her shoulders and slipped into the hallway.

The porter was not at his usual place beside the gate, but since no one expected visitors at this early hour, Morgan thought nothing of it. He was probably in the kitchen having his breakfast, she decided.

Richards met them as they crossed the yard. "Come inside, mistress," he said quietly, casting an anxious look at the blank windows of the house. He led the way into the shadows of the stable.

"What is it, Richards?" Morgan asked, anxiously.

"The master has given orders that you canna ride unless he or Master Giles is with ye."

"When did he tell you this?" Morgan flared.

"Samuels did it. This morning, early like."

"But you did manage to get the coach?"

"Oh, aye," he responded. "It was done long afore. It's waitin' now two streets over. But we'll have to slip out the back, and not ride like you said."

"It doesn't matter," Morgan reassured him. "Is there another way out of the stables?"

"Aye, that there is! This way."

Richards led them into the grain room where metal-lined bins held the horses' feed. In the back wall wide door gave onto an alley where carts could come when they delivered fodder. It was a short walk from there to the coach. There were six armed outriders as well as a driver.

Richards climbed onto the box beside the driver after he had seen Morgan and Bridy safely inside the vehicle. He would accompany her to Billingsgate Market, before heading south with Bridy. Morgan's journey would take her north.

The two women were snug and warm under the rugs Bridy had the foresight to slip out the day before. There was also a large hamper of food, since one never knew what the inns along the way would have to offer.

Despite Morgan's fears that he would have second thoughts, James was waiting at the market. He sat astride a bay thoroughbred, attended by his manservant on a dun-colored cob.

"Miss," Bridy said hesitantly. "I'll remember ye in my prayers always."

"Thank you, Bridy. The letter I gave you should help you find a new position. I wish you could come with me."

"I will, if you need me."

"No. Your future is with Richards."

Bridy sighed happily. "'Tis indeed." She climbed down from the coach wearing smile for her intended, and Morgan realized she would be all right with the stalwart groom.

She watched as Richards mounted a horse he'd purchased the day before. Bridy was lifted up to ride on a pillion behind him. With a last wave, they were gone.

James exchanged words with the driver before dropping back to speak with Morgan.

"We will try to cover as much ground as possible before dark. I hope you will be comfortable?"

"I don't expect comfort," she replied. "But I agree we should get far away from London as quickly as we can."

"Good. Let's be off then."

Morgan waited a second, then realized he intended to ride outside. At first she was nettled, but then realized it was his way of showing his honorable intentions. With a rueful sigh she settled back in the seat, trying to get comfortable as the vehicle jolted over ruts and stones. She managed to convince James Challoner to rescue her, but he certainly wasn't the kind of husband she would have chosen if she'd been given a choice! Her mind strayed to Daniel Harris, and she passed the time trying to imagine what he would have done in a similar situation.

The sky was overcast as they left the city and started across the heath. The heavy coach rocked and lurched over every bump in the road as the coachman kept his team at a canter. Morgan knew the horses wouldn't be good for many miles at this rate. They would have to be changed for fresh ones at every opportunity.

She pulled her cloak closer and curled up under the rug, trying to stay warm. Once again she wondered at the circumstances that led her to take such a rash step. She was running away to marry a man she barely knew. It also meant, she told herself, that she would have to remain in England, unless ... Surely he would want to see the property in the Indies. Once he had seen how beautiful, how green and warm it was, perhaps he could be convinced to live there. Yes, Morgan thought, that would be her next plan.

She let her mind go, daydreaming about the Indies and her old life. Such thoughts always made her sad, so she didn't often allow her mind to dwell there. Still she was so miserable now that a little more couldn't make it any worse.

The rhythmic thunder of the horses' hooves seemed to grow louder as she mused. Suddenly the coach lurched and she was almost thrown from the seat. The crack of the coachman's whip sounded and the obedient horses increased their speed. There were dark blurs in the windows on either side as the forward guards dropped back.

Morgan leaned her head out the window so she could she see what was going on. They were being pursued! When another lurch almost tipped her out onto the road, she pulled her head back inside, bracing herself as best she could. Whoever they were, it was only a matter of time before they overtook her. Pulling a heavy coach, the team was no match for saddle horses.

There was a possibility their pursuers were simply

highwaymen, but in her heart Morgan knew better. Oh how she wished she had made James give her a weapon of some kind!

The hoof beats drew closer and there was the sound of pistols fired. Morgan didn't know who was being foolish, for they didn't have any hope of hitting a moving target from the back of a galloping horse. Then there were shouts and a clash of steel, the sounds dropping rapidly to the rear. Morgan almost braved the window again as she realized the two forces had stopped to engage each other in hand to hand combat. The coach continued on its way, and she wondered if maybe they would escape after all.

But that hope was in vain. Minutes later the sound of hooves came again and two riders drew up on either side of the coach. There were loud pistol reports followed by a string of curses. The horses pulled up, and the coach slowed and came to a stop. When they were standing, Morgan reached for the door handle, but the sound of another pistol shot started the horses into motion again. She tried to keep her balance as the coach began to move, but she was flung back on the seat. Then someone took the reins and brought the frightened team to a standstill.

Morgan pulled herself up, opened the door and dropped onto the ground. Looking down at her from the back of a big gray hunter was her cousin Oliver. He climbed laboriously down from his mount and slowly walked over to where she stood. Without a word he hit her, an open handed slap with enough force to knock her to the ground.

"I think it's time you were taught obedience," he said, breathing heavily.

Morgan lay where she had fallen, her hand on her cheek, her eyes wide with shock and fright. Then she saw the bloodied body of the coachman where he had fallen beside the wheel, almost close enough for her to touch.

"Get to your feet, you little harlot!" Oliver shouted. "Get back in the coach!"

"I ..." she began but got no further before Oliver's riding whip came down on her shoulders. She shrieked in terror and turned over, covering her head with her hands.

The blows fell one after another and although her heavy cloak kept her from real harm, Oliver kept hitting her until he had taken the edge off his rage. When the whip finally stilled Morgan didn't move. She lay huddled on the ground, too frightened to do anything else. No one had ever treated her so! Silence stretched and she ventured a peek up at her cousin. Oliver still stood there, his chest heaving as he fought to catch his breath, his eyes glazed, and the long lash of the whip dangling from his wrist. He stared at her for a long minute until the sound of horses drew his attention.

Giles rode up on a lathered horse. James stumbled behind him, tied by a rope around his wrists. His clothes were torn and muddy and a trickle of blood ran from his forehead. In the rear rode a small troop of horsemen, a motley assortment of hired bullies as well as grooms and housemen.

Morgan got to her feet and started toward James, but Oliver swung the whip again. The blow caught her in the stomach and startled her as much as it hurt.

"Into the coach," he growled.

She opened her lips to object, but the look on his face as well as the whip made her reconsider rebellion. As she turned to the door, her foot on the step, she paused and looked one more time at James.

"Obey me, you shameless whore!" Oliver roared, slashing at her with the whip again.

She tumbled into the coach, just avoiding the lash. Never in her wildest imaginings had she thought Oliver would behave thus. Morgan was frightened, but she was also angry at being intercepted in her flight. She climbed onto the back-facing seat so she could see what was happening outside.

The horsemen halted when they reached the coach.

"Are you in charge here?" James asked, pulling himself together and glaring at Oliver.

"I am, indeed," Oliver replied, his face a mask of fury.

"Then I demand you release me. You have no right …"

"Rights!" Oliver yelled. "How dare you speak to me of rights, you insolent puppy! You elope with my ward and expect me to condone your actions? I ought to ..." He sputtered as he sought for words.

Giles dismounted and gave his reins to one of the grooms. "Father, allow me to rid you of this problem," he said with a smile.

"No," Oliver replied. "You got into enough trouble last time with your dueling."

Giles frowned. "I'll be careful. No one will have to know."

"I said no and I mean no!" Oliver snapped. He nodded to Samuels who was mounted on a big-boned roan horse, the animal as tall and lean as his rider's philosophy. "Where are the guards?"

"Dead or fled," the servant replied.

"Good." He nodded at James. "Now get rid of him too."
"Yes, sir."

Chapter 18

Oliver turned his back and beckoned to one of the grooms. While they spoke together, Giles and Samuels dragged a protesting James off the road. His conversation finished, Oliver climbed into the coach. He seemed oblivious to what was happening to their prisoner.

Morgan watched in horror until James and his captors were out of sight. She clenched her hands into fists, wanting desperately to do something to help. Once again she wished for a pistol, but by now it was too late. There were the sounds of thrashing and blows, and then a very loud gunshot shattered the air. When the echoes died away there was complete silence. Even the birds and insects had stopped their noises. When the shrubbery rustled and parted, two men emerged. Giles approached the coach as Samuels remounted his roan.

Oliver looked at his son, one eyebrow raised.

"It's done," Giles told him.

"Good," Oliver said softly. "Return to London and wait on your mother. As soon as she can make herself ready, bring her home."

"To Haverton?"

"Yes, to Haverton." Oliver flicked Morgan with a glance. "Your little cousin and I will wait for you there. We have some pressing business to attend to in the mean time."

Giles looked at Morgan and grinned knowingly. "Certainly, father. Have a pleasant trip." He stood back from the coach and waved to the groom who was now in the driver's box. The horses were set in motion and the coach started on its way. Six mounted men surrounded them, guarding them from the dangers of the road.

Morgan sat back in her corner and glared at her cousin with unconcealed hatred. "You killed him. You killed James!" she accused.

"I?" Oliver managed to look surprised. "Not at all. I was here the whole time. You are my witness. If anyone is responsible for the death of that unfortunate young man, it is you."

"Me? What do you mean by that?"

"You were the one who brought him here."

"I ..." she began, trying to think past the feelings of guilt. "No, you cannot put that on me. What you have done is wicked!"

Oliver shrugged. "I could care less what you think," he said, and then abruptly changed the subject. "You didn't drink your chocolate this morning?"

159

"Chocolate?" she said, confused. "No. There wasn't time."

"Pity. It would have saved a lot of trouble." He seemed bored by the whole subject. Reaching into a pocket he produced a flask. "You will drink this."

"What is it? My chocolate?" she sneered. "You really didn't have to go to all the trouble of bringing it."

"No, this isn't your chocolate," he replied. "Drink it." He shoved the flask into her hands.

Morgan opened the cap and gingerly sniffed the contents. "What is it?"

"Just a cordial. Drink it."

She sniffed and took a very tiny sip. The alcohol content was very high and the mixture much too sweet. "No thank you. It's not to my taste." She held the flask out to him.

Oliver leaned forward and slapped Morgan across the face, catching the flask when it dropped from her hand. He held it in front of her. "Drink it!" he shouted. "Or, by God, I'll pour it down your throat!"

"I don't," she began as tears ran from her eyes. As Oliver reached for her she quickly took the flask and sipped the sweet liquor.

"All of it."

She drank and when the flask was empty threw it at him. He smiled as he caught it.

"So, now are you happy?" she asked in despair. "What was in the flask? Poison?"

"No. Just a sleeping draught. It will to save me the trouble of having to look after you on the journey."

Morgan could feel it working already. Her eyelids wanted to close and her head felt too heavy.

"The poison," Oliver told her, his voice coming through a thickening haze, "was in the chocolate."

His words went on, but she wasn't there to hear. The coach trundled down the road, working its way west, to Bristol.

Morgan slept most of the trip. The drug wore off, but before she could protest or even gather enough strength to fight him, Oliver gave her another dose. She vaguely remembered stumbling into an inn and being solicitously cared for by the innkeeper's wife. She spent the night in the comfort of a feather bed, but the next day they were off again. She didn't begin to regain her senses until the afternoon of the third day and by then they were approaching Bristol.

"I want you to listen to me," Oliver told her carefully. "Pay attention!"

Morgan was propped in the corner staring dully at nothing. She turned her head toward the voice and tried to focus her eyes.

"Morgan, can you hear me?" Oliver demanded.

"I ... I hear you," she managed through parched lips. Oliver made a sound of disgust and removed a bottle from the basket under the seat. He poured a pewter mug half full and held it out to her.

"I don't want any more of your potions," she whispered, closing her eyes and turning her face away.

"This is just ale. Drink it."

Morgan eyed the cup. She was terribly thirsty. After a second she took it and drank. It was ale and it did quench her

161

thirst. What else it would do remained to be seen.

Oliver took the empty cup away from her. "We'll be in Bristol before long. My solicitor is expecting us."

"Your solicitor?" Morgan frowned, trying to pierce the fog that filled her brain. "I don't understand."

"There is nothing for you to understand," Oliver informed her. "All you have to do is sign some documents he has prepared."

"What documents?"

"Concerning your inheritance."

Morgan mulled this over, her thoughts coming clearer as the minutes passed. "My inheritance? I thought we already took care of that. Didn't you give me papers to sign before we went to London?"

"This is another matter entirely. These papers weren't ready before we left for town," Oliver said with a strange smile.

Morgan was still feeling weak and her cousin's expression made her feel very uneasy. She subsided into silence.

The horses' hooves rang on cobbles as the coach entered Bristol. There was the usual miasma of a populated center, but over it all came the sharp salty tang of the sea. Morgan breathed it in, remembering her home and wishing once again that she could be there. The solicitor's address was a building on the waterfront, and Morgan stared out the window as they passed the ships moored along the quay. It was a bustling scene as cargo was unloaded while other ships were provisioned and stocked with trade goods.

The coach threaded its way carefully all through this activity, being stopped only once. There was a group of excited onlookers crowding around the door to a tavern. By craning her neck, Morgan could see what everyone found so interesting -- a couple of barmaids locked in combat, their hair and clothing in wild disarray. They fought, wrestling, clawing and biting, all the while screaming invective at each other and at the crowd that egged them on.

Oliver stuck his head out of the window and called something to the coachman. There was the sound of the whip and more shouts. With curses and waved fists, the crowd parted to let them through.

Soon they came to a halt in front of a building whose sign proclaimed it to be the offices of Messieurs Paulson and Gregory, Solicitors. Oliver climbed down and reached up for her hand to steady her down the steps.

"Listen carefully," he said softly when she was standing beside him. He didn't release her and his grip tightened painfully. "I want you to behave while we are here. I want you to say nothing and do nothing except sign the papers I give you. Do you understand me?"

"Yes," she responded, startled by the pain in her hand.

"Good."

Oliver let her go and led the way inside.

They went through the outer office, a large dim space where two clerks sat, their backs to the door, busy writing in huge ledgers propped up before them. A third occupant, who had been copying a document, rose politely to greet them. Upon learning their identity, he escorted them through one of the doors piercing the far wall. A short, thin man, his hooked nose supporting a pair of spectacles, was inside.

"Mr. Haverton. I am happy to see you again, sir. Madam," he added, giving a short bow. "Please be seated. How can I serve you today?"

Oliver held a chair for Morgan before seating himself. "We corresponded about the documents disposing of certain of my cousin's properties. Are they ready? She is here to sign them."

"Ah, yes. Yes. We have them prepared." Paulson looked at his clerk. "You know the papers of which Mr. Haverton spoke. Bring them."

"Yes, sir." And the clerk scurried.

Paulson beamed on his clients.

"Dispose of what ..." Morgan began, but Oliver interrupted.

"'Tis is the matter I spoke of in the coach, my dear." He took her hand in both of his and holding it where Paulson couldn't see, squeezed until the bones cracked. "Remember?"

Morgan turned her eyes away. "Yes," she whispered.

He released her as the clerk returned. Paulson spread the papers on his desk so Oliver could read them. Morgan leaned forward and looked as well.

She pushed the top sheet aside and stared for a moment at the one underneath. "This is a will!" she said, surprised.

"And a very wise precaution, too, I might say," Paulson said, beaming. "A woman in your position, about to be wed, should make such provisions. It prevents misunderstandings in the future."

"About to wed?"

"Here," Oliver said, getting to his feet and taking a quill from the pot on Paulson's desk. He moistened the point with ink. "Sign."

Morgan took the quill and looked at the papers. "I think ..."

"Sign the papers!"

Morgan looked up at her cousin and something in her eyes made him turn to the attorney. "May I have a moment alone to speak with my cousin?" he asked with a smile as false as his heart.

"Of course, of course!" Paulson responded, and went out the door.

"Listen to me, bitch," Oliver hissed through clenched teeth when they were alone. "You will sign these papers."

"No." She wasn't sure what her options were, but she wasn't about to sign what might well be her death warrant.

"You will sign or regret the consequences."

"No, I will not sign them."

He moved as if the strike her, but caught himself. "Listen carefully," he told her, his face contorted in anger. "You will sign these papers if you want to continue to live."

"What do you mean?" she gasped. What more could he do to her, she thought?

Oliver sat back in his chair, trying to bring his rage under control. "We have been feeding you a slow poison for the past month."

Morgan shrank back from him and barely breathed her reply. "No."

"Oh, yes. We have been giving you small amounts so you wouldn't notice, but you are poisoned just the same."

Morgan was speechless.

"If you sign these papers without anymore to-do," Oliver continued, "I will give you the antidote. If you do not sign them …" he smiled at her, but it was not nice to see.

The past three days had been too much for Morgan. Her eyes closed and tears began to run from under the lids. Not a sound, not even a whimper came from her lips.

"Stop that," Oliver demanded.

"I can't," she managed in a weak voice.

Oliver slapped her and she gasped, her head coming up. She stared at him for a second, then put her head on the edge of the desk and began to cry in earnest.

"Damn," he breathed. He paced to the door and back again, standing and looking down at Morgan. Perhaps the past three days had been too much for her. Still, if he gave her a chance to recover from the drugs, she would only give him more trouble. "I'll be right back," he told her. Not caring whether she heard or not he left the room searching for brandy or something else to serve as a restorative.

As soon as the door closed behind him, Morgan was on her feet. She brushed the tears from her face and took a deep breath. She knew crying could be an effective weapon against a man, but she never expected it to save her life.

The room contained a desk, three chairs and a rather handsome modern cabinet stuffed every which way with books and folios of papers, but none of this was any use to her. There was only one door and Oliver was on the other side of it. She went to the window, and was looking for a catch when something in the street caught her eye. A wagon was loading casks and crates of produce under the direction of a warmly dressed individual, a bright scarf wrapped around his head in place of a hat. She had seen that scarf before, she thought. There was something familiar about the man too, but he was deep in conversation with the carrier, his back turned. Morgan only caught a fleeting glimpse of his face, but she was certain it was Juan Smyth.

But if Juan was here ... Her eyes swiftly scanned the ships moored alongside the quay. There! Her breath caught as she glimpsed the familiar spars and rigging of the *Kestrel*.

At that second there came the sound of a hand on the door latch and she quickly resumed her seat.

Morgan was daubing at her eyes when Oliver and Paulson returned to the room.

"We will return the papers in the morning," Oliver was saying. "With my cousin's signature," he added, glaring at Morgan.

"Yes. Certainly," the attorney agreed smiling. He called to his clerk and the man came, gathered up the papers and put them into a leather case.

With a show of concern, Oliver took Morgan by the arm and helped her out of the building. His grip was like iron, his fingers digging into her flesh. After bundling her into the coach, he took the case of documents from the clerk. "To-morrow morning," he told the attorney.

"We await your pleasure," the man returned, bowing.

Oliver climbed onto the seat, carefully placing the document case beside him. The clerk put up the steps and closed the coach door. Horseshoes scraped on the cobbles for a moment as the vehicles was set into motion.

"I think you will regret this day," was all her cousin said to her when they were on their way.

Morgan didn't reply but stared out of the window at the black spars of the *Kestrel* as it made ready to sail.

Chapter 19

The house that generations of Havertons called home was icy cold, as if it contained the accumulation of a hundred frigid winters within its walls. There probably hadn't been a fire in any of the rooms since the family left for London. Oliver raged through the empty house, slamming doors and shouting for the caretaker, while Morgan shivered on the settle by the front door. It quickly grew dark outside, and the fine drizzle that started earlier in the afternoon turned into a driving rain. She could hear drops spattering on the other side of the door, and a thin line of moisture crept under the edge.

The caretaker and his wife scurried through the cold house, bringing kindling and logs to light a fire in the sitting room. Oliver dragged Morgan into the room after him, thrusting her into a chair before he went to stand in front of the fireplace. He watched the fire crackle into life, rubbing his hands greedily in the meager warmth.

Morgan looked at the papers he had dropped beside her on the table and knew she was of no more importance to him than those sheets, something to be attended to and then, when they had served their purpose, put away and forgotten, or perhaps burned in the fireplace.

She was still shivering even though a little warmth began to penetrate where she sat. The caretaker and his wife returned, each with a tray piled high with dishes of what Morgan suspected was their own dinner. Hands trembling with fear, they quickly laid two places on the table by the window and withdrew to stand by the door, waiting further orders.

Oliver approached the table and surveyed their efforts with a disdainful lift of his eyebrow.

"And," he said speaking with deceptive softness, "what do you call this?"

The caretaker and his wife exchanged a quick glance. "Dinner, sir," the man stammered, wringing his hands. "'Tis all that's prepared, sir, us not knowin' you were comin', that is. 'Tis a meat pie and a capon, sir."

Oliver ignored him and splashed wine from a squat earthenware bottle into a tarnished silver goblet. He sniffed it before he took a tentative sip. "No doubt this wine came from my cellars here?"

The caretaker stared at him, his eyes wide, lips trembling with terror.

"My own wine graces your miserable table?" Oliver continued, spacing his words for added emphasis.

The caretaker's mouth opened and closed but no sound came out. His face was as white as his shirt. Morgan wondered what Oliver did to his servants to inspire such terror.

"Get your whoresons carcass out of my sight," Oliver exploded, reaching for the nearest object to throw after the fleeing couple. He hefted the pie and it hit the doorsill with a crash, splashing gravy and chunks of meat over the wall and floor. A side dish of potatoes and winter vegetables followed the plate shattering on the flagstones. Oliver's rage was so great that he threw everything he could reach, not stopping until his hand wrapped around the bottle of wine. He looked at it for a long moment before lifting it up and pouring a generous amount into his goblet. He drank it off and poured a second draught.

Morgan watched him, silent and anxious. Oliver was drinking a third goblet full when he caught her eyes on him.

"What are you looking at you graceless slut?"

Morgan dropped her eyes.

"Answer me, bitch," he roared, spilling a trickle of wine on the front of his coat.

"Nothing," she responded.

"Nothing," he sneered. "'Tis a goodly word to describe you. Nothing. You do nothing. You give nothing. You say nothing -- nothing that is of any use to me and mine, that is. What use you have been to others, though, remains to be seen."

Morgan flared at his insinuation. "What do you mean by that, sir?"

"Do you actually pretend you cannot guess?" he asked his lip curled in contempt. "Your paramour, your precious

James. Giles and I did attempt to dissuade him from such folly. I can only imagine what means you employed to induce him to run away with you." He laughed, making a very ugly sound.

Morgan flushed hotly. Oliver knew precisely that she used her fortune to tempt James, but he liked to torment her. On top of everything else that had happened to her in the past days, his words didn't have the sting that he might have wished.

"Since there doesn't seem to be a prospect of dinner," she informed him, "I think I'll retire. It's been a long journey."

"Sit down!"

Oliver filled the goblet again and Morgan hesitated. "I said sit, damme!" he roared, flinging the goblet at her.

It hit Morgan on the shoulder spilling wine down her cloak. She looked at it with distaste and removed the garment, hanging it over the back of the chair before she reseated herself. She stared at him then, her face stormy.

Oliver stood, his head thrust forward, his eyes slitted. He was breathing hard and looked to Morgan like a mad animal. Moments passed.

"Yes," said her cousin slowly. "You appear to obey, don't you? You like to fool people into thinking you are a dutiful young woman. But you don't fool me." His hands clenched into fists. "You need to be taught," he whispered. "You need to be taught who's your master."

When he took a step forward his eyes fell on the papers that had been pushed aside and forgotten during his more pressing concern for warmth and sustenance. He paused and then went to a writing desk that stood against one wall. From this he obtained an inkpot and quill. He put the pot down beside the papers and set about mending the point on the quill.

Morgan rose to her feet and moved over beside the fire, but still kept all her attention on her cousin. She could never tell what he would do and she needed to be ready.

"For once in your miserable life," he said as he worked on the quill with a penknife, "you are going to be of use to someone else."

"And how is that?"

Oliver paused in his task and looked at her. "You're going to sign these papers."

"For what purpose?" she asked, amazed at her own boldness. She had a distinct feeling that as soon as the papers were signed, her life would be worth less than nothing. "Since I am to be of benefit, I would like to know in what way I am serving," she added.

"One of them is your will, as you have already seen. The other is a transfer of ownership for your property in the Caymans."

"Transfer? To whom?"

"To a buyer. It isn't necessary for you to know whom or any of the details."

"You mean you sold my plantation?"

"Not yet. Not until you sign this paper." Oliver set the quill aside and lowered himself into the chair where she had been sitting. He stretched his legs out comfortably.

"I refuse!" Morgan said, her voice rising, and her fists clenched at her sides. "I will never agree to the sale! You may be my guardian, but I know you can't sell my property."

"It is true. I cannot sell you property unless you agree to it. But you will agree, I think." He smiled at her, a smug self-satisfied smile she found both disgusting and frightening.

"Then perhaps you'd better think again," she retorted with false bravado. She was quaking inside, but desperation formed her words. She would not, could not sign those hated papers!

"I have already begun negotiations to sell the plantation. All that remains is for you to sign these papers," Oliver told her. "And you cannot refuse since I have already received a down payment."

"How much did you get for it? And where's the money?"

"The money is what has paid for your little excursion to London."

"Don't you mean *your* little excursion," she snarled, her eyes blazing with fury.

"The money covered certain necessary expenses for the whole family."

"Oh, aye," Morgan said her voice filed with sarcasm. "I can see that it did! And after all of those necessary expenses, how much is left?"

"Nothing is left. But," he added, forestalling Morgan's protest, "I only received a down payment. Before the buyer will transfer the rest of the funds he wants the deed. That document requires your signature."

"And yet I refuse to sign." Her chin was up and her lips in an uncompromising line.

"But you will. Remember what I said about the poison?"

Her words were still defiant even though she went pale. "I don't believe you would do that."

Oliver laughed. "Then you don't know me very well. Remember James? It was no trouble to kill him."

"Giles did it."

"Certainly," Oliver agreed. "He derives a great deal of pleasure from killing. And inflicting pain. But the poison was my idea."

Morgan moved restlessly, her gaze wandering to the window pane where she and her cousin were reflected on the glass like actors on a stage. She only wished what was happening in the room was so divorced from reality. She looked at Oliver again. "What was the poison?"

"Arsenic. 'Tis easy enough to obtain, and the results are infallible."

"Then why am I not dead?"

Oliver was silent and Morgan felt a stirring of relief.

"The only poison was in my morning chocolate, wasn't it?" she asked and saw the answer in the flicker of his eyes. "That's it then. I only had the poison one morning, but I was sick and spewed it out." It was Morgan's turn to laugh. "You can't use that to frighten me."

Oliver got to his feet and came to her side, taking her arm in a tight grip. "I don't intend to. Nor do I intend to waste anymore time bandying words with you, bitch. You'll sign these papers if I have to beat you bloody." He reached for the riding whip that he had laid on the mantle.

Morgan struggled in his hold, but he was much stronger than she.

174

"Are you ready to obey me?" Oliver asked, the whip raised.

"Never."

"Worthless whore!" Oliver screamed as he struck at her. The whip fell across her shoulders, the lash hurting her this time since she no longer wore the fur-lined cloak. Oliver flung her from him and she landed on her hands and knees on the stones of the fireplace. Morgan gasped as the lash found her again and again. When she opened her eyes, a basket of iron tools for the fireplace was in front of her, a poker leaning conveniently forward. She grasped it and struggled to her feet. As she turned the lash caught and tangled on the iron rod. It stuck only momentarily, but still it was enough to make Oliver pause in his frenzy.

Morgan was never sure how it happened. All she remembers is that the lash came down, hitting her hand and arm with a strip of fire. She must have swung the poker, for the next thing she knew Oliver was laying on the floor, his periwig in disarray and a trickle of blood running down his forehead and gathering in a pool beneath him.

The poker slipped from Morgan's fingers and clattered on the stones of the hearth. She stood and gazed at her cousin in horror, his sightless eyes seeming to stare right back at her.

"Oh my God! I've killed him," she whispered aghast.

Rain beat against the windows, blown by a stiff wind, and the fire snapped and hissed in the grate. Oliver lay deathly still. Morgan moved away from him, walking backwards until she came up short against the edge of the table. The inkpot and mended quill were still lying beside the docu-

175

ments she was supposed to sign. She took the papers up and carefully avoiding Oliver's body, dropped them into the fire. The papers began to curl along the edges. Then an area blackened before a thin flame appeared, working its way through the thick paper. Morgan watched the documents burn, concentrating on the fire and trying not to think of her cousin laying dead beside her. Soon there was nothing left of the documents but some ash that fell between the logs.

And that took care of the damned papers, she thought. The next thing she had to do was get away from the house.

Morgan caught up her cloak and swung it around her shoulders as she went to the door. Tapers flickered in the hall, but the rest of the house was in darkness. There was no sign of the caretaker or his wife. Morgan went swiftly to the front door and drew the bolt.

Outside it was black as pitch, and the wind tugged at her cloak. Morgan held it tightly around her as she went down the shallow steps of the porch and into the rain. If she remembered correctly the stables were around the left side of the building. There was a coachman and the grooms, but no doubt they would all be in the warm kitchen having their supper.

The stables were dark and deserted except for the weary coach horses, and a couple of big farm animals. Beyond them was the only riding horse, a short-legged chestnut cob who dozed, one hind foot cocked in the straw. He looked around at Morgan as she took his bridle from its peg and moved up beside him.

"Easy, lad," she whispered as she slipped the bit into his mouth and pulled the headstall over his ears. This done she untied the rope around his neck holding him in the stall. Backing him into the aisle, she realized she wasn't sure where the saddles were kept and she didn't want to waste any time looking. Fortunately one of the things her father had taught her was to ride bareback and astride. He never guessed this might one day save her life.

The cob was reluctant to go out into the rainy night, but Morgan didn't give him a chance to refuse. She led him swiftly to the mounting block in the yard and climbed onto his back. He gave one grunt of protest before obeying the urging of her heels and heading into the night.

Haverton was approximately twelve miles from Bristol, and by riding steadily, Morgan hoped to reach the town before morning came and the tide turned. She couldn't imagine what had brought Daniel Harris to England, but with any luck he and the *Kestrel* would still be at the docks. She didn't even try to think what she would say to get him to take her back to the Indies, but she still had sixteen gold pieces stitched in the hem of her petticoat, and it might be enough to buy her passage home.

Chapter 20

Please! Please be there!

The words repeated over and over in her mind, a litany punctuated by the clop of the horse's hoofs. The words were a focal point for Morgan as she rode the cold wet miles. Fortunately the horse was soon as tired as she, for her seat was so weak that any sudden movement would have had her off. She sat slumped on the cob's back, her hands clenched in his mane and the reins as if this tiny point of contact was all that kept her mounted. And thus they traveled through the rain drenched night.

Please be there, Morgan whispered to herself through lips so cold that they didn't feel like part of her face anymore. She was hardly aware of it when the city appeared ahead, a deeper shadow in the black, cloudy night. Bristol slept in darkness unbroken except at the taverns and other places where insomniacs gathered. Other than these, the only ones awake were the watchmen who walked their rounds. Each had a lantern bobbing above him on the end of a long pole, and that enabled Morgan to see them in time to hide. She did have one tense moment, hiding in an alley while a particularly slow moving watchman went by.

The rain had stopped sometime ago, although she wasn't sure when, and the exhausted cob splashed through puddles as he carried her toward the waterfront. Morgan slumped wearily on his back, soaked through and shivering within the bedraggled fur she still wore. Despite her miserable state, however, she didn't swerve from her goal.

The smell of the harbor was strong in her nostrils when she finally found a fairly decent-looking inn. The lamp that should have been lighting the courtyard through the night had gone out and everyone there appeared to be fast asleep. This made it perfect. Morgan slid off the cob before leading him across the courtyard, his shoes clacking on the cobbles. She pushed open the barn door and took him into the dark shelter. Here there were neither grooms nor dogs, which surprised her, but, taking advantage of this bit of good fortune, she took time to make the cob comfortable. After their miserable ride he deserved it. By the time anyone got around to questioning his presence, she would be far away. Morgan turned him into an empty box stall and brought him an armful of hay from the pile in the corner. He nosed it and, even though he was too tired to eat, he pulled out a few strands and held them in his mouth as he cocked his hip, dropped his head, and gave a heavy sigh of relief.

Morgan left him there and slipped into the street. She

didn't feel secure alone and on foot in this part of the city, but the wharf wasn't far. Afraid someone would try to interfere with her she kept to the shadows and walked as quickly as she could. Along the docks a number of taverns were still open, light spilling from their windows. She could hear drunken singing inside one of them as she hurried past. She looked ahead now, trying to see the spars of Daniel's ship against the sky, not daring to breathe lest they not be here.

"Please," she said under her breath. "Please be there."

She had to pick her way carefully around a pile of crates and barrels that had been stacked, waiting for transport. There was a guard leaning against them, his musket beside him, his head down as he dozed. Her breath caught in her throat as she eased by, but he didn't stir. She could just make out the familiar sign for Messers Paulson and Gregory on the building as she passed. Using it to orient herself, she searched the ships moored along the wide paved wharf.

Then she saw it, the familiar raking spars. The *Kestrel* was still at her berth! The sight changed everything for Morgan.

A wind blew up the channel smelling of the sea, and the sky was growing lighter in the east. Morgan knew dawn was coming soon and that the tide would turn. There were lights on the *Kestrel* as a few members of the crew moved about, getting ready to sail. She didn't have a moment to lose!

Morgan hurried forward and crossed the plank that gave access to the ship. A couple of the crew stopped and stared at her as she stepped down onto the deck.

"Please," she said. "I have to see Captain Harris."

"Bet you do, my beauty" one of them replied with a

grin. "But 'es not here now, so you'll have to make do with the likes of us." He gave a loud laugh and dug his companion in the ribs with his elbow.

The other man licked his lips and came forward. "'Ere's a pretty thing come to bid a sailor a fond farewell." He slipped his arm around her waist and turned her to face him. "Give us a kiss, lovey."

"Take your hands off of me!" Morgan cried, twisting free and striking out. Her hand resounded on his face with a loud crack.

With a muttered curse the sailor reached for her again, but suddenly there was an interruption.

"Here, now. What's going on?" a familiar voice asked, and Juan stepped from the hatchway. The two sailors quickly moved away from Morgan.

"Juan," she called relief plain in her voice.

"Mistress Moorhouse?" He couldn't have looked more surprised. She was the last person on earth he expected to see. "What are you doing here?" Juan was shocked at her bedraggled appearance, but he remembered his manners. "How can I help you?"

"I have to see Captain Harris. Please, it's urgent."

"Back to work!" Juan snapped at the two men who slunk off. He gave Morgan a graceful bow. "Please follow me. The captain's below."

"Thank you," she managed through frozen lips.

Morgan's knees were trembling as she followed Juan down the steps. Was it really only three months ago she had walked here? Tears pricked the insides of her lids and she fought back the urge to cry. She huddled inside the wet cloak while Juan knocked on the cabin door.

"Yes," a familiar voice called.

"You have a visitor, sir," Juan responded, throwing open the door to reveal Morgan.

Daniel looked up from the charts spread out on the desk in front of him. He half rose from his chair when he saw who was standing there. "Morgan?" he whispered.

How many times had he dreamed of something like this? How many times had he imagined her here with him, back on his ship once again. He closed his eyes, but opened them immediately lest she disappear. She was still there. She was real.

Morgan moved into the light as he got to his feet, coming quickly around the table to her. Juan quietly closed the door on them and withdrew back up to the deck, a small, knowing smile on his lips.

"Morgan? What has happened? Why are you here?" Daniel asked.

"I need -- I have to go home," she managed, her teeth chattering.

He suddenly realized her condition and reached out to take the cloak from around her shoulders. "You're soaked," he stated. He went to a locker and poured a glass full of amber liquid from a bottle he kept there. "Drink this," he said, holding the glass out to her. "'Twill warm you. And then you'd better get out of these wet clothes."

Morgan sniffed the contents of the glass, the alcohol making her nose wrinkle.

"It's brandy," he told her.

Her teeth chattered against the glass as she sipped. The

warmth started on her tongue and then burned its way through her body as the liquid went down her throat.

"If this were the Indies, I could give you rum," he said lightly as his eyes went over her. What he saw appalled him. She was not only wet through to the skin and obviously very cold, but there was a livid welt on her hand and arm, and bruises marred her pale skin. Another welt laced the back of her neck. Her brown eyes were huge in her white face and circled with dark shadows above prominent cheek bones. He pulled a chair away from the table and she sank gratefully into it.

"What happened," he asked. "Where's your husband."

"Husband?" Her brow furrowed in confusion. "I don't have a husband. I'm not married."

Daniel leaned against the bulkhead and crossed his arms, looking down at her. Although this really wasn't the time, there was a lot he needed to know. "Did your cousin tell you I came to see you in London?"

"You were in London?" she asked incredulously. She shook her head on wonder. That would have changed everything, she thought, but it was just like Oliver to keep the information from her. "No! I wasn't told of it!"

"I came to find you. They told me you were engaged to be married to your cousin's son, Giles."

"That was a lie," she said firmly, her hand tightening on the glass. She met his gray eyes with her huge brown ones, warmth that had nothing to do with brandy coursing through her veins. She felt safe for the first time in months. "Oliver, my cousin, wanted me to marry Giles so he could control my property. As it was I discovered he'd been selling off parts of

183

it all along. Then he brought me here, to Bristol, so I could sign more papers." Her voice faltered and stopped as she remembered.

Daniel just watched, holding himself in check. He wanted to hold her, but she had obviously been through so much! He didn't dare move or touch her until he was certain what she wanted from him.

The lamp on the table hissed softly in the silence, its flame flickering, making shadows dance on the bulkhead.

"Morgan?"

Her eyes were enormous, golden in the lamp light.

"I want to go home," she said simply, plaintively. She set the glass aside and came to her feet, facing him. "I have money. Gold. I can pay you for my passage."

"And what will your cousin have to say to this?" he asked.

She shook her head, a tear slipping from under her eyelid and sliding down her cheek. "He's dead."

Daniel didn't ask to hear the details. His finger touched the glistening drop of moisture and then withdrew. "You're certain that this is what you want? Once we're at sea there's no turning back."

"More than anything," she said fervently. "Oh, please, oh please!" she begged. "Take me away from here."

"All right." He moved to the table and rolled up the charts, putting them away. "We're sailing with the tide, and I need to be on deck. I suggest you get out of your wet clothes. And get some sleep." He paused and looked back at her.

"I never thought I'd see you again," he said mostly to himself, drinking in the face that only an hour ago had been a memory. My darling, my love, he called her in his thoughts. "You're safe now," he said aloud.

"I know," she replied with a little smile.

It was the smile that got to him, cutting through his defenses. The cabin was small and he was standing close enough that the faint scent of her. His hand came up and hovered a moment as he looked deep into the brown eyes that gazed so trustingly back at him. Very carefully he brushed back her hair, his palm warm for a second against her cheek. Her eyes closed and she leaned toward him, but his hand withdrew as he turned away and went out the door.

Morgan stood swaying as weariness hit her like a blow. She staggered to the bunk and dropped down, asleep almost before she touched the mattress. Her sleep was deep and dreamless, bred of both emotional and physical exhaustion. She didn't feel the ship begin to move, starting on the long voyage back to the Caribbean.

Chapter 21

When Morgan woke she was ravenously hungry and something smelled absolutely divine. In her first groggy moments she thought she was still dreaming, but then realized she really did smell food. She opened her eyes wide and took a deep breath of the wonderful odor, banishing the fog of sleep.

Sunlight poured through the wide windows over the bunk, dazzling her eyes and leaving the rest of the cabin into a black shadow. She was tucked into a nest of pillows and warm blankets, and as she started to sit up she realized that she was naked. She didn't remember undressing herself! She pulled the blanket around her shoulders.

"Have you finally decided to rejoin us?" Daniel asked, his voice coming from the darkness. She shaded her eyes with her hand and saw him standing beside a table where he just set a tray from the galley.

"Only if those dishes are filled with food and that wonderful smell is real," she replied. "I'm starving."

"I'd be surprised if you weren't," he replied. "Put this on and get up. Or would you rather dine in bed?" He handed her a huge shirt and a long bed gown of dull golden brocade. The shirt was silk and would serve as a shift.

"No, I'll come to the table," she responded taking the garments from him.

"Your clothes are dry," he continued. "But I'm afraid they may have been ruined by the rain. They'll need some attention before you can wear them again."

"Turn your back," she said as she pulled the shirt under the covers with her. He obliged with a grin. She managed to get dressed while preserving her modesty, even though she suspected it was Daniel who undressed her while she slept. The sleeves of both of the garments were too long and she folded them back before sliding off the bunk. "Is that breakfast?" she asked.

Daniel turned catching sight of her in the gold robe, her long red hair in tangles around her shoulders. The sleep had done wonders; the haunted look had disappeared from her face and the shadows were gone from her eyes. To him she had never looked more beautiful.

"Breakfast was hours ago," he told her. "This is dinner."

"Dinner? How long did I sleep?"

"One day and most of another."

"Days?" she gasped. "Why didn't you wake me?"

"You did wake up a couple of times, but I doubt you'd remember much."

"It seems strange to sleep so long."

She came to the table and looked at the food there. Daniel's cook had done his usual wonderful job. There was a stew of chickens and vegetables as well as a loaf of crusty bread and butter. Daniel poured two glasses of wine and held a chair for her to seat herself.

"We're two days into the Atlantic. We'll reach the Caribbean in three weeks, God willing."

Morgan raised her glass as if in a toast. "God willing."

"Now," Daniel began, setting his wineglass aside. He served her a generous helping of stew. "See if you can eat this."

"I don't know why I couldn't," she replied. She tasted the thick broth and it was as good as the tantalizing odor promised. "I think I will have to steal your cook," she commented.

Daniel grinned and shrugged. "He's free to go where he chooses. If he's tired of the life of a buccaneer he's welcome to go with you."

"I'll do my best to persuade him."

Daniel laughed again and broke an end off of the bread. Between the two of them, they managed to finish most of the loaf and the big bowl of stew.

Finally Morgan sat back and sighed, her eyelids drooping, a satisfied grin on her lips.

"Do you want more?" Daniel asked.

She shook her head. "I wouldn't know what to do with it."

Daniel refilled his wine glass and leaned back in his chair. "Now we have to discuss your future," he told her.

"My future?" she inquired, looking surprised.

Daniel nodded. "Have you thought of what you'll do when you get to the Indies? It's no place for a gentlewoman alone."

"But ..." Her eyes were wide as she gazed at him, the implication of his words hitting her. She took a deep breath. "I still have the plantation. I'll go there."

"And what makes you think you'll be permitted to live there now, if you weren't allowed to do so before?"

"It was Oliver who prevented me last time. Now he's dead, and I will do as I please."

"And Giles?"

"Giles can go to the devil," Morgan spat, her face reflecting her hatred.

"What happened to you in England to have given you such a distaste for your family?" Daniel watched her carefully as he spoke.

"Family?" she replied, anger and the sunlight turning her eyes a gleaming gold. "Kin they might be by blood, but they're no family of mine. Their behavior proved that!" She paused and drew in a deep shuddering breath before telling Daniel everything that had happened in London.

"The poison," Daniel interrupted, alarmed. "Do you know what kind it was?"

"Arsenic. But I didn't get much." Her eyes were frightened as she looked up at him. "You don't think ...?"

"Nay, lass. I don't know anything about poisons. You would be the best one to know."

"Me?"

"Aye. How do you feel?"

189

Morgan thought about it before she answered. "I feel well. A little stiff perhaps, but that could be from the ride last ... no, two nights ago."

"Then I'll wager he was bluffing, using the threat of poison to force you to do his will."

"That sounds like Oliver." Morgan only hesitated a brief moment before continuing her story.

She paused again when she came to the part about James, but, locking her eyes on his gray ones the words came out. I don't know what prompted me to go with him," she ended "There was nothing between us. We were not in love, and I'm not sure he even liked me. It was the money, you see."

"So what the two of you had was one of the most compelling reasons for a marriage."

Her brow furrowed as she thought about it. "You mean that he wanted my money and I needed his help to escape?"

"Precisely." Daniel rose to his feet and came over to where she was sitting. "Your eyes are almost closed. You should go back to bed."

"I can't spend the whole voyage sleeping," Morgan protested. She looked at the empty glass in her hand. "Must be the wine," she suggested ruefully.

"Must be." Daniel reached down and taking her glass from her hand carefully set it aside. He lifted her from the chair and as she swayed against him, his arms tightened around her.

"You will take me home, won't you," she asked softly.

He couldn't help but laugh. "I already seem to be committed, lass," he responded. "Unless you think you can swim back to shore?"

She didn't answer but looked up at him, her eyes huge and golden.

He was acutely aware of her body against his and fought against the desire that threatened to break out of his control ... and lost.

"Daniel," she whispered. "I'm so glad I found you. I was so afraid you had gone, that I would never ..."

Daniel's arms tightened and his mouth came down on hers, his lips more than demanding. They took, plundering, awakening something primal that had only been hinted at before.

Morgan felt the fire kindle inside of her, a fire that only Daniel seemed to be able to call forth. She felt the heat start somewhere in her belly and spread downwards, pulsing. The heat built and grew, as wave after wave of desire washed over her. She was swept away from all reality except the incredible intensity of the two of them locked in an embrace. She strained against him, wanting to melt into his body, to become one with him, with Daniel, her beloved.

Morgan's mouth opened under his and she surrendered, offering herself completely. His left hand slid under the heavy mane of hair, his fingers following the curve of her head as his lips moved against hers. Then his mouth softened, becoming gentle, teasing. His tongue traced the curve of her upper lip calling forth exquisite sensations before his kisses trailed off to her cheek, her eyelids. She felt as if she didn't dare breathe for fear of shattering the moment.

His right hand brushed lightly over her breast before traveling down her back to caress her softly rounded bottom, pulling her even closer.

She could feel him, hard and ready as she clung, moving slowly, seductively. She wanted more, she wanted ... she didn't know what she wanted, only that she wanted Daniel, his hands on her and his mouth ....

Daniel was breathing harshly, his eyes closed. "Morgan," he whispered into her hair. "Do you really want this? I don't want to ... to force you."

"This is what I've always wanted," she told him, gazing into his eyes.

"But is this the first time?"

She nodded.

"You may regret ..."

"Never," she said fiercely, coming up on tiptoe so that she could reach his mouth. As she kissed him he drew her against him again.

"So be it," Daniel whispered. He pushed the brocade dressing gown off her shoulders and she lowered her arms to let it drop to the floor. His hands traced the shape of her back through the thin silk of the shirt before they trailed around to her breasts. He teased her nipples and felt them stiffen at his touch.

She ached with wanting him, wanting his hands on her, on her bare skin. Morgan reached down to pull the shirt up over her head. Then her hands went to tug Daniel's jacket from his shoulders. She untied the cord that held his shirt and he helped her pull it off. There were soft, brown curls on his chest and she shivered with delight as she rubbed her swollen nipples against them.

Daniel kissed her again, then suddenly lifted her in his

192

arms and carried her to the bunk. He knelt over her, looking down at her beautiful face amid the frame of blazing red hair. Her skin was gleaming white against her hair, and she was as soft as satin to his touch.

"Please," she whispered, her hand on his shoulder, trying to pull him down on her. "I want you so much."

"There's time," he replied, taking her hand away and kissing the palm, her wrist, the soft tender place inside her elbow. His tongue burned her skin, so intense was her reaction. "We need to go slowly," he whispered.

Her hands trailed slowly down his sides, over the lean, hard muscles of his belly to his belt. He inhaled sharply and his eyes closed as she released the buckle. Then he kissed her, his lips gentle as his hands were busy shedding his boots and breeches.

He was hard and ready. As he lay down beside Morgan, her hand slipped down his belly again, curious to know that part of him. Daniel gasped as she touched him and he reached down to take her hand away.

"For a virgin, you're pretty bold," he murmured in her ear.

"I may not have had experience," she said, "but that doesn't mean I don't know anything." She lay facing him, their bodies all but touching in the narrow bunk.

"No?" he mocked.

"No." she retorted, not wanting to admit her ignorance.

"Do you know about this," he whispered as his hand slid down her body and lightly stroked the insides of her thighs.

She drew a deep shuddering breath, and her eyes closed

in delight as his fingers found the slippery warmth between her legs. His lips were a sweet torment as they spread kisses down her neck, across her shoulder and onto the soft mound of her breast. His tongue licked at her nipple before his mouth explored further.

Morgan had never felt anything like this. It was almost agony just to try to contain it all. She wound her fingers in Daniel's thick brown hair as her body strained against him, gasping a soundless scream.

Daniel gathered her into his arms, his mouth on hers again.

Anything he wanted to do now was all right, she thought. Even unto death, she was his, totally, completely without any reservation whatsoever.

Daniel trembled, holding himself under control as he moved his body over hers. His weight supported on one elbow, he used his other hand to spread Morgan's thighs. When he hovered between them, he let his chest brush lightly against hers as his mouth sought her lips yet again. He moved slowly carefully against her, pressing until the last barrier gave way, and he slid into her hot velvet depths.

Morgan cried out as he entered.

"Are you all right?" he whispered.

"Oh, God, yes! Please," she begged although she had no idea what she was asking for. There had been a moment of sharp pain, but now, with Daniel filling her, the pleasure swamped her. All she knew was that she didn't want him to stop.

Morgan arched her body against him, taking him deeper. She shuddered as each sensation layered itself, each one more glorious than the last.

Her arms held on to him, fingers digging into his shoulders as she followed his lead, moving as he did. Daniel gave himself up to it. She was more wonderful than his wildest dreams. She was powerful in her own way, a wanton, not caring for anything beyond the intensity of their union.

Suddenly her eyes opened wide as she felt something growing inside of her, a sudden increase in the sensitivity of her body, as if every feeling was magnified until she thought she could no longer bear it. He could feel her begin to crest, and as she bucked against him, he let himself go. Together they rode to the crest as it peaked, and very slowly ebbed, leaving them spent and gasping for breath in each other's arms.

Chapter 22

Three weeks passed as the *Kestrel* sailed westward, and for three weeks Morgan experienced more happiness than she ever imagined possible.

One night, she woke bathed by bright moonlight. She was alone in the bunk and realized Daniel had gone on deck. The weather had grown steadily warmer as they neared the Caribbean, leaving the harsh damp English winter behind. Soon they would be in Port Royal.

Everyone on board said this was the easiest crossing they had ever experienced. For Morgan it had been weeks of bliss. She loved Daniel and he loved her. They were together all the time and never seemed to tire of each other's company. And every night they expressed their love in more physical ways. She felt filled with contentment, fat with it, like a sun-warmed cat, she decided.

She stretched out in the bunk, imagining the feel of him

196

and gave a shiver of delight. How wonderful he was, his body, his mind ... everything about him. Now she understood the happiness her parents had shared, and she vowed her life with Daniel would be just as wonderful. Morgan spent long minutes imagining what their future would hold, her eyes closed to contented slits, a happy smile on her lips. But why imagine, she asked herself, when Daniel was just a few feet away. There were beads of sweat on her forehead and she wiped them away. It was warm in the cabin, but there would be a cool breeze up on deck.

Morgan slipped out of bed and donned one of Daniel's big silk shirts. She tied it at her waist with an embroidered sash whose fringes fell down to the shirt hem just above her ankles. Not bothering with a comb, Morgan used both of her hands to push her heavy hair back over her shoulders and out of the way. Her simple toilet completed, she slipped out the doorway and up the stairs to the deck.

The bright light of the full moon washed the *Kestrel* with silver, making the golden glow of the lanterns hanging in the rigging superfluous. Above the ship the sky was a deep black of midnight spread with millions of bright stars. Morgan went to the rail and stood there, breathing in the sharp salty tang, letting the wind cool her cheeks. Daniel was behind her up on the quarterdeck, and although she could feel his eyes on her, she didn't turn around or move to go to him. Tension grew from her need for him and built inside her, and she knew that he felt the same, but still she resisted, holding herself apart until she could stand it no longer. Then very slowly she turned and looked up.

Daniel stood at the wheel, his body sharply defined by

moonlight, his long brown hair ruffled by the wind. His eyes were in shadow, but she knew that he watched her. She leaned back against the rail, looking at him for a long time. Then, drawn by a compulsion she did not wish to resist, she moved across the deck and up the short flight of steps.

One of the crew had been there, standing watch with the captain. When Morgan appeared he slipped away without a word, taking up a position on the foredeck with the night watch.

"I couldn't sleep," Morgan whispered breaking the silence that stretched between them.

"Come here," Daniel said, speaking just as softly. He held the wheel with one hand while he released the other to make room for her. Morgan moved to stand in front of him, her back pressed against him as he closed her within the circle of his arms and the *Kestrel's* great wheel.

Together they stood, alone in the night as the wind drove them ever westward. She could feel the wonderful warmth of his body against her back, while the great wooden ship rose and fell beneath her feet, carrying them westward.

"There," Daniel said suddenly. "Did you see that flash? Off to port side beyond the edge of the main mast?"

"Yes! What was it?"

"A shooting star. You see a lot of them in spring time."

"Do you sail by the stars?" Morgan wanted to know.

"I can if I have to." Daniel lifted his right hand and pointed beyond the main mast. "Those three stars close together are Orion's belt."

"Orion?"

"The hunter. His dog, Sirius is just beyond. They're

from Greek mythology," he added.

Morgan laughed softly. "How do you know that?"

"I had a tutor when I was a lad. He encouraged me to read about such things."

"Encouraged?"

"With a hazel stick," Daniel replied with a grin. "But now and then I find I am grateful for the experience."

"But not the hazel stick!"

"No, not the hazel stick," he agreed.

"And what did you learn about Orion?" she wanted to know.

"He was the greatest hunter in the world, or thought he was. He boasted that no animal could overcome him. "

"Was it true?"

"No, it never is. And boasting about it was an even bigger mistake."

"What happened?"

"Zeus, king of the gods, was angered by Orion's arrogance. My tutor said it was the sin of pride, and warned me never to do the same."

"What happened to Orion?" Morgan prompted.

"Zeus sent a scorpion that stung him in the foot. You can see the scorpion right over there."

"Those stars?"

"No," he pointed, his cheek against hers as he helped her find the right constellation. "Right there." His lips breathed a delicate kiss before he drew back.

"Did he die?" Morgan asked, delighted with the tale. Although classical mythology was in vogue, she had never heard this story.

"Yes, he died."

"That's sad."

Daniel laughed softly. "As are most of the myths."

"Don't any of them have happy endings?"

"Some of them do. Orion didn't end up too badly. He was placed in the sky, along with his hunting dogs, the hare he was chasing and the scorpion that bit him."

"And that's his belt." Morgan leaned her head back against Daniel's chest as she looked over the mainmast at the three stars."

"Yes."

She frowned. "There are so many stars. How do you remember them all?"

"Practice," Daniel told her. He leaned forward and kissed the soft skin of her neck. "But I'll never remember anything with you around to distract me."

"I can go away," she teased and his arms tightened around her.

"That would distract me even more," he promised.

Morgan giggled. "Then teach me some more about stars."

"All right. Do you know anything about astrology?"

"My maid, Hana, told me a little. She said I'm a Scorpio."

"I might have guessed," he murmured.

"Why?"

He laughed and avoided the issue. "I'm going to teach you to sail my ship," he told her. "Put your hands next to mine."

She did as he bid, her hands just big enough to grasp the

heavy wooden spokes.

"She's a light lady," Daniel told her speaking in her ear. "Can you feel her moving?"

Morgan nodded, entranced by the sensation of the powerful vessel lifting and surging under her hands. Above her head the rigging hummed as the great sails tugged and pulled as if they were alive.

"Look at the compass," Daniel instructed. "We're on a heading of south, south west. See where the needle points?"

"Yes."

"Keep the ship as close to that heading as you can. And keep the wind on the back of your head. Do you think you can do that?"

"Yes, I can," she responded, delighted by this new experience. Daniel slowly removed his hands and waited for a moment, ready to take the wheel again. When Morgan appeared to have no problems with the ship, he moved away to lean against the rail.

Bare feet planted on the wooden deck, Morgan stood tall behind the wheel as Daniel watched her, amazed that fortune had brought her back into his life. There had been other women, women of all sorts, but except for one time, he was always careful not to become involved. The only time he ever toyed with the idea of marrying, it was Robert, Morgan's father, who pointed out that he already had a wife and she was his ship. Maybe Robert had been right, for then his life was on the sea. But this was different. He'd never felt like this before. Morgan changed everything. Without her, he realized, life would have lost the thing that gave it all meaning.

Daniel had known her for years, as a little girl growing up on her father's plantation, more of a red haired sprite than a child. He remembered seeing her once riding down the beach at breakneck speed on her pony. He held his breath, sure she would fall, but Robert laughed at him, saying that Morgan was more resilient than most boys her age.

Robert had been right about that too, Daniel thought as he remembered Morgan's story of the abuse she'd experienced at the hands of her cousin. She was resilient. Still it was just as well that the man was dead. If not, Daniel would have felt the need to kill him.

A crewman came quietly up the steps from the ship's waist, and Daniel moved to take the wheel from Morgan.

"It's time to change watch," he told her.

After a few soft words, the seaman replaced the captain at the wheel. Daniel bade his replacement good night and held his hand out to Morgan. Together they went below deck.

The wide windows in the stern were open and a cool breeze came into the cabin. Daniel stopped just inside the door and took Morgan into his arms, kissing her gently.

She wrapped her arms around his neck and pressed her body hard against his, wanting him. Daniel grinned down at her, kissing her heavy lidded eyes.

"Aren't you sleepy?" he asked, his lips tracing a line from the corner of her mouth to her ear.

Morgan didn't respond with words but ran her hands slowly down his back. She reached around and felt the warm bulge in the front of his breeches.

"You're not sleepy either," she said.

Daniel gasped when she touched him, and took her hand away. "Slowly," he whispered. His hands were busy with the knot of the scarf around her waist. It dropped to the floor as he gathered her up in his arms, carrying her to the bunk.

Moonlight was their blanket and the slap of waves the music that accompanied their lovemaking. When they were finished they lay side by side, relaxing in the warm night. Morgan's head was cradled on Daniel's shoulder while his arms held her close.

"Where are we going to live?" he whispered.

"Hummm?"

"After we're married. We have to decide where to live," he repeated.

Morgan rose up on her elbow and looked down at him. His gray eyes were soft. "You never said anything about a wedding," she said.

"You didn't think I'd not marry you after this?" he asked.

"I didn't think about it at all," she admitted.

"Then perhaps it is time. Would you like to be a baroness?" he asked her.

"A baroness? But then you'd have to be a baron! I thought you were a ..." Her words trailed off.

"A pirate? A landless buccaneer?" He laughed at her confusion. "I have to admit that right now the title means more problems than glory, but it has been mine since my father and my older brother died. And now it will be yours if you'll have me. Will you marry me?"

"Yes, of course I will! I just didn't think you would

want to."

Daniel kissed her. "I once asked you father if I could court you. Did you know that?"

"No, he never told me."

Daniel looked away, a shadow of sadness crossing his face. "It doesn't matter now. You were very young. Too young." He laughed again. "And so was I."

"But it does matter," she insisted. "I used to watch you, you know."

He stared, then laughed. "What?"

"I used to listen when they talked ... my parents. I pretended I wasn't interested so they wouldn't send me away. That's how I always knew when your ship was coming in."

"You little ..."

"It meant nothing," she assured him. "Just a childish fancy. I used to think you were handsome."

"Used to think?"

"Well, you were so much older than I, and ..."

"Am I so much older now?" he demanded.

"Oh, no. Well, not much older," she teased, her golden eyes wide and innocent.

Daniel lunged at her. "I'll show you!"

Morgan shrieked and tried to dive under the covers, but Daniel caught her. Her wrists immobile in his hands, he used his weight to pin her body to the mattress. Looking down at her his expression changed and his lips came down on hers. Her body arched to meet him.

In two more days they would be in Port Royal.

Chapter 23

"Captain!" There was a knocking on the cabin door and the voice repeated its summons. "Captain!"

Daniel opened his eyes reluctantly. It was morning and the Caribbean's bright sun filled the cabin. Morgan was nestled in his arms, her head tucked under his chin, her breath soft and warm on his bare chest.

"Captain." Juan knocked again and Daniel knew the crew wouldn't disturb him unless it was of the utmost importance.

He disentangled himself and slipped out of the bunk. Padding across the cabin he opened the door a crack. "What is it?"

"Ship, captain," was all that Juan said. The look on his face said the rest.

"I'll be right there." Daniel closed the door and began to

dress. The ship could be any of a number of vessels, friendly or hostile. It might even be prey, but the look on Juan's face implied they were Spanish.

The ocean is a vast place and a chance encounter by two vessels is slim. That the *Kestrel* happened into the path of a Spanish ship at just this moment was unfortunate. They had sailed to England with about a third of the crew, and very few of the regular fighting men were on board.

"Daniel?" Morgan's sleepy voice came from the bunk.

"You need to get up and dress," he told her. "A ship's been sighted."

"A ship? Whose?" She brushed the heavy hair back from her face.

"That's what I mean to find out."

She felt slow and stupid from sleep. "Daniel, what's going on?"

"I don't know. Perhaps nothing. Come on, snug-a-bed. Get up and make yourself decent."

"Certainly. But ..."

His mouth stopped her words, stealing a swift kiss. "May like 'tis nothing," he told her, pulling away. "But I have to go see to it." With another swift hard kiss he was gone.

Morgan sat up and yawned. Throwing aside the sheet she swung her legs over the side of the bunk. Digging into the cabinet that held Daniel's clothing, she appropriated a shirt, the last one, she noted. She'd managed to clean her riding habit and slipped that on without petticoats. Attacking her tangled hair with a horn comb, she looked out of the stern windows, hoping to see the ship, but the view held nothing except rolling sea.

"God's fish!" She muttered the exclamation popular in London as she hit a particularly difficult tangle. She yanked at it and wished again for Bridy, or better yet, Hana. For a moment she wondered where her maid was and how she fared. Then returning to the task at hand she worked until her hair was combed. Pulling the copper masses over her shoulder, she braided them. Her toilet completed, Morgan went to the door.

After the muted light of the cabin, Morgan had to squint in the intense sunlight. Everything gleamed as bright as glass and just as brittle, she told herself as the distant ship threatened to shatter her happiness as well as the safety of the *Kestrel*.

Morgan could just make it out, a dark outline in the distance. She stared, trying to see more, when a shout from the quarterdeck caught her attention. She turned to see Daniel there with members of his crew. He was looking toward the other ship through a long tube she realized was a spyglass. Closing the instrument with a snap he turned and said something to a crewmember who shouted up into the rigging.

Morgan followed his glance and saw the spars filled with men. At the word they began unfurling more sail. The *Kestrel* was going to run for it.

As the wind caught the new expanse of canvas, the *Kestrel* leaned over in the water and her speed increased. The men continued to work until every inch of sail was pulling. The sounds were loud in Morgan's ears, the roar of water against, the hull and the snap of canvas in the wind. They combined to create an energy that was palpable. Morgan looked at the other ship and thought it looked smaller. Was it possible they were going to outrun it?

"Captain!"

The call came from up the mainmast where one of the men was on watch.

"Another ship off the forward bow!"

Everyone ran to see, many of those on the quarter deck swinging through the rigging to cross the waist with greater speed. Morgan climbed the shallow steps and strained her eyes into the distance.

"Battle stations," Daniel said, his voice quiet and controlled. He handed the spyglass to Juan and turned to Morgan. "Come with me."

She followed him back to the cabin where he crossed to a locker in the bulkhead. He opened the door and removed his sword, a fine Clemens Horn in a scabbard attached to a sword belt by two light chains. He buckled this on and adjusted the second scabbard holding a *main-gauche*, a left-handed dagger that tapered two feet to a wicked point.

"I need your help," he told her as he did this.

"Me? What can I do?" she asked, bewildered.

"Something especially important to me. I need you to stay in the cabin and under no circumstances come up on deck."

"There's going to be fighting, isn't there," she stated.

"It appears that way."

"Why? Who are they?"

"Spaniards."

"But why are they after the *Kestrel*?"

Daniel grinned but there was no humor in his face. "The

Kestrel is something of a bane to the Spanish. They would like nothing better than to see her sunk and me dead. There's one ship in particular, the *Santa Clara* ..." His voice trailed off.

Morgan drew in her breath in something like a gasp. "But Daniel ..."

"Will you do as I bid?" he insisted.

She drew in a deep breath. "Yes. If you insist."

"I do insist. There is nothing you can do on deck, and your presence will make it all the more dangerous for the rest of us."

"Then I will most certainly remain out of sight!"

Daniel smiled briefly. "Good."

He kissed her, his arms around her like steel bands holding her tightly against him. The buckles of his sword belt dug into her flesh but she didn't care -- this might be the last time she ever held him.

Don't even think it, the voice in her mind cried out. She clung to him, her mouth open and pliant beneath his until he pushed her away. His breathing was harsh as he looked at her one moment more. Then without another word he was gone.

Morgan went to the bunk and looked out the windows, bracing herself against the movements of the ship, trying to see, but not even the pursuing vessel was visible. She turned over and flopped down, her back against the bulkhead as she stared at the cabin, the space she had shared with Daniel all these weeks, the place where she had been so happy. They had made plans together, designing a future with each other, and now all of it might be lost!

She was terrified, but more than that, she was angry. After the horror that stalked her in England, to have found such joy and now to have it stolen from her was more than she would endure. Not only was there the possibility of losing Daniel, but her own life was in danger too. Well, that was something she would never surrender without a fight!

Morgan pushed herself off the bunk and went to the cabinet where Daniel kept his sword. Another weapon hung there, and she took it out. It was a slender fencing sword. It had a simple cross piece for a guard and was lighter in weight, thus more easily handled by a woman. Morgan drew the bright steel from its scabbard. She knew nothing of swordplay and she cursed her inadequacy. She hefted the blade and made a few tentative swings. It didn't seem beyond her strength to maneuver, but whether or not she could hit anyone with enough force to cause hurt she didn't know. At least the point was sharp, and she knew she could stick it in someone. It would do, although, sometime in the future she vowed to have Daniel teach her to fence -- if they survived this.

She set the sword aside for the moment and went to explore the cabinet further. Hanging from a peg was a small sheathed dagger. Morgan drew it forth and admired the slender blade etched with intricate designs. The hilt was bright brass in the shape of dragons, the creatures so carefully sculpted that even their scales and talons were visible. Morgan liked the weapon and decided to keep it as well.

She turned back to the table where the sword lay when the ship lurched, suddenly loosing speed. Morgan could feel the change even in the cabin. The *Kestrel* rocked in the water, going slower and slower. Morgan heard voices and the sounds of running feet. There was a heavy dragging sound and slamming of wood against wood. She didn't know it, but the guns were being run out and prepared for battle.

In the future, Morgan would say this was the worst moment of her life. She promised Daniel she would remain below, but hearing strange noises and not knowing what they meant was a torment. Then there came the boom of the ship's guns firing accompanied by the acrid smell of gunpowder. There was an enormous crashing sound followed by a rending noise. Then more shouts, the clash of steel and a loud confusion of footsteps overhead.

The last told Morgan that the battle had come to the decks of the *Kestrel*. At first she barred the door to the cabin and stood behind it, clutching the sword and dagger, listening. When it seemed as if there was relative silence in the companionway, she unbarred the door again and peered outside. All was in shadow and empty, but she couldn't see the deck. Still holding her weapons she moved slowly toward the light. The noises were -- louder, curses, shouts and, frighteningly now and then a cry of agony. With the bright sun behind them, she couldn't distinguish individuals, but watched as silhouetted figures in violent motion passed the hatchway.

Morgan gasped as she peered up the shallow steps to the deck. The Spanish ship was beside them, held to the *Kestrel* by lines and grappling hooks. On the decks men were fighting hand-to-hand with swords, daggers, belaying pins, anything they had. Morgan saw Juan swinging a cutlass with one hand while in the other he held a smoking pistol. While she watched he smashed the gun barrel against the head of his adversary.

Then Daniel was before her, sword in one hand, dagger in the other, both liberally stained with blood. He was on the foredeck fighting a tall man dressed in black velvet lined with scarlet silk, his linen trimmed with gold lace. The Spaniard was handsome, his hawk-like features set off by a thin curling moustache and a well groomed beard. He wore diamond earrings, and a rosette of the gems decorated the hat surmounting his glossy black periwig. Beside Daniel in his simple cotton shirt and loose breeches, the Spaniard was magnificent, but Morgan couldn't appreciate him, not when he threatened the man she loved!

While Morgan watched there came a shout from the Spanish ship. "They're coming," was the call and Morgan looked where the watchman pointed to see yet another ship approaching. She couldn't imagine whose side this newcomer would be on and was desperate lest Daniel was unaware of it.

The Spanish captain, however, was not unaware. He shouted something to his crew as he continued his wary fencing with Daniel. For just a moment the two of them were alone on the foredeck, and Morgan felt as if she watched a play on a stage. What happened next was also unreal, and the horror of it left her breathless. One of the Spaniard's crew came up behind Daniel, who had all of his attention on the duel. The crewman loomed almost impossibly large as he struck the English captain a wicked blow across the back of his head. Without a sound Daniel fell unconscious.

Morgan must have screamed for the Spanish captain

turned in her direction. He watched as she came out of the companionway, a sword and dagger gleaming in her hands. He grinned, his teeth white against his dark skin. With an ironic salute of his sword, he turned and leapt back to his ship. His giant crewman followed, Daniel's unconscious form slung over his shoulder.

Chapter 24

Chaos prevailed. Orders were shouted in Spanish and English as two crews tried to sort themselves out. Men ran and leapt for the rail, sails were deployed, rigging adjusted. Soon other shouts came from the starboard side as the new ship came into range. Morgan didn't recognize her, but she was the *India Princess*, a ship Daniel had taken not a year before. The ship was now captained by Daniel's good friend, William Curran.

Morgan didn't care about any of this. As far as she was concerned, the strange ship might be another enemy, except the sight of it had driven the Spaniards into flight. At that moment all she cared about was going after the Spanish ship and rescuing Daniel.

Morgan dropped the sword and rushed to the rail as the two ships parted. A couple of the Spanish crew members swung across the widening space, trying desperately to get back to their own vessel before it went too far. Juan managed to get his pistol reloaded and discharged it after them, missing his target. The Spanish captain called an order and musket barrels appeared over the rail. With a rattling bang and cloud of smoke they discharged, balls digging white scars in the *Kestrel's* deck. One ball whizzed perilously close to Morgan, but she didn't move until Juan dragged her away from the rail.

"No!" she screamed, fighting him, blind with panic.

"*Senorita, senorita*," he begged, ducking her blows. "Please. Come away."

"Juan," she panted. "I can't. I can't. They've got Daniel."

"I know, *senorita*," he soothed. "But we'll get him back. Just wait. We'll get him back."

"How?" she demanded. She pulled loose from his grip and went back to the rail.

"Watch." Juan pointed to the *Princess* sailing past their stern, intent on the Spanish ship. One of the *Kestrel's* crew leaned from the rigging, calling out to the other ship, telling them about Daniel's capture.

Morgan saw the big man she would later know as Little Billy nod in response. "Aye," he yelled back. And the *Princess* was past, swift on the trail of the Spaniard.

Morgan remained at the rail, Juan beside her, watching.

Behind them the rest of the *Kestrel's* crew were busy moving among those who had fallen, finding and aiding their comrades. Dead enemy seamen were dumped over the rail, while the wounded were dragged off to the side to await the captain's pleasure.

The captain. Morgan brushed away a tear that slipped down her cheek and swallowed, trying not to give way to emotion, but she wasn't winning this battle either. She and Daniel had so little time together. Could it really be ending like this? Was he really gone?

She thought of going back to the cabin and giving way to tears, but she couldn't drag herself from the deck. She wanted to be there when the *India Princess* came back -- with Daniel. He would come back, she insisted to herself. She couldn't imagine what she would do if he did not!

The hot sun beat down on her head. The afternoon passed, time slipping by like waves under the *Kestrel's* hull, but to Morgan, everything happened in slow motion. Time had never moved so stubbornly!

Evening just darkened the sky when a ship was sighted on the western horizon. The watch rang his bell and called the crew back on deck. Armed, they waited, prepared for anything since there was no way to know if the ship was the *Princess* until it drew nearer. Morgan gripped the rail with fingertips that turned white with strain. It was the *Princess*, she told herself. It had to be! And Daniel was safe on board her.

The *India Princess* flowed toward them from the west, her sails spread like great billowing wings. Foam hissed from her bow as she drew ever closer, and when she was within hailing distance the wind was let out of the sails and she slowed.

Morgan stood in silence, trying to be patient, although her eyes scanned the distant deck for any sign of her lost love. Juan came from his place on the aft deck and stood beside her. He looked sideways at the intense figure of his captain's lady and shook his head, his mouth in a tight, bitter line. The *Princess* had come back much too soon to have stopped the Spanish ship. He was afraid Morgan was in for a disappointment. He too would miss Daniel Harris. He had never sailed under a better captain.

A longboat lowered from the other ship and a pair of sailors manned the oars, transporting a big black-haired man in a rather fantastic-looking costume from the *Princess*. But Morgan didn't concern herself with his dress. One look at his face as he climbed on board the *Kestrel* was enough to tell her Daniel hadn't been rescued.

"Who are you?" she demanded as soon as his boots touched the deck. "And where is Daniel? Why didn't you bring him back?"

Billy stopped dead in his tracks, visibly confused since he was not accustomed to having to answer to a woman. He looked at Juan who stepped forward.

"May I introduce Captain William Curran," he said to her. "This is Mistress Morgan Moorhouse," he told the buccaneer. "She's Robert Moorhouse's daughter, and she is Captain Harris' lady." The last was by way of a warning.

Billy nodded to her and then remembering himself, swept off his hat and made a gallant bow. "Madam," he began. "We followed the Spaniard and would have been able to overtake her before sunset, but that she fell in with two other ships, both frigates."

"And you didn't stay to fight?" Morgan demanded, her eyes blazing.

217

Billy opened his mouth to answer and then closed it again. He looked distinctly uncomfortable. Daniel was his friend and he owed him much more than his command. But he wasn't accustomed to defending himself against a girl. Hands on her hips, Morgan looked as if she was going to fly at him any minute.

"They were frigates," he repeated. "Frigates! The *Princess* could take one, maybe even two of them, but not all three."

"It wouldn't help the captain if the *Princess* was captured," Juan added quickly.

Morgan turned her stricken face to him. "Then what do we do now?" she asked. "How can we save him?"

Juan and Billy exchanged uncomfortable glances.

"I don't know ..." Billy began at the same time Juan spoke.

"There's nothing ..." Then Juan stopped speaking too.

Silence fell and the sound of waves slapping on side of the ship were loud.

"You aren't going to do anything?" Morgan exclaimed. "You're going to just abandon him!"

"He was aboard the *Sangre de Christo*," Billy said quietly. "Everyone knows that ship."

"I don't!" Morgan looked from one man to the other.

Neither one would meet her eyes.

"What is it? Tell me!"

"The *Sangre de Christo* is based in Cartagena."

"Its captain is an officer of the Inquisition," Juan added softly. "There is nothing to be done. I'm sorry."

"Nothing?"

218

He shook his head. "No. Nothing."

"We can petition the governor back in Port Royal," Billy began. "That's the logical thing to do."

"Petition? And just how long is that going to take?" Morgan demanded.

Little Billy and Juan exchanged glances.

"And all the while Daniel's in the hands of his sworn enemies," Morgan continued.

"Mistress, you don't understand..." Billy began.

"Oh, but I do," she replied, tears choking her. "I understand all too well!" She whirled and raced down the steps to the dark passageway below decks. Slamming the cabin door behind her, she collapsed on the bunk, giving way to tears.

The *India Princess* departed the next morning, resuming her voyage to Port Royal. The *Kestrel* followed, sailing more slowly as her crew patched and began repairs. Although most of the work would be completed in port, the ship still had to be able to fight if necessary.

Morgan came on deck the next day wearing one of Daniel's coats wrapped around her against a chill more of emotions than the weather. She looked around at the familiar deck, lit by lanterns in the dim early morning, staring as if she was seeing everything for the first time. After a moment she shivered, pulling herself together, and went quickly up the steps to the quarterdeck. Here she found Juan standing by the helmsman, watching the sails, judging the wind.

"Juan," she began.

He came to her immediately.

"Who's in charge now?" she asked.

"I am, until we get into Port Royal," he told her.

She nodded. "Good. That's good. You and I will be able to deal with each other."

"*Senorita*?" he asked, not sure what she meant, but positive he wasn't going to like it.

"Turn the ship around," she told him. "We're going after the captain."

Juan opened his eyes wide and stared at her. "We're going to do what?"

"I have a plan. We're going to rescue Daniel."

"He's in Cartagena. We can't go there. It would be sailing straight to our deaths!" he exclaimed.

"No, it won't," she assured him. "As I said, I have a plan."

"Eh?" he grunted not sure if he wanted to hear it. What was this plan, and more important, what part would he have to play in it? Horrified, his hair practically stood on end.

"Listen," she began. "Of course we won't sail into Cartagena. That would be foolish. But there's no reason why one or two people can't be put ashore down the coast, in some secluded place where the ship can be hidden. From there we could make our way into the town and find Daniel."

"Make our way? You mean just walk into town?" Juan repeated, not sure if he liked the sound of any of this. "And who is the 'we' you refer to?"

Morgan's chin came up stubbornly. "If you're afraid, I'll go alone," she said. "I speak Spanish fluently, and there is no reason anyone should know I don't belong there."

"You can't go alone," Juan protested.

"You can't stop me."

"You can't go without the ship, and I ... I ... I don't know," he concluded lamely, visible shaken by her intensity. "*Senorita*, you don't know what you're getting into."

"It doesn't matter. Nothing matters except rescuing Daniel. Whatever I have to do, I will do it."

"You could be killed. I could be killed!" He scowled. "No. There has to be another way. A safer way."

"I thought about it all night, and there isn't. We have to act, and we have to act now. We can't let Daniel to die at the hands of those butchers." But he still looked skeptical. "Juan, you have to help me. This is Daniel. Remember how he saved you from a similar fate?" she pointed out cannily.

Juan scowled and looked away. He couldn't argue about his debt to the captain. And he couldn't let her go into the city alone. God only knew what she would come up against! And he could see she was determined.

"I want to think about it," he said, playing for time.

"Of course," she allowed graciously. "But don't take too long. We're sailing farther in the wrong direction every minute."

Juan looked at the helmsman, who studiously avoided his eye.

"Well," Morgan prompted.

" *Senorita*," he protested. "You aren't giving me enough time! I will need until morning at least."

"That's too long," she said firmly. "You must decide now."

And, he realized later, she was so determined to get her way it never occurred to him to insist that she give up her foolishness and accept his word as final. The woman actually convinced him to be a part of her insane plan! But never, not to anyone, not even to himself would he ever admit how terrified he was.

Chapter 25

The white stone buildings of Cartagena shone in the early morning sunlight. One of Spain's principle holdings in the New World, the city was governed by the Viceroy of Peru, as was all of South America. In fact, the inhabitants of the city considered themselves Peruvians.

Inside the walls, shops opened for business and vendors set up their stalls early so they could do most of their business in the cool morning. They closed down during the heat of the day, but would open again at dusk when folks came out to enjoy the evening air. This morning, torches still flared outside the huge gates to the city. Some late-comers hurried into town, hoping they would be lucky to find a place in the market to display their goods. Morgan and Juan blended in with them. She kept her head down, her hair covered by a black *rebozo* as she walked slightly behind Juan as was proper. She kept her eyes on the ground, and didn't respond to the guard's quips.

Juan, however, laughed and returned their jokes.

"And where are you going with that?" one of the guards asked, commenting on the guitar slung over his shoulder.

"To the market, of course, *senors*," Juan responded. "I thought maybe I could make a few pesos. For our mother, you know, *senors*. She has been ill."

The man snickered and bent to peer at Morgan's face in the shadows. "You might make more selling your sister," he commented. "If one could see her, that is. What's wrong with her? Is she deformed?"

"My little sister is a good girl, *senors*," Juan protested. "She's just shy."

They laughed at this. "Then you shouldn't be taking her to market." But they left it at that, their attention focused on an Indian in a wooden cart drawn by a pair of staid oxen.

"I thought we'd never get inside," Morgan hissed. "Why did you have to spend so much time talking to them?"

"Did you want to make them suspicious?"

"Suspicious? Don't you think they'll be suspicious when they see me dancing?"

Juan paused. "I still don't think that's a good idea," he said, returning to what was obviously an old argument between them. "I think you should be content to pretend to be my sister. My bashful, quiet little sister."

"As your sister I would be little more than baggage, of less use to anyone than your guitar," Morgan complained. "No. I want to help."

"By making yourself conspicuous?"

"How else do you think we're going to get information?"

"By listening."

"Good. You listen then," she growled, adjusting the black shawl around her. The black skirt swirling around her ankles over three petticoats was full of dust from the road. The upper part of her body was covered by a loose white cotton smock. Over this she wore another black shawl with the ends crossed over her breasts and tied around her waist. It was not a costume that recommended itself to her. It was bulky and hot.

"Where did you get these clothes?"

"What's wrong with them?" Juan looked at her. "You're dressed like a modest young Spanish woman."

"I'm like to drop dead from the heat," Morgan complained. "My mother never wore anything like this."

"Your mother was a hidalga. And," he added, pressing for an advantage, "she would not have been walking into an enemy city to rescue her lover."

"Hah!" Morgan let the *rebozo* slip further back on her head as she gazed at the twin spires that rose high about the other buildings. "That's the cathedral?" she asked.

"Yes. The prison will be somewhere nearby," Juan replied quietly.

"And that's where Daniel will be?"

"That's where he'll be. Unless they're keeping him in the military prison. And he might also be at the fort."

"Fort? What fort?"

"Fort Lazaro. It's a hell hole by the harbor. It's only half completed. I've heard they're cutting costs by using prisoners to do all the work."

"And Daniel might be there?" Morgan asked, her heart constricting in her chest.

Juan glanced at her. " *Senorita*," he began softly. "You have to be prepared for the worst. It's been six days since they captured the captain. Although we know the ship brought him to Cartagena, we have no way of knowing where he is or what has happened to him."

Morgan shuddered, then drew a resolute breath. "All the more reason I need to help you find him. And I can't do that if I sit meekly in a corner."

Juan gritted his teeth. This woman was determined to get her own way. "And while you dance, who will protect you from impropriety?" he demanded in a last ditch effort.

"My good brother will protect me," she said sweetly with a grin. "Or I will protect myself. Look." She pulled a metal object from the waistband of her skirt. Juan saw the flash of brass and recognized the dragon hilted dagger.

"*Diablo*! Put that away," he hissed, looking around to see if anyone else had noticed. "Innocent young girls don't carry daggers!"

"Then I don't see how they remain innocent," she protested as she wrapped the *rebozo* around her shoulders again. "Especially not with those guards around. How should I protect myself? As a proper young woman?"

"By not making yourself conspicuous." He huffed out an exasperated breath. "Young unmarried girls have brothers," he told her. "Brothers who will protect them," Juan informed her, regretting for the hundredth time that he had agreed with the crazy plan. It wasn't going to work!

"Good. You are my brother, and you will protect me.

And I am going to dance," she announced. "It will give us an excuse to be in the tavern. We just need to find the one frequented by prison guards."

They had come to the huge open square in front of the cathedral where the market was in progress. Spanish settlers, Indians, mestizos and black slaves were all there, buying and selling fish, meat, garden produce and fruit as well as locally made crafts and more expensive imported goods.

While Juan made inquiries, Morgan wandered through the stalls, looking with delight at the wares that were, for the most part, exotic to her. As she wandered, her *rebozo* slid back exposing her face and shining red hair. Despite her peasant clothing, her refinement and beauty stood out in the common market among the dark-haired locals, but she was unaware of the attention she attracted.

Don Luis sat on the back of a gray stallion, his dark eyes following the lovely girl and her companion. Richly dressed in silks and a velvet coat, Luis was attended by a small troop of his house soldiers. He wore a neatly trimmed black beard and mustache beneath his proud hawk-like nose.

"Who is she?" he whispered softly to himself.

"Cover your hair," Juan told her, finding her at a stall selling bright hand woven fabrics.

"Did you find it?" she asked pulling at her head covering. "Did you find the tavern?"

"Yes. It's there." He nodded toward the front of a cantina just visible on a side street leading toward the cathedral. "I will try to find work there."

"*We* will find work there," Morgan corrected.

Juan frowned at her. "Very well, we," he corrected him-

227

self. "But I suggest you allow me to do the talking. Properly raised Spanish girls do not ..."

"Do not do anything, it seems," Morgan interrupted. "But very well. You may get us the job."

Juan was torn between irritation and amusement at her high handed manner. "*Si, senorita,*" he said softly.

The name of the cantina was *La Tecolote*, the owl, and its owner Ben Ortega, a surly man whose first inclination was to boot the pair out of his establishment. Juan talked fast, his face set in an ingratiating smile and when he offered to entertain the afternoon patrons for free, Ben agreed to a trial. During all of these negotiations Morgan stood meekly aside, an anonymous figure hidden in a black *rebozo*.

Under the cover of the thin black wool she looked around. The air reeked of the mingled smells of unwashed bodies, cheap wine and a local beer called *chicha* made from maize. The cantina had a low ceiling supported by pillars that were no more than peeled logs set at intervals down its length. It felt like a cave, an impression further heightened by the unpainted stone walls. The dirt floor, watered by years of spilled drinks and worse, had been packed hard as rock by the pounding of a thousand feet. Nothing would ever again penetrate its smooth surface. Candles set in crudely carved wall sconces and a number of primitive oil lamps were the only light.

Juan unwrapped his guitar and, taking a seat on a low stool, carefully tuned the strings. Ben watched impatiently, wiping his hands on the dirty apron that strained across his belly. Juan struck a chord as he mentally tested his audience and then broke into a simple rendition of a popular folk tune.

He played it a second time, adding embellishments and again, decorating the melody line until it was almost unrecognizable.

Ben nodded his head and went down the bar to fill a jug held by the stout Indian girl who served the customers. The customers applauded when Juan was finished playing. Someone shouted "More!"

Juan grinned at Morgan and obligingly began to play another tune. When he was finished the owner was standing at his side.

"Very well," he conceded. "You can play here. I pay two pesos for the evening and your dinner."

"Two pesos?"

"And tips," Ben added. "And you can sleep around back, above the stable."

"My sister ..." Juan began.

"Eh?" Ben looked at Morgan still standing in the shadows. "I have a serving girl. I don't need her."

"She's a dancer," Juan said reluctantly.

Ben looked at her again. "How can she dance, wrapped up like that? I can't even see her face."

Morgan dropped the *rebozo* and stepped into the light and Ben was momentarily confused. Here was no peasant maid! There was good blood in the girl. She had to be some hidalgo's bastard daughter, and he wasn't sure if he wanted her around. A face such as hers might cause more trouble than it was worth.

"I don't know," he began.

"Please, *senor*," she said softly in her flawless Spanish. She didn't know it, but her Castilian accent instantly decided

229

him against her.

All the while Don Luis sat quietly at a table by the door. He listened to Juan playing and his subsequent conversation with Ben Ortega. Now he felt it time to intervene.

"A dancer would considerably enhance your establishment," he said quietly to Ben. "And one so lovely as the *senorita* will probably bring you many new and influential patrons."

Ben was not impervious to the implications of Don Luis' words. "As you say, *senor*," he agreed quickly, bowing. "A dancer is just what we need at *La Tecolote*. You will begin tonight," he told Morgan.

Don Luis smiled and bowed, taking her hand in his and lightly kissing the finger tips. "I will be here, *senorita*, to see you dance."

"Thank you for your intervention, *senor*," she said shyly. "My brother and I are grateful."

"It is my pleasure, *senorita*." Don Luis looked carefully at her. "Have I seen you before?"

"No, senor. I don't think so," Morgan assured him, taking her hand back.

"What is your name, pretty one?"

Morgan lowered her eyelashes. "Anna, *Senor*," she replied using the name she and Juan had agreed upon. "Anna Leyba. My brother is Juan."

Don Luis, reminded of the presence of the brother took a step back. "Until this evening." With a smile he was gone into the sunlight.

Juan insisted they remain out of sight in the barn until evening. He took the opportunity to doze in a pile of hay, but

Morgan paced, unhappy to waste even this little bit of time when she was so close to rescuing Daniel. Where was he? How was he? Her nervous movements disturbed a crow that had been scavenging for dropped grain. He cawed at her before lifting to the rafters. The sound was her only answer.

At last the long afternoon drew to a close and a sunset streaked the sky with orange and rose. Once again Juan sat on the low stool in the cantina, picking out popular melodies and singing in a low voice. The room was crowded now, and an older, heavy-set woman with streaks of gray in her dark hair joined the Indian girl serving drinks from the bar. Morgan sat cross-legged on the floor beside Juan, the *rebozo* once again covering her. This time she was grateful for its shelter. There were a few women present, but they were mostly whores of the cheapest kind, and she was appalled by their behavior as well as the smells emanating from their soiled clothing.

"I told you," Juan whispered as she leaned close to him to avoid a woman who staggered past in a rank wave of perfume that Morgan found nauseating. The woman laughed raucously at something her escort said.

"Told me what?" Morgan asked quietly.

Juan scowled at her and jerked his head toward the door. "It's time for you to dance. Your new patron just arrived."

She had seen the commotion as Don Luis and a party of young hidalgos came into the cantina. She drew a deep breath. "You know what I can do. We should start with the country dances."

Juan rippled a chord and Morgan rose to her feet. There

231

were catcalls from a woman ensconced in the lap of a swarthy, bearded man brandishing an earthenware mug of beer. She whispered something to him and they laughed uproariously, showing a lot of bad teeth.

Morgan shot them a look from narrowed eyes, and dropped her *rebozo* in the dust beside Juan. Dressed in just the tunic and dark skirt, she walked into the center of the clear space and took a pose as Juan began a melody. In keeping with her disguise as a simple peasant, her long hair was bound in a single long braid that swirled around her as she moved. The sound of Juan's guitar was her partner, and she and the music curled around each other in the torchlight, making magic the like of which her audience had never seen.

When the final chord was vibrating to its end and Morgan was still, the patrons came alive, throwing coins onto the dance floor, stamping their approval, and shouting for more. Juan obliged and started another song. Morgan danced on. Later, when Ben counted his profits for the evening he realized that he was about to improve his financial standing.

Don Luis was mesmerized by the woman he knew as Anna Leyba. Her body was as slender and finely bred as any of the well-born maidens he knew, but she was not surrounded by *duenas* and family honor. This woman was available to him, and he wanted her with a lust that surprised even him by its intensity.

Luis watched the slender figure dancing in candlelight, blazing like a flame. Anna Leyba. He said the name to himself. Her brother looked like a reasonable man. Since she was obviously of marriageable age, the only reason he would have brought her into town would be to see her suitably settled in life. Luis would speak to him and make a generous offer. Anna would be worth what he expected to pay for her, and Juan would be more than happy with the price. Luis would settle her in a small house, a secure place he could visit when time and his family obligations permitted. Yes, the future suddenly looked much brighter for Don Luis de Caravaga.

Chapter 26

Morgan wasn't used to dancing this long and trembled with exhaustion when she finally took a break. She huddled on a stool in the kitchen, sipping bitter wine from a fairly clean mug, letting the crowd entertain themselves for a while. She was glad when Juan suggested they retire for the night. They slipped out of the cantina through the kitchen door to escape the noisy crowd out front and, more important, to avoid any patron who might want the beautiful dancer's company for the rest of the evening. Juan couldn't help but notice Don Luis and his party. They were generous with the coins they tossed along with quips and invitations, but Juan didn't consider them any more dangerous than the other patrons. That is, not until the next morning.

For what was left of the night, however, Morgan slept on a bed of straw, wrapped in her *rebozo* and a fairly clean blanket Juan found somewhere. He didn't sleep as much as doze beside her, his hand on his dagger, ready to defend her if the need arose.

Sunlight reached through gaping holes in the barn's walls, but it wasn't until almost noon that Morgan stirred. She yawned and sat up, the *rebozo* and blanket falling away. Juan was already awake.

"I slept well," she commented. "But I like a bed with a mattress and sheets much better."

"We don't need to be here much longer," Juan said. "Just one more night. I think I've found the man we need."

"You did? Who is he?" She yawned again.

"The keeper of the prison behind the cathedral. He was at the cantina last night."

"Are you sure Daniel's there? You said there were three prisons in the city. He might be in any one of them."

"When the jailer drinks he forgets to hold his tongue." Juan shook his head. "He was bragging to his lady friend about his special English prisoner."

"Daniel," Morgan breathed. "He's alive." A wave of relief swept over her. Alive! But for how long? She shivered with anxiety. "We have to go. We have to get him out of there!"

"If it is him, he's safe for now," Juan said, calling her back to earth. "They're waiting for the Grand Inquisitor to return from the Northern provinces. We have another couple of days."

"I don't care if we have days! I want him out of there. I want him out of there now!"

"So do I. But it isn't going to happen at all if we don't

235

move carefully. We might even end up in a cell with him."

"We need a plan," she told him.

"Yes. That's what I've been doing all morning, trying to figure out a way to get into jail and then back out again."

"But it's easy," Morgan said quickly. "We go to the prison and hold a knife at the jailer's throat until he takes us to Daniel's cell."

Juan stared at her in amazement. "And then what," he asked, exasperated.

"Then we cut his throat," she responded sweetly.

Juan realized that she was perfectly serious. "What about the guards? And the other prisoners? Do you think they'll do nothing while we help the captain escape? You cannot be serious."

"We'll think of something to do about the guards," Morgan told him. "Distract them -- something. And the other prisoners won't have to know what's happening."

Juan shook his head. "I knew your father, *senorita*. I don't think he would approve of such a plan."

"I too knew my father," Morgan reminded him. "And I think he would have liked my plan very much."

She yawned again. "I'm hungry. And I want water for washing."

Juan laughed. "We can wash at the watering trough like everyone else," he told her.

"What about breakfast?"

"We will get something in the market."

"Good. Then we can talk about my plan some more."

Don Luis was not pleased to have missed the beautiful dancer that first evening. He waited after her performance ended,
but she did not reappear and no one would tell him where
she had gone. Frustrated, he went home to toss and turn in
his bed for the rest of the night. In the morning, he was short
with his servants and family, and they were glad when he
finally left the house.

When he found the cantina closed, the door bolted, he
went to the market where he had seen her the first time. He
left his horse and wandered up and down between the
booths, scanning the crowd. There were many women present, but none of them was Anna Leyba. His guards moved
carefully around him, fearful of rousing his famous temper.

Fortunately before any of them felt his wrath, Morgan
and Juan appeared, eating thin pancakes made of cornmeal.
They were spread with honey and rolled up into little tubes
called *flautas* - flutes.

"*Senorita*," Don Luis said, placing himself in their path.
"*Senor*," he added, looking at Juan. "I would have a word
with you."

"Of course, my lord. We are at your service," Juan told
him, giving a short bow. "How can we serve you?"

Luis looked at Morgan. She was even more beautiful
than he remembered. She dropped her eyes under his scruti-
ny, and pulled the black *rebozo* close, shadowing her face.

"I think your name is Juan? Juan Leyba?" Don Luis
asked. "Leave you sister in the care of my guards. They will
see she comes to no harm. I would have a word with you in

237

private."

Juan gave Morgan a surprised look. "They'll look after her?" he asked reluctantly.

"I have said so," Don Luis snapped. He turned on his heel and led the way into the shadows cast by the cathedral, away from the crowds. He was so accustomed to having his orders followed that he didn't even look to see if Juan was behind him.

With a shrug toward Morgan, Juan left her and followed the hidalgo, wondering what the man wanted and at the same time afraid he might know.

"I imagine you have come to the city to earn some money?" Don Luis asked.

"Yes, *senor*."

Don Luis nodded. "Then I have an offer that will bring you more than your wildest dreams."

"*Senor*?"

"Your sister, Anna. I want her."

"But, *Senor*! She is ... she's my sister. I can't just sell her!" Juan stammered.

"Why not? It's a common enough transaction." Don Luis smiled. "I will give you a hundred golden doubloons for her."

"Doub ... doubloons?" Juan stammered.

"Doubloons. Pistoles." Don Luis repeated, his frayed temper threatening to snap.

"But *senor*, I can't ..."

"Why are you so reluctant? Are you afraid she won't be well treated? I assure you, she will live in luxury for the rest of her life. She will have everything she desires."

"No, *senor*. It isn't that. It's ..." Juan thought fast. "My sister, she has a temper, *senor*. Oh, not a big one, nothing that you would find troublesome, but she ..."

"She has fire, eh?" Don Luis liked the idea. He had seen flashes of it in her dancing. He could imagine that fire burning in his bed, and the thought made him dizzy with desire. He must have -- no, he *would* have this woman!

"What would she say, *senor*," Juan continued, "if she knew I had sold her, like a ... like a chicken or a cow?"

Don Luis came down to earth with a crash. "She doesn't have to know, you fool," he growled. "Just take the money and leave the rest to me."

"But I have to tell her something," Juan insisted.

"Then think of something that will make her happy. But I want her tonight."

"Tonight?"

"Yes, imbecile. Tonight. She will never set foot in *La Tecolote* again."

"No, *senor*. Not if you say so." Juan wasn't sure of a way out of this. He knew he had to get back to Morgan and warn her of this new danger. "Will you give me some time to prepare her?"

"Until this afternoon. I will wait that long."

"No. I ..."

"Did you just say 'no'?" Don Luis couldn't believe what he had heard. Was this peasant presuming to deny him?

"I don't mean 'no'." Juan was at haste to correct himself when he saw the flash of rage in the grandee's eyes. "I mean, I have a better idea. She will come to you with no suspicions at all."

"And what is that," Don Luis demanded from between clenched teeth.

"I will tell her we are to entertain at your house this evening. "

"Ah, yes," Don Luis said slowly. "Yes, I like the sound of that. Bring her to my house at sunset. It is one street beyond the cathedral there. The house with a blue gate in the wall. A servant will be waiting for you. At sunset." Juan didn't have to know that Don Luis' main residence, where his family resided, was located on the outskirts of the city.

"With a blue gate?" Juan asked, pretending stupidity.

"Yes. A blue gate." Don Luis took a gold coin from the pouch at his belt. "This is just one of many," he said with a thin smile. "When your sister has come to my house I will give you the rest."

Juan couldn't keep the gleam from his eyes. A hundred gold doubloons was a fortune for anyone.

"Thank you, *senor*," he said with a low bow as he made the coin disappear. "I thank you a million times." He bowed again. "Ten million times. May the good Lord and the blessed Virgin and all the Saints bless you and your house."

"Enough!" Don Luis snapped. "Sunset. Don't be late." He stepped from the shadows and strode to where his horse was waiting.

Juan hurried back to Morgan with the gold coin and his startling news.

"'Tis an added complication," he told her as they made their way into the alley behind the cantina. "And so, if we're going to do anything here, we have to act quickly."

"Oh, we're going to do it, all right," Morgan assured

him. "But I don't understand. What does the Don want with me? Does he want me to dance?"

"No, not dance, exactly." Juan heaved a sigh of exasperation. "He wants what any man wants of a woman."

"Oh." Her mind circled his meaning. "OH!" she repeated more loudly. "He wants me for his …"

"… mistress," Juan supplied.

"Mistress!" she repeated, scandalized, realizing she'd just been sold like some property. Her voice rose mirroring her outrage. "Who does he think I am!"

"Shush," Juan warned. "A peasant girl. Nothing more."

"Well, it's insulting!"

"Perhaps, but we should have suspected something like this might happen."

"So now we have to evade an amorous Don along with everything else?"

"Aye. And if you not at his house this evening, by tomorrow he'll have the city militia searching for you. And me," he added, thoughtfully. "And we won't have any problem getting into the prison. Because we'll already be there. In a cell," he added pointedly.

Morgan remained silent. Oh, Gods, he realized. She's thinking again.

"So how many days do we have left?" she asked after a moment.

"For what?" he demanded, wondering how much longer they could survive this insane charade.

"We planned for the *Kestrel* to wait in the cove for seven days. This is day …"

"… day three," he said. "We have four more days."

241

"Yes, but we won't need them. We're going to get Daniel free tonight."

"Nothing to it," Juan groaned. Just now, however, it seemed impossible.

"I wonder when the jailer eats his dinner. And where," Morgan mused.

"Does it matter?"

"Of course. Can you find out?"

"Of course," Juan echoed. Morgan was assuming leadership again. She was developing a horrible habit of taking decisions out of his hands.

"So how will you do it?"

"What?" he asked, abandoning his paranoid musing.

"How will you get the information?"

Juan sighed. "I will just step into *La Tecolote*, into the kitchen and ask about our dinner. Then I will try to get one of the servants talking. I think the little Indian maid likes me."

"No, I think the other one likes you. The fat one," Morgan said, grinning.

Juan scowled. "Either way, one of them will know something."

"I'll go with you."

Juan opened his mouth to protest then closed it again. He already learned that arguing with Morgan never got him anywhere.

The fat maid's name was Aurelia, and she was more than willing to gossip with Juan while his sister sat quietly in the corner.

"Rosita ... Rosy, that's the whore who was with him last

night," Aurelia said as she bustled about her tasks. She filled a bowl full of beans mixed with corn and meat chunks, and handed it to Juan. He passed it to Morgan as he listened. Aurelia filled another bowl, then splashed some beer into a mug for him.

"She comes every day, after siesta. I think she hopes if she takes good care of him, Chacon will marry her. Ha!" She broke off laughing.

Morgan looked around for a spoon. She found one carved from a piece of horn. Wiping it on her *rebozo* she began to eat, listening carefully.

"No one would marry her!" Aurelia snorted. "No one told her a man's not gonna pay for something he can get for free!" She chuckled again as she poured milky-colored liquid into the floor drain from a huge kettle of beans. Adding fresh water, she hung the kettle from a hook in the fireplace. After poking the embers to a blaze, she dropped a hunk of greasy meat on the work table and began cutting it into smaller pieces. Only then did she resume her narrative. "But Rosy was never very smart. She has a temper and she can fight, but she was never one for thinking things out."

Juan sipped the beer and ate his stew. "But she is the jailer's woman," he prompted.

"And him no better than ... Well, who else would want him?" Aurelia glanced up from her task. "She fought for him, you know," she continued, changing the subject. "He had his eye on one of the maids from a cantina across town. *Los Brazos*. Tall, skinny wench. One night Rosy cut her up." She brandished the knife she held. "Sliced her up just like this." The knife blade fell and separated another piece of

243

pork. "Since then, no other woman's dared to so much as look at him."

"Where does she get his supper?" Morgan wanted to know.

"Eh?" Aurelia looked up. Juan smiled at her and she returned to her task. "Here, of course. Rosy takes it to him. She should be waking up about now. She'll be here soon."

Morgan grinned at Juan, and then nodded to Aurelia. "You have so much to do here. Maybe I can help you?"

"Now wait," Juan began.

Aurelia stared at Morgan, her eyes furrowed in surprise. "I could use some help. But I thought you were a dancer."

"That doesn't mean I can't do other work. I know, I'll get Chacon's dinner ready for Rosy."

"You need to be careful with her," Aurelia warned. "I told you how she is with a knife."

"I'm not going to do anything except help you get a tray ready." Morgan smiled. "What does Chacon usually eat?"

"Rosy won't like it," Aurelia began, looking at Juan for support. When he just shrugged, she conceded. "It's on your head," she warned.

"*Senorita*, this is folly," Juan whispered to Morgan when the cook went into the storeroom.

"We have to do it," she insisted. "This might be our only chance."

"Oh, aye." Juan couldn't think of an argument.

Morgan left her stool and spoke quietly into his ear. "When I was in England my cousin gave me something to drink, a drug of some kind. It made me sleep for almost three days. Do you know what it could have been?"

Juan realized what she was thinking. "For the guards?"

"And the jailer. And probably Rosy too. It would get them out of the way and keep them from giving alarm until we're at sea."

"Aye. That might work. But what did your cousin give you?"

"I don't know." Morgan frowned as Juan sighed. "There was an apothecary at the market," she added quickly. "His stall was near where we bought the *flautas*."

"I remember," Juan said.

"Could you go there and ask him what to use? Tell him that you're having trouble sleeping. Ask him to sell you something, something strong."

"Maybe. It might work."

"Good." Morgan smiled accepting this tepid comment for agreement. "While I wait, I'll help Aurelia. Oh, and we'll need a lot of wine. For the guards."

Chapter 27

Morgan put a clean cloth over a full bowl of the corn and bean stew. A half loaf of corn bread was beside it, and three earthenware bottles of wine.

Juan came back from the market with a small, hand-blown glass vial half full of a white powder. It was stopped with a piece of cork and sealed with lead. He waited until Aurelia had her back to him, busy tending the big kettle over the fire, before giving the drug to Morgan.

"How do we do it?" she asked looking at the vial

"Put some in a cup of wine and mix it up. Then add that to the bottles. If we put the corks back in, no one will know anything thing is amiss."

Morgan cast a quick glance at Aurelia who was still busy at the fireplace. She opened one of the bottles and ges-tured to Juan to do the same to the rest of them. Then after pouring a little of the dark red liquid into a clay cup, she started to dump in all of the powder.

"Stop!" Juan warned in a low voice, grabbing her wrist. "Don't use all of it."

"Why not? I want to be sure it works."

"Don't worry. It'll work! The old man assured me just a few grains will give a good night's sleep. You've already used enough to have them unconscious for a week."

"Good." Morgan stirred briskly, mixing the powder into the wine. She then poured a third of it into each bottle. "Put the corks back in and let's get out of here," she whispered.

"What's going on?!" a harsh female voice demanded from the doorway. "Who in hell are you?"

Morgan dropped the vial into a deep pocket under her skirt as Rosy came into the kitchen accompanied by the smell of sweat and cheap scent. It was the same woman who had been sitting on the lap of the huge bearded man in the cantina the night before. Morgan stepped back from the tray that held the jailor's dinner as Rosy approached. She whipped off the cloth and looked at the stew and bread. Grunting reluctant approval she replaced the cloth.

"What are you trying to do," she growled at Morgan. "Take my man?"

"No, *senorita*," Morgan protested. "I was only helping Aurelia ..."

"Huh!" Rosy looked Morgan up and down as if sizing her up for a fight.

"I will help you, *senorita*," Juan offered, quickly interrupting what might get out of hand. "I can carry the wine."

Rosy looked at the bottles standing beside the tray.

247

"Three bottles?" she asked. "Why are there three bottles?"

"For the jailer. And surely the guards will want to quench their thirst too?" Juan put on his most winning smile.

Rosy let loose with a bellow of laughter. "Be hard to keep them from it," she cackled. She hefted the tray and turned toward the door. "Come on then," she said to Juan.

He picked up the bottles and bent down to Morgan, whispering quickly. "Be sure she doesn't see you following us. Keep your face hidden. And be careful! I'll let you into the jail as soon as they've all had some of the wine."

"*You* be careful," she whispered.

Clutching the squat bottles, Juan went into the alley. Morgan watched from the doorway until he and Rosy disappeared around the corner before she followed.

The sun was low, almost touching the distant mountain peaks, lengthening the shadows of the buildings to deep purple puddles in golden light. The last vendors at the market were closing their booths, packing up their wares for another day. A young boy drove a small flock of sheep past Morgan, taking them home for the night. She had to dodge around a donkey loaded with bundles of firewood as someone else was returning to the city after a day working in the foothills. Somewhere a pig was squealing, and from the cathedral came the sound of bells and chanting.

Morgan moved through the crowds as quickly as she could, careful to keep Juan and Rosy in sight. Even though she knew where they were going, she wanted to time her arrival at the jail to theirs. She was so intent on not being seen, however, that she didn't notice someone was following her.

Not wanting to be disappointed again, Don Luis sent one of his house soldiers to keep watch on Morgan. Tonio spent a boring afternoon sitting at the end of the alley behind *La Tecolote*. The only occupation he had was watching both the back and front entrances to the cantina while trying to stay in the shade at the same time.

He had seen Rosy and Juan come out, and assumed they were going off somewhere to be alone with each other. This idea was reinforced when Morgan came out of the cantina, obviously following them, but trying to be discreet. He watched, amused at what he interpreted as her disapproval of her brother's tryst.

The sun sank lower in the sky. Tonio's instructions were to stay with the dancer until sunset. Then he was to bring her to his master's house. He measured the light that was left in the sky. Another few minutes ...

Morgan paused, sheltered by an angle of wall around a tall narrow gate. From her hiding place, she could see the door to the prison. It was almost half again as tall and broad as any other door would be. It was so tall, she decided, that it would be possible for a man to ride a horse into the jail and not have to duck his head at all. The vertical wooden planks were reinforced by three thick horizontal bars, and studded with enormous bolt heads. The jail, it seemed, would be as hard to get into as it would be to get out of.

Tonio was momentarily concerned as he watched his quarry disappear around the angle of the wall. He wasn't sure she hadn't gone into the house beyond. Then, when the door to the jail opened and a hand beckoned, she darted across the street and disappeared into the ecclesiastical fortress. This

249

was an added complication. Tonio wasn't about to enter the domain of the Jesuits!

"There were four guards," Juan told Morgan in a low voice.

"Did they drink the wine?" Morgan asked.

"All of them. Rosy too, although I didn't think she would at first. She had less than the others."

"But she's asleep?"

"Soundly. You mixed a strong dose of the sleeping powder."

Morgan's breath caught in her throat. "Where's Daniel?"

"Down there." Juan nodded at a long hallway that disappeared into darkness. "They've got him in one of the back cells."

"Where are the keys? Give them to me. Get him out. Hurry!" Morgan said in a tumble of words. Her heart was pounding so loudly she was amazed Juan couldn't hear it. She started down into the darkness, unconcerned that she couldn't see.

"Wait," Juan said. He grabbed a lantern from the table, lit a spill in the corner fireplace and quickly kindled the wick. Holding the light high, he set off into the darkness after the impetuous young woman. He passed her, and when he reached what he believed was the right door, touched her arm. "Here."

Morgan took the keys from him and fit one of them in the lock. Juan held the light aloft and peered through the small barred window into the dark cell. The lock clicked and door swung open on emptiness. There was no one inside.

Morgan gave a little cry of despair and turned a stricken

face to Juan. Her eyes filled and without a sound, a single tear slid down her cheek.

"Easy now," he cautioned. "There's another cell."

Morgan wiped her eyes and drew in a deep shuddering breath. Again Juan looked inside while she worked the lock. There was someone in this cell. He just hoped it was the right someone. The door at last swung wide and light flooded the space within, causing the figure inside raise his arm to shield his eyes. A chain from his wrist clanked as he moved.

"Daniel?" Morgan whispered. "Daniel!"

He was dirty and bearded, rips in his clothing as well as bruises and welts telling of the rough handling he had suffered, but Morgan cared nothing except that he was alive. She flew into his arms and he held her to him.

"Morgan?" he asked, not believing the evidence of his own senses. His eyes devoured her face, taking in every beloved feature as his hands felt the heavy silk of her long hair.

"What in God's name are you doing here?" Daniel asked. "How did you get here?" He looked over her shoulder at Juan who stood in the doorway.

"It's a long story, captain," Juan said dryly. "And one I'm not so sure you'll like. But before I tell it, I think we should get out of here."

Daniel grinned down at his impetuous love, and gave her one hard kiss and a promise of many more to come. "Get these chains off me," he said. "And then I'll need weapons."

The key ring yielded a rod that unlocked the chains. Daniel went from the cell, his arm around Morgan's waist, wanting never to let her go again.

"In here," Juan said, leading the way to the guard room

251

where five men were snoring. Daniel glanced at them, but didn't ask questions.

Morgan appropriated a sword and a dagger from the sheath hanging at the jailer's side. Daniel took them from her with a kiss. He stripped off his filthy ripped shirt, replacing it with clothing from one of the guards.

"They aren't much cleaner," he commented. "But I'll look a lot more respectable." He put on the guard's hat and grinned at his rescuers. "What do you say?"

"We'd better go," Juan told him. He couldn't understand the captain's euphoria.

Daniel lifted one of the bottles and was about to drink when Morgan pulled his hand away. "No! No, don't! It's drugged."

Daniel looked from the wine to the sleeping forms.

"I won't ask whose idea that was," he said with a grin. He put the bottle back on the table. "I'll forgo a drink then, until later. And I think you both have quite a story to tell me."

"Later," Juan repeated, looking out into the street. "It's sunset." He turned to Morgan, but she was too busy looking at Daniel to see the concern on his face. Juan was thinking of Don Luis and wondering if they could avoid him long enough to get out of the city. Well, he said to himself, we can only try. "We should split up," he told the pair. "I'll go first and signal the captain from the corner when the way is clear. *Senorita*," he nodded at Morgan, "you should follow us as you did before."

"Why," she began, but he interrupted.

"Just until we are out in the street and away from the

jail. Then we can go to the gate together."

"Lead the way," Daniel told him.

Juan nodded and disappeared through the door.

Morgan rose up on her tiptoes to put her arms around Daniel. Her body molded to his as their lips met. She knew this wasn't the time, but she couldn't help it. She'd been so frightened, and she missed him so much!

Daniel kissed her back with equal fervor, but then, with an effort took her arms away. He held her hands a second more and kissed her again, quickly. "Just a little while longer," he said.

He stepped to the door, holding it open a crack so he could look out. Juan waved to him.

"Come after us as soon as I reach the corner there," Daniel told Morgan. He kissed her again and then slipped out into the night.

Morgan nodded at his back, her eyes filling with tears. She had been brave before, but now that Daniel was safe, she didn't want to leave him even for the short time it would take to cross the square in front of the cathedral.

Morgan shook off her fears peered into the street. She saw Daniel walking through the lowering darkness. There were a few people about, but no one seemed to pay attention to him as he crossed the square. Then he disappeared around the far corner.

Morgan pulled the door open and stepped outside. She wrapped the *rebozo* around her, thinking how happy she would be when she could throw it away. As she started into the street a heavy hand fell on her shoulder.

"One moment, *senorita*," Tonio said. "I believe you

have an appointment with my master. He sent me to bring you to him."

Chapter 28

Daniel and Juan hid in a narrow street between tall stone buildings. The air was thick with odors, a mélange of cooking, sewage from the open gutter running down the center of the street, and some strongly scented flowers growing heavens knew where in that maze of buildings. Small shops lined the roadway, while above them heavily grilled windows opened into apartments. Past the shutters, open to catch the evening's breezes, they could hear voices, people talking and laughing. Somewhere a baby cried.

Daniel rubbed the bruises on his wrists. He was having trouble catching his breath as the deprivations of the past week caught up to him. He hadn't been harmed or badly treated as yet, but the lack of fresh air, food, and freedom was debilitating. Daniel would drive himself as far as need be to escape, but right now, he took a moment to just breathe some clean air.

Leaning casually against a wall in the shadows, he and Juan waited. In the time it took to get Daniel out of prison the sun had disappeared below the mountains. Darkness fell over the city like a great black cape.

Morgan didn't appear.

"She should be here by now," Juan admitted.

"We shouldn't have left her."

"It was too dangerous for all of us together," Juan insisted. "What if someone had tried to stop us? What if there was fighting?"

"She would have been in worse danger. I know." Daniel paced forward to get a better view of the road.

Juan watched him thinking how little he knew his lady. If there was fighting, Morgan would have been in the middle of it.

He gave a low snort at the thought. And realized Daniel was staring at him.

"You know something," the captain stated.

Juan grimaced unhappily. "I'm afraid … Yes. Don Luis."

"Don Luis?" Daniel waited for an explanation.

Juan drew a deep resolute breath. "Don Luis took an interest in Mistress Moorhouse," he explained.

"He did, did he?" Daniel asked, his voice filled with menace. "And just who is this Don Luis, and what form did that interest take, pray tell me?"

"He, er, offered me money for her."

"Money? How much?"

"One hundred. Doubloons." Juan took a deep breath.

"Gold," he added

"And for this, he expected what?" Daniel's voice was soft, without inflection, and Juan cringed at the rage he could feel seething underneath.

"Well, you know. He *wanted* her."

"Yes? And?"

"I don't know. We planned to elude him -- to break you out of prison and get out of the city before Don Luis, er, took possession."

"And just what did you do with one hundred gold doubloons?"

"I only received one. A down payment." Juan plucked the shining coin from his sash, but Daniel made no move to take it.

"Truly nothing happened between them, captain," Juan hastened to assure him. "They spoke only one time. The Don thought Mistress Moorhouse was my sister. He saw her when she danced. In the cantina."

"She danced in a cantina?" Daniel repeated. He took a deep exasperated breath. "Apparently there is a lot more to this story, but we have no time to go into it now. Where is Morgan?"

"I told her you wouldn't be happy," Juan protested. "But she would have everything her way!"

Daniel glared.

Juan sighed. "I was to bring her to Don Luis at sunset. But I suspect he didn't trust me. Well, I *know* he didn't trust me. He probably sent some of his own people to bring her to him."

"So now we have to go and find her." Daniel started for

the mouth of the alley.

"No! Wait. Wait! You can't!" Juan protested taking his arm and trying to hold him back. "If they see you it will be over. For all of us. We'll all end up in prison." Reluctantly Daniel stopped. "I will go" Juan continued. "I know where he is."

"And what should I do while you are gone?"

"Get yourself outside the gate. I will bring Mistress Morehouse. We'll meet you outside."

Daniel pondered, and then shook his head. "No. We go together."

"Captain, please. We don't have much time. I can move around this city easier than you can. I will find Mistress Moorhouse. I promise."

"You say you know where she is?"

Juan swore silently. They were a fitting pair, he told himself. Two stubborn ... "Yes. Yes, I can find her, but we're wasting time. Look, I have to do this alone. Don Luis knows me. It won't seem strange if I come demanding my money. In fact, he would think it odd if I do not."

Daniel closed his eyes and nodded, giving in. "All right. Bring Morgan out safely," he whispered, clapping the quartermaster on the shoulder. "I'm depending on you. God speed."

"And to you, captain. Wait. Take my guitar. It will be safer with you. And if anyone notices, it will give you a reason to be out so late."

Daniel took the instrument and slung it over his back, settling the strap across his chest.

They parted at the street, one man heading for the huge

gates that guarded the city, the other back into the heart of town.

Juan slowly retraced his steps to the prison, keeping a watchful eye out for Morgan. There were few people about but none of them were her.

He went to *La Tecolote* first, and pausing in the kitchen doorway, asked the Indian maid if she'd seen his sister. The girl cast a look toward the noisy main room before she shook her head, no. Juan returned to the street knowing his worst fears had come true. When the great hulk of the cathedral was before him, he turned to the right, heading in the direction of the house with the blue gate.

Lights shone from between clinks in the shutters on the second floor, but the gate was securely fastened. Juan worked his way around to the back, looking for another entrance. He would wager anything Morgan was inside.

Morgan protested, but Tonio wouldn't listen. He fastened his hand on her arm and started for his master's house dragging her along with him. She thought of screaming, but remembered Juan's warnings not to call attention to herself. There had to be a way out of this. She had to think!

Don Luis sat at the head of the dining room table on the second floor of his *pied-à-terre*. The polished creamy plaster walls reflected light, small flames flickering in sconces and above gleaming silver candleholders. Places for two were set at the table, but the Don sat alone, his long fingers toying with the stem of a glass, moving it so light reflected through the deep red wine, casting ruby reflections on the white table cloth. He raised his head when he heard footsteps outside the door. A smile of satisfaction twitched the ends of his moustache. At last!

Tonio pushed Morgan into the room ahead of him. Don Luis looked at her for a second from under his lowered brows. "Leave us," he said to Tonio.

The man servant bowed and fled.

Don Luis came slowly to his feet and approached the girl.

"Why have you brought me here?" Morgan began, clutching the *rebozo* tightly around her head and shoulders like armor against his advances. She fought to keep her voice even as feelings of apprehension, frustration, and anger jarred inside her. "What do you want of me?"

"Your brother didn't tell you?" he asked, raising his hand toward her face. Her beautiful face. Her soft skin ...

Morgan flinched, and his hand stopped moving.

"Don't be afraid of me, little one," he said as soothingly as he would to gentle one of his precious horses. "I won't hurt you." He tugged the *rebozo* from her fists and lifted the material from her head, dropping it to the floor.

The candlelight caught in Morgan's red hair, the color brightening into flame. Her huge eyes were flecked with gold within a frame of dark silky lashes. She stared back at him, her chin at a defiant angle.

"You still haven't told me what you want," Morgan protested. "You can't keep me here against my will."

Luis chuckled. "But of course I can. I have bought you. You belong to me." His hands reached for her and she dodged back.

"I belong to no one," she spat.

"Perhaps we should discuss that," he said, dropping his hands to his sides. He would have to go carefully with this one. "Come. I mean you no harm. Look, dinner is waiting. Won't you join me?"

Morgan looked at the table, at two places set in candlelight. She started to shake her head, but suddenly a thought came to her. Maybe there was a way she could get herself out of this. But first she had to pretend. She drew a deep breath. "Yes, but please ..." She looked up at him, making her eyes as wide as possible, trying to seem innocent and bewildered. "Please give me some time to get use to this, to ..." She spread her hands wide and looked around at the splendor of the room. "This happened so fast. I need time to become accustomed."

"Take all the time you need," Don Luis offered generously. He bowed her to the table and carefully held the chair as she seated herself. He resumed his place beside her and rang a small silver bell set near his plate.

Two silent Indian slaves brought dishes to the table. They presented them, one by one. Don Luis nodded or shook his head to indicate which of them met with his approval. Soon the plate before Morgan was laden with steaming rice and peppers, and slices of pork, roasted and seasoned with apples and cloves. There were bowls of fruit, dishes of olives and a plate of cheese as well as crusty bread made from wheat flour.

Without a word the slaves disappeared, closing the door behind them. Don Luis poured wine into Morgan's glass and sat back looking at her. All the while dinner was being served she neither spoke nor moved. She just sat at the table, her hands in her lap, her brown eyes never leaving his face.

"Well," he prompted. "Don't you like your dinner?"

She gave a little smile and picked up her fork.

"You said you were going to explain my situation to me," she murmured.

"Your accent," he commented, sipping from his glass. "I'm curious to know who your parents are. Where were you raised?"

"*Senor*?" She feigned confusion.

"You're no peasant! Who was your father?"

Morgan dropped her eyes, not knowing what to say. Had he seen through her disguise or was this some invention of his own mind? Her thoughts raced. She had no idea what Daniel and Juan might be doing. She was terrified Daniel might come looking for her and be caught again. Escape might not be so easy a second time. She had to get away from Don Luis!

The Don leaned forward and started to place his hand on her arm when someone knocked on the door. He pulled back angrily. "What is it!" he yelled, his black brows drawn together in a thunderous scowl.

Tonio opened the door a crack and stuck his head inside. "Master. A man is here. He says he is ..." he jerked his head toward Morgan and silently mouthed the rest of the sentence, "this woman's brother."

"Ah." Luis looked at Morgan and then rose to his feet.

"I'll only be a moment, my dear. We'll finish this conversation when I return."

Juan was waiting downstairs in the portal surrounding the courtyard. He had his hat in his hands, the perfect picture of subservience.

"You've come for your money?" Don Luis asked as he appeared.

"Yes, your lordship. I was afraid you had forgotten."

"I don't know if I should pay you," Luis said. "Since it appears you weren't about to keep your end of the bargain."

"Sire! My sister isn't here?" Juan asked.

"Oh, she's here. But it was my man who brought her."

"I was so worried, your worship. I didn't think I convinced her. She's so stubborn. Maybe if I talk to her again?"

"That won't be necessary." Luis wanted nothing more than to be finished with this tiresome peasant. "Come with me. I'll give you your pieces of silver."

"But, sire," Juan protested. "You said golden doubloons!"

Luis smiled. "And so I did." Leading the way to his office he unlocked a strongbox and removed two leather sacks that clinked as he tossed them on the desk. "One hundred golden doubloons," he said. "Take them and be gone."

"May I just say good bye to Anna?" Juan asked.

"She's no longer any concern of yours," Don Luis told him. "Tonio! Show this visitor out."

"Thank you, Senor," Juan said bowing. His hand under his hat reached for his dagger. When Tonio came he bowed again and followed the servant toward the gate.

Morgan still sat at the table when Luis returned to the

dining room. Food had been moved about on her plate, but he couldn't see if she had eaten anything. He resumed his seat.

"Forgive me," he said softly. "It was business that wouldn't wait."

"Was it my brother?"

"It was."

"You bought me from him, didn't you? You paid him off?"

"Think of it as a kind of dowry," Don Luis told her.

"But my family would pay a dowry to you," she protested.

"Yes. But there are other settlements paid to the bride's family as well. But come, do not worry yourself about such things. You future is settled, and I'm sure you will be very happy."

"Will I really live here now?"

"Yes, you will."

"And can I have new clothes, nice ones like the ladies wear?"

Luis laughed. This was going to be easier than he imagined. "You will have anything you desire."

Morgan picked up her glass and sipped the wine, looking at him over the rim. Silence stretched, and Luis could feel the heat building inside of him. She was so beautiful and he desired her so much. The swelling in his breeches neared discomfort. Well, he would soon alleviate that! He picked up his glass and drank deeply.

"Jewels too," she asked, her eyes alight with something he mistook for avarice.

"Jewels you shall have," he promised. "Servants to wait on you, a carriage of your own and more gowns than you can ever wear."

Morgan laughed. "Why would I want so many gowns?"

"I don't know. Women seem to enjoy having clothes." He smiled back at her and wiped the sweat from his forehead.

"I guess that's true," she commented. She peered closely at him. "You look warm. Do you feel well?"

"I'm feeling ..."

Don Luis stared at Morgan, a very strange look on his face before he slowly put his head down on the table. She rose to her feet and examined him. Although his eyes were closed and his breath came with a deep snoring sound, she thought he seemed asleep rather than dying. That was just as well, for, while she was not flattered by his desire to possess her, she did not want to kill him. All she wanted to do now was to get out of Cartagena.

But first to escape from the house. Morgan drew a dagger from the sheath under her skirt, went to the door. She turned the handle and began to pull it open when she heard swift footsteps coming toward the room. She flattened herself against the wall, hoping whoever was coming would pass on by.

They didn't. As Morgan watched as the latch was pressed downward and the door slowly opened. She couldn't see who it was, but they gave a gasp of surprise when they saw Don Luis sprawled on the table. Morgan clutched the dagger in a sweaty palm, but then recognized the intruder.

"Juan?" she whispered. "What are you doing here?"

265

"I've come for you," the quartermaster replied. "What did you do to Don Luis?"

"I had some of the sleeping drug left."

Juan laughed softly. "Bravo, *senorita*!" he applauded. "Now let's make good our escape. The captain is waiting, and I'm afraid he's not very patient."

Chapter 29

No one appeared to be interested as Morgan and Juan made their way to the city gates. They kept to a swift walk that might seem natural for someone hurrying home after a long day in the city, but it was nerve-shattering nonetheless. Morgan couldn't help but feel that any minute they would hear sounds of pursuit or shouts to halt. She had to resist the urge to run. She hunched her shoulders, the *rebozo* tight around her head, her arms pressed closely to her sides as she tried to make herself invisible. Despite Morgan's fears, however, she and Juan passed out of the city without further incident. It was as if ill fortune had exhausted itself and had nothing left to do to them.

Daniel waited impatiently behind a thicket of palmetto bordering the road. Without pausing, Morgan went straight into his arms. He held her almost too tightly, his mouth devouring hers in a kiss filled with all of the longing and pain of their separation.

Juan politely turned his back and kept watch.

"I was afraid I'd never see you again," Morgan murmured, tears glistening on the ends of her long lashes.

Daniel brushed them away with gentle finger tips. "I can't believe you're here. I can't believe you came to find me," he whispered. He gazed down at the woman held in the curve of his arms, filled with awe and wonder that anyone would do this for him. His lips grazed her forehead and then eyelids before finding her mouth again.

Morgan didn't answer. She couldn't speak for all the emotions exploding insider her. She couldn't get enough of the feel of him in her arms, and clung to him, her body molded to his.

"Captain," Juan interrupted quietly. "We still have some distance to go before we're safe."

At his words the couple came reluctantly apart, although Daniel kept Morgan's hand in his.

"I want to thank you too, Juan," he said. "Coming after me was more than a man could expect. I owe you a debt I may not be able to repay."

Juan looked at Morgan, then back to the captain. He remembered the threatening, bullying girl who would probably have taken the ship and gone to Cartagena by herself if he hadn't agreed to help her. And he still thought it was a foolhardy adventure. "It had to be done," was all he managed to say, embarrassed by the captain's appreciation. "Let's finish it then."

"How far do we have to go?" Daniel asked.

"Three miles. Maybe a little more."

Daniel was showing strain in the shadows under his eyes and the gray pallor beneath his tan. Still, having his freedom had done much to raise his spirits and strengthen his will.

He looked down at Morgan who stood silently beside him, her hand clasped to his as if she would never let it go again.

"You're tired," he said with love and concern in his voice. "Can you walk that far?"

She answered with a chuckle. "I got here, didn't I? And," she looked up at him, her eyes a twinkle in the moonlight. "Now that I'm with you," her whisper trailed off against his lips. "I can do anything."

Daniel never let go of Morgan's hand as they walked to the cove. Her heart was light, even as her footsteps grew heavier. After the events of the past days, even Juan was soon flagging. They followed a narrow path through dark jungle for most of the journey. Roots and branches seemed determined to bar their way, making the going even more difficult. But they had to hurry.

The time was an hour after midnight. Nerves were wound tight when they finally saw a gleam of moonlight through an opening in the trees. Daniel shoved Morgan behind him when the underbrush rustled and armed men stepped onto the path ahead and behind them. The men held swords as well as muskets primed and ready.

"Hold off, you blind sons of ..." Juan began, stepping into their path.

This was just too much, Morgan decided. She swayed

and would have fallen if Daniel hadn't caught her. I will not faint, she told herself, firmly. After everything else that had happened, fainting would be stupid! She braced her knees and stood up straight. "I'm okay, she told him."

He smiled at her and released her hands.

"Captain?" a sailor said, peering at them.

"Yes," Daniel replied. "And I suggest you lower your weapons."

"Captain! We're glad you're alive," one of the men exclaimed. A ragged chorus of "Ayes," echoed his sentiments.

"I'm glad to be here, too. But I suggest we get on board and cast off. We don't know when they'll discover I've escaped."

"And that's not all," Juan murmured to himself thinking of Don Luis, the gold coins a delightful burden in his sash.

The band of sentinels escorted them the last steps back to the ship. There were unasked questions on everyone's lips, but the nearness of their enemy was wearing on nerves, and they were more than happy to finally be away.

The ship was hidden in a wide cove in a creek that emptied into the ocean. The humid night air blanketed them. Insects filled the air with sound. An alligator barked somewhere nearby while a night bird skimmed the surface near the trees, hunting for his dinner. Although the moon wouldn't be full for some days yet, still it shone brightly enough to outline the *Kestrel* in silver against the dark jungle. To Morgan she was a welcome sight as the longboat carried them across the water. It meant her terrifying adventures were over at last.

As they climbed onboard, the crew jumped to their

tasks, stowing the longboat and getting the ship ready to depart. Morgan followed Daniel onto the quarterdeck, but kept apart, content to lean against the rail and watch him reassume command.

Captain Harris stood beside the helmsman, legs braced against the ship's movement, his hands clasped behind his back. The crew scurried to do his bidding, some leaping into the rigging to drop a delicate spread of canvas while the others raised the anchor and stowed it away.

Black jungle pressed in on them as they began to move, branches sometimes scraping the ship's sides. The trees seemed to be trying to keep them there, but they soon fell away as the *Kestrel* carefully maneuvered into a wider channel leading to the sea. The ship moved more swiftly as open water beckoned. More sail was deployed and her speed increased. Soon the trim brigantine crested the waves, freedom ahead. Now all they had to do was avoid Spanish shipping. Fortunately it was a big ocean.

At a word from the captain all canvas spread to the wind and the *Kestrel*, stretched her wings like her namesake and flew.

Daniel swayed as the ship rode the waves, picking up speed. The wind was chill on his back and he imagined it blew away the stench of his captivity.

"Barney," he said to the watch.

"Aye, captain?"

"I'll be below. Call me immediately if we sight another ship."

"Aye, captain."

Daniel turned in the moonlight and held out his hand to

271

Morgan. She placed her fingers in his and went below.

A salt fresh breeze came in the open windows of the cabin, and Daniel couldn't get enough of it. He breathed it in, more than glad to be away from the stench of prisons. There was a brass canister of water and he poured some of it into a wash bowl. Taking out his good razor, he shaved off his beard. Even though he was very tired, Daniel dumped the dirty water and refilled the basin. Then he stripped and washed away the grime of his captivity. Morgan helped, scrubbing his back. Somehow her clothes came off and Daniel ended up washing her as well. Soap slick, their bodies came together, flesh warm on flesh, their arms locked around each other in the dark cabin. Daniel's lips trailed kisses across her face, neck and shoulders as Morgan clung to him, shivering with delight at the sensations racing through her body.

The towel dropped to the deck as they fell into the bunk, arms and legs intertwined. But tonight Daniel was subtly different, as if captivity made him realize each second with her might be his last. He demanded and plundered, making love with an intensity that surprised her. She could feel the strength in him, and she reveled in his masculinity. She responded, roused to new heights and when she finally reached the peak and plunged down from that dizzying place, her body shuddered and bucked against him as a scream rose from her throat. He took it into his mouth and let himself go, his own moan of pleasure escaping against her lips.

Still tangled together, they drifted into sleep. Their rest was as deep and fulfilling as their love making had been, rocked by the *Kestrel* in her swift flight across the sea.

Morning came and grew into noon unnoticed, but when the afternoon sun slanted through the open windows, Morgan came awake to find Daniel staring down at her. She smiled and stretched like a cat.

He bent to kiss her gently. "I've been thinking," he said.

"Ummm," Morgan purred back.

"We have things to talk about," he said softly.

"What sorts of things?" she asked.

"The future, for starters." He regarded her gravely. "I don't know where we'll live or what we'll do, but you did promise to become my wife."

"You said I would be a baroness."

"I did. And you can be a baroness if you want."

"Well, then, I suppose I'll marry you."

He grinned as he gathered her to him and kissed her deeply, and then just held her.

Time slipped by and finally Daniel recalled himself from whatever sweet dreams were passing through his mind. He released her and smiled. "I have a ship I've been neglecting. Do you see what a bad influence you've been?"

"I?"

"It's past noon and the captain's still abed. And he's in bed with a woman. 'Tis a monstrously bad influence." Daniel shook his head. "It leads to all kinds of carelessness among the crew. They'll begin to think their captain's too easy." His hand caressed her smooth skin, lingering on her breast, his thumb slowly circling the nipple until it came erect.

"So you have to go and assert your authority?" Morgan whispered as her eyelids drooped with pleasure. She could

273

feel the heat building at his touch.

"Aye, lass. I think it would be a good thing, don't you? If I assert my authority, that is." He shifted his body until it was over her as his mouth descended deliciously.

They made love again, in the sunlight, this time gently, peacefully. Daniel was suspended above her, holding her trapped within the barriers of his arms moving slowly, very slowly within her until she moaned aloud and reared up against him, her heart beating fast, her breath coming in gasps. His eyes closed and he collapsed, burying his face against her neck as he trembled and released.

They rested, the sun making hot patterns on Daniel's back, draining the last bit of tension from him.

"You said you were going on deck," Morgan reminded him. "You said your crew was getting lazy."

"They are," he agreed, not raising his face from her hair. "They are that."

"You're not moving very fast yourself," she commented.

"No, that's true. For some reason, I feel loath to move just now. It could be this wondrous couch." He kissed her neck. "Perhaps I'll sleep just a little."

"As you will, my love. But will you be so good as to let me up first?"

"What and loose this lovely pillow?" His hand caressed her breast. "Nay, lass. Ye must think me daft."

"Aye, daft," she returned, copying his lilt. "But if you don't let me up ..."

"You're a hard woman, Morgan Moorhouse," he complained rolling over on his side.

"I thought you just said I was a wondrous couch," she

pointed out. "How can I be soft and yet hard at the same time?"

"A shrew," he complained. "My love is a shrew." Daniel shook his head and climbed to his feet. He padded to a clothes chest and began to dress. Morgan followed him, the towel wrapped around her.

"One of the first things we'll do when we reach Port Royal is find you some women's clothes," Daniel commented as she appropriated another one of his shirts. "You're leaving me nothing to wear." He quickly slipped into a coarse cotton shirt and a seaman's loose trousers.

"You don't look naked to me," Morgan laughed. She belted her shift with a brightly patterned scarf. The water-stained skirt of her riding habit completed the outfit. "The thing I want most right now though, is food," she confessed.

"That won't be difficult." Daniel brushed his hair smooth and fastened it at the back of his neck with a narrow black ribbon. Although he was still a little pale, he felt himself again.

He led the way onto the deck and, after looking up at the broad expanse of sail against the blue sky, swung onto the stern. The watch greeted him and within seconds they were deep in conversation.

Juan came up from the forward hold, and Morgan went to speak to him.

"Good morrow, *senorita*," he greeted her.

"Good day, Juan. Is there anything left over in the galley? I'm awfully hungry. And I'll wager the captain would like to eat as well."

"I'll bring you something. There are biscuits and some

cold meat, I think. But I know the cook is planning a special dinner for tonight."

Morgan's eyes sparkled. "Thank you. I'll be with the captain."

"*Senorita*," he called, stopping her as she turned to go.

"Yes, Juan."

"It was well done," he said simply before he turned to the hatchway. "Crazy and insane," he added as he moved away. "But well done."

"I couldn't have done it without your help. I am in your debt," Morgan called after him.

"Yes, I know." He grinned and nodded, and went about his task.

Morgan smiled as she moved to where Daniel stood at the helm, holding the speeding ship on her course, a look of contentment on his face.

Yes, it was well done, she thought. Still, looking back at it now, she was amazed at what had passed. She would never have thought herself brave enough to do those things. But at the time it seemed the only thing she could do. She couldn't imagine a life without Daniel. Even if she died trying get him back, she would be better off than trying to live without him. She loved him with an intensity she could barely contain. No wonder she behaved so boldly!

As if sensing her thoughts, Daniel smiled over at her. She moved to stand beside him, the wind pushing against her like some living thing. This was where she wanted to be; this was where she belonged.

Chapter 30

"Spring weddings are said to be propitious," Morgan commented. She stood against the rail in the waist of the ship, Daniel beside her as they watched Port Royal grow in the distance.

"Our wedding couldn't be otherwise, no matter when it occurred. But I propose we wed as soon as it can be arranged. I don't want to wait too long to claim my bride."

"And then we'll go to Cayman Brac? To the plantation there?" Morgan asked.

"If you wish. Perhaps it would be best to see the plantation before we decide where to settle." Daniel grinned down at her. "But after that we'll go to the Carolinas. I want to show you the *Bright Folly*. Would you like to go sailing with me for a while?"

"I've always loved being on the sea."

Daniel kissed her. "As soon as we land I'll talk to the governor about our wedding. And we must see about getting you some clothes."

"But I can do that," Morgan argued. "I still have some of the money you gave me."

"I gave you money? When was this?"

"It was the money for the *Bright Folly*. Unless, of course, you want me to give it back?" She looked at him teasingly. "I mean, if you marry me, everything I own will be yours."

"Nay, lass. It's your money. I'm just surprised you still have it."

"Well, I don't have all of it. But here should be enough to buy a trousseau."

"Can you find what you need in Port Royal?"

"All I need to find is Hana -- my maid," she explained. "She'll know where I need to go."

"She's here, in Port Royal?"

"Somewhere. I just have to find her."

"This town isn't a place a lady can wander at will," Daniel warned her. "I think it would be best if Juan finds your Hana. He will know who to ask. You can wait on board the *Kestrel* where it's safe."

"But I want to go with him. I can help."

Daniel laughed. "I had a long talk with Juan yesterday. He's still too unsettled from your last adventure to feel comfortable going anywhere with you again this soon."

"I don't know why he would feel that way," Morgan complained, piqued that anyone would see humor in it.

"Perhaps you wouldn't. But we owe him a great deal.

We need to consider his feelings."

"Very well then," Morgan conceded. She subsided, watching the activity in the harbor as the *Kestrel* moved slowly to her berth.

It was early in the afternoon a number of small craft sailing toward the town. Daniel identified them as local fishermen returning after a long day on the water. There were three larger vessels in port. One was careened, her bottom being cleaned of an accumulation of barnacles and other ocean growth. Another was anchored further out in the water, two guards clearly visible on her deck, muskets in their hands. The third ship rode against the wharf, her name, the *Cumberland*, clearly visible across the stern. Morgan noted considerable activity on her decks.

"She's just arrived," Daniel commented. "Probably from England. That means mail and news."

"It seems strange that less than two months ago, I was in England, in the cold and fog," Morgan said.

"Did you dislike it so much?"

She shrugged. "I didn't have a chance to like anything. I was always in the company of my cousins."

"Not always," Daniel reminded her.

"No. But even that was unhappy."

"Perhaps we will go there again someday," Daniel said, his eyes on the ship as they passed her. "I could show you different parts of the country. There are places of incomparable beauty."

Although he spoke lightly as ever, Morgan knew him well enough to recognize a wistful note in his voice. "You mean your home in Wales?"

"That. And some other places."

"I would like to go there with you."

"Then we will do it. But not yet." Daniel stood up. "It's time for me to go to work. We've arrived.

Morgan remembered Hana said she was going to her old friend Maximillian DePaul. Juan knew him as an enterprising coastal trader, and conducted Morgan to his shop which was barely a three minute walk from the *Kestrel's* berth.

A tall black man stood behind a long counter, where bolts of cloth and other merchandise were arranged for sale.

"May I help you, mistress," he asked, his voice accented with an islander's melodious lilt.

"I'm looking for a woman called Hana. She said she was going to ..."

"Mistress Morgan?" Hearing a familiar voice, Hana stepped from the back of the store, and Morgan flew into her arms.

"Hana! Oh Hana! I found you. I'm so glad! Are you all right?" The words tumbled out.

"Of course, child!" Hana pulled back and held her erstwhile charge at arm's length. "Let me look at you." She frowned. "How come you're dressed like that? And what are you doing here? Where's your cousin?"

"Dead," Morgan said. "Oh, Hana, I have so much to tell you. And that's why I came. So you could tell me where to go to buy some clothes."

"Where's your own clothes?" Hana asked suspiciously.

"In England, I guess. Will you ..."

"And why didn't you bring them?" Hana interrupted.

"I couldn't. There was no time."

Hana glared.

"I ran away," Morgan confessed.

"Uh, huh." Hana looked at DePaul who was staring curiously at them, and then at Juan who was lounging in the doorway. "I remember you," she said to him. "You were on that pirate ship."

"Hana!" Morgan chided.

"*Si*! I am that very same pirate." Juan agreed readily and in perfectly good humor.

"So what are you doing here with Mistress Morgan?"

"Daniel sent him to help me find you," Morgan told her.

"To be sure she stays safe," Juan added.

"Huh," Hana grunted. "And who's gonna keep her safe from you," she asked fiercely.

"You have it all wrong," Juan complained. "What you should ask is who will keep me safe from Mistress Moorhouse!"

Hana looked at her old charge. "What have you been up to, child?" she asked.

"Adventures," Juan supplied, with a grin.

"Missus." DePaul interrupted what promised to be a protracted exchange. "Maybe you should take our guests roun' back and give them some refreshment while you talk. Customers be comin' here soon."

"Morgan," Hana responded. "This is my old friend,

Maximillian. He's my husband now."

"Oh, Hana, that's wonderful!" Morgan smiled with surprised delight and nodded to DePaul. "Thank you for helping Hana. I was so worried about her when my cousin sent her away."

"My pleasure, mistress," he replied. "Good thing, as it turned out. Only way I get to marry dis wonderful woman."

"You hush. You just married me for my money," Hana chided him, but she was smiling and obviously happy with her new life.

Hana stood back for Morgan and Juan to precede her into the back of the shop. Through a storeroom was a small apartment, and beyond that a walled terrace shaded by a trellis supporting a riot of tropical flowers.

Morgan sank down in a chair while Hana brought fruit juice. She had just taken a sip when everything started to tip and shake around her. For an uncomfortable second she thought she was going to be violently ill. Then she realized everyone else was having the same experience. Juan was holding onto one of the posts supporting the trellis, looking up at it with great concern. Hana was standing with her back against the stone wall of the building, her eyes closed, her lips moving without making any sound. In a second, though, it was all over.

"What was that," Morgan asked, still feeling a little sick.

"Earthquake," Hana told her. "We've been having a lot of them this past month. Big one last week knocked some houses down."

Juan shook his head. "This one did some damage too, if

I'm not mistaken." He pointed to where a dust cloud was filling the sky. There was the sound of running footsteps outside the wall and excited voices.

"Everyone all right back here?" DePaul stuck his head through the door.

"We're fine," Hana told him. "Better go back up front before someone decides to come and help themselves."

"Has there been much trouble with looting?" Juan asked.

"Some," she replied. "But you go on, child," she said to Morgan. "I want to hear everything that happened to you since you went to England."

Everyone settled themselves comfortably and Morgan told her tale.

"Captain Harris," the governor said by way of greeting as Daniel came into his office. "You certainly took you time getting here."

"I came as soon as we docked," Daniel replied, not certain what this greeting presaged.

His relationship with Governor Sikes was tenuous at best. The Governor was an unimaginative stickler for the letter of the law as it came to him from England, while Daniel preferred to live by his own laws. As a result he and the governor were often at loggerheads, even though Daniel now and then conducted business for him. All in all it was a very uneasy relationship.

"You left Bristol some seven weeks ago. Seven weeks is overly long for a voyage across the Atlantic, especially in this season," Sikes commented.

"I never said we came straight away," Daniel protested. "What is the purpose of this? And how do you know when the *Kestrel* left Bristol?"

"Perhaps you saw the *Cumberland* when you came into harbor?"

Daniel nodded.

"She carried a passenger who came all this way, in part, to see you."

"And what would he want with me?" Daniel asked, wishing Sikes would come to the point.

"He will tell you himself. I sent for him as soon as you arrived and he should be here ... Ah, here he is now."

Juan and Morgan returned to the ship followed by a young boy pushing a hand cart filled with packages. Morgan had been shopping, and Hana promised to visit her in the morning to help organize her purchases. Back at the shop a seamstress was already busy sewing new dresses and other garments.

Four soldiers in scarlet uniforms stood on the wharf beside the *Kestrel's* gangway. The sergeant stepped forward at they drew near.

"Mistress Moorhouse?" he asked.

"Yes," Morgan replied, looking at the men curiously.

"Sorry, mistress," the man apologized. He felt uncomfortable arresting a woman who was both so young and obviously well-bred. "I have orders to place you under arrest. You have to come with me."

"Why? I don't understand," she said.

"What's this all about?" Juan asked, stepping in front of Morgan.

"I have my orders," the sergeant insisted. "I'm to bring Mistress Moorhouse to the governor straight away."

"On what charge?" Morgan demanded.

"I don't rightly know if I can say, miss," the sergeant told her.

"But I haven't done anything," she insisted.

"That's for the courts to decide, mistress. Come along now."

"But ..."

The sergeant took Morgan by the arm.

"Here now, unhand her," Juan protested.

The other soldiers moved between him and their sergeant.

"No, Juan. Don't," Morgan said quickly. "This is a mistake. I'll be all right. Just go find Daniel and tell him what's happened."

With soldiers surrounding them, the sergeant led Morgan away.

"Tell the captain," Morgan called back to Juan.

She wasn't so much afraid as she was bemused by her arrest since she couldn't see any reason for it. She was certain there'd been some mistake. Daniel would soon set everything right again.

Daniel was in the governor's office when the soldiers brought Morgan into the room. She started to go to him when she recognized two of the other people with him.

"Oliver!" she gasped, her face going white.

"'Tis well you recognize me," he sneered. "Thought I was dead, didn't you, you murderous little ..." He pressed his lips together, controlling what would have become an angry tirade.

He looked the same as always except for a livid scar crossing his forehead and disappearing under his periwig.

"I'm glad you're not. Dead, that is," she stammered.

"Let's hope so," he replied. "You see," he said to Governor Sikes, who regarded her with a mixture of pity and revulsion. "With the proper care, perhaps she can be saved."

"Perhaps you are right," Sikes agreed slowly.

"Look here," Daniel began but the governor cut him off.

"You've seen the papers. I understand your objections, but there's nothing you or I can do about this."

"Do about what?" Morgan asked, looking from one to the other of them, her eyes wide with shock. "Why am I here? What's happening?" She started forward but the sergeant and one of the other soldiers held her back.

"We obviously can't put her in the common goal," the governor said, ignoring her. "But there's a small room in the basement where we can keep her until you are ready to embark."

"If it's a stout room with a lock and no windows, I think it would be best," Oliver said. "We can't be too careful. She's dangerous."

"Dangerous?" Morgan repeated. "What have I done?

286

Why am I dangerous?"

"You will be silent," Oliver snapped.

"I demand to know what I'm accused of," she continued. "You can't just detain me this way!"

"You're accused of murder and attempted murder," Daniel told her, in a quiet voice.

"Murder?" she gasped. "But I didn't kill anyone!"

"Does the name James Challoner mean anything to you?" Governor Sikes asked.

"James? Of course ..." Then she realized how convenient this would be for Oliver.

"We know you couldn't help yourself, poor child," Oliver said with false concern. "And when I tried to help you, to take you away where you would be safe and cared for, you attacked me. Don't you remember any of it?"

"Remember? Of course I remember!" Morgan exclaimed. "I remember that Giles killed James. I remember that when you tried to kill me, I hit you with the poker and escaped."

"There," Oliver said to the governor. "Do you see how the poor thing twists the truth in her tormented mind?"

"It would seem so," he answered, looking at her with undisguised pity.

"So young, so beautiful, and so very mad," Oliver continued softly. "Had we not found out when we did, who knows what other young men she might have lured to their deaths. You are very lucky," he told Daniel. "We were just in time to save you from a similar fate."

Morgan looked at Daniel who had been standing aside all this time. "Daniel?" she asked. "Won't you help me? You

287

know what they're saying isn't true!"

Daniel looked at her, his face without expression, and then slowly turned and walked out of the room.

Chapter 31

Morgan was thrust into a small storeroom in the basement. There was one window, a tiny slit with iron bars opening onto the ground and further blocked by a thick growth of bougainvillea. The floor and walls were mortar and stone, and the door a stout wooden structure, reinforced with huge nail heads. A big hand-wrought iron lock on the outside held the door securely closed.

Oliver followed the soldiers as they took her down the wide stone stairs. He smiled as they thrust her into this makeshift cell. One of the soldiers held the lamp, the only source of light in the dark basement. He and his companion stepped out of the way as Oliver swung the door almost closed.

"It didn't have to come to this," he said, blocking the opening. "You should have signed the papers when you had a chance."

Morgan glared at him, refusing to give him the satisfaction of a conversation. He had manipulated everything, and he had ruined her life. But the greatest hurt had come not from his machinations, but from Daniel's defection. How could Daniel have believed these terrible things about her? How could he!

Tears welled up, threatening to spill, but she forced them back. She wouldn't cry. Not in front of Oliver!

"Stubborn yet? We'll see about that. You'll be glad enough to do whatever I want before we're through with you, my girl."

"I'm not 'your girl'," Morgan spat, choosing to give vent to anger instead of tears.

Suddenly, as if a giant hand struck her she was flung to the floor. She tried to steady herself as the room shook and rocked around her. Somewhere in the building a woman screamed, and there were the sounds of running feet. Oliver clung to the door frame with one hand and the door with the other, his face white beneath his wig. Somewhere above them came the sound of a great crash, loud shouting and more screams.

"Find out what's happening," Oliver yelled to the soldiers.

They needed no more invitation than this. The soldiers turned and raced pell-mell up the stone stairs to the relative safety of the ground floor.

The shaking ceased as abruptly as it started.

Morgan rolled over managed to get into a sitting position. She began to get to her feet when there was a scurrying sound outside and a dull thud.

"Morgan?" a voice called.

"Daniel?" she cried. "Daniel!"

His strong hands pulled her to her feet and clasped her to him. "Are you all right?" he asked anxiously. "They didn't hurt you, did they?"

"No. I'm fine. But please get me out of here."

"With pleasure, my love."

Daniel led her around Oliver's recumbent form and up the steps. He paused at the top and peered around the wall. A fire burned somewhere in back of the building, and everyone's attention was focused there.

"This way," Juan called from the front hall.

They went swiftly out into the courtyard in front of the governor's house. Panicked people were running back and forth apparently at random, and no one paid them any attention. As they approached the front gate, aloud shout from the house called the guard away from his post. Thus they were able to walk outside without being questioned.

Beyond the wrought iron gates, Daniel led Morgan and Juan into the maze of cobblestone streets. It was downhill to the wharf, and although the temptation to run was strong, Daniel kept them to a more decorous pace.

"We'll move the *Kestrel* out immediately. Did you finish provisioning her?" Daniel asked Juan.

"No, there wasn't time. But the magazine has been replenished."

"Power and ball?"

"Plus a goodly weight of shot for the muskets. If we get into a fight we'll be able to hold our own, if nothing else."

Juan looked satisfied at this.

"We can put into one of the Cays for water." Daniel commented. He looked down at Morgan. "Did you think I'd abandoned you?" he asked.

"Of course not," she began, but then caught the look in his eye. "Well, it was cruel of you to leave me like that in the governor's office. I didn't know what to think!"

"Aye. But do you understand it was the only thing I could do? Governor Sikes knows me too well. If he thought I even imagined rescuing you, I would have been kept in irons until after the *Cumberland* sailed." Daniel grinned. "We seem to spend a lot of time rescuing each other."

"I don't think we should make a habit of it," Morgan warned. "And I do wish you could have found some way to reassure me."

Daniel swung her around into his arms and, regardless of curious stares, kissed her hard and thoroughly.

Juan busied himself contemplating the roofline on the opposite side of the street.

"Never doubt my love for you," Daniel whispered fiercely. "That is the one and only constant in this world."

Morgan gazed up at him with damp eyes. "Daniel," she began, but whatever she was about to say was interrupted by the sound of many running feet.

"There!" a voice shouted from the top of the street. "There they are!"

As one Daniel, Morgan and Juan turned and ran toward the harbor. They could hold off an army from the decks of the *Kestrel*, but here on the street with only Daniel's sword and Juan's dagger they would soon be lost.

Fortunately the steepness of the street allowed them to see the ship long before they reached her. While they watched, a troop of red coats came from between two warehouses and took up positions at the gangplank.

Escape on the *Kestrel* was no longer an option.

Daniel pulled Morgan into an alley and Juan followed, hoping it wasn't a dead end. There was a wall with a gate that swung open at Daniel's touch. Juan recognized the backyard of the Devil's Trident. Daniel quickly closed and latched the gate behind them.

The sun lowered itself into the western sea and shadows lengthened. Daniel took them into the darkness cast by a stone staircase. There was a small opening, a storage place under the steps. They crouched there and listened as their pursuer's footsteps came down the alley.

"Here," someone called, having discovered the gate.

"It's locked, you looby," another voice chided. "I say they went down the alley."

The footsteps went on and Juan let go his breath in a long grateful, sigh. But it was still too soon to celebrate. "Now what do we do?" he asked.

"Hana," Morgan said.

She could feel their eyes as both of the men looked toward her in the darkness.

"She'll hide us. I know she will," she explained.

"Hiding us is one thing," Daniel told her. "We need some way to get off the island. The climate here will be unhealthy for both of us until your cousin is gone and the governor has a chance to forget I had a hand in rescuing you."

"I agree," Morgan said. "But a place to hide is the first

of our problems. We can worry about transportation later."

Although Hana lived with her husband in a small apartment behind their shop, DePaul's three sons lived with their wives in a larger house outside of town. The fugitives were taken there in a cart, filled with baskets of fruit. Port Royal was still trying to recover from the latest series of earthquakes, and since there was a lot of traffic to and from the town, no one questioned the cart.

"We need a plan," Daniel said, pacing the veranda of DePaul's house. He went to stand, his hand on one of the pillars, looking out through the darkness toward the brightly lit town. A couple of small fires still burned in the poorer sections, but even they were being brought under control.

It was a singularly hot June, but a breeze blowing in from the sea brought them relief from the day's heat. Morgan sat beside Hana, and Juan perched on the railing, a tankard of rum and fruit punch in his hand.

"You need information first," DePaul pointed out.

Daniel turned back to him. "I need my ship." He didn't like losing control of the *Kestrel* even for a short time.

"It may be some time before it's returned to you. Where is your crew?" DePaul asked.

"On shore leave, most of them. I only keep a skeleton crew. I hire other seamen as I need them."

DePaul understood what this meant. He was familiar with the practices of the buccaneers who made Port Royal their home. But DePaul also knew that there was no way the *Kestrel* could sail less than ten and, even better, twenty able bodied seamen. It would take that many just to get her huge sails aloft.

"You'll need something smaller, then, to get away," he said in his lilting voice. "Tomorrow, before light, my little sloop, the *Sabina*, is leaving for the other side of the bay. I have another son who lives on the big island. He will give you shelter for as long as you need it."

Despite Daniel's reluctance to leave the *Kestrel*, he had to admit this presented the best option. But once Morgan was safely with DePaul's son in the foothills, he intended to come back for his ship. In the meantime, Juan could gather a crew so they'd be ready to sail immediately.

Everyone's sleep was fitful that night. There was something in the air, a tension or foreboding. Hana said her prayers, secretly invoking her gods and the saints, and asking them to protect her family and friends. She could never decide whether or not they heard her, for early the next morning the city of Port Royal was gripped by another earthquake, this one much larger than the last.

Morgan, sleeping in Daniel's arms, awakened when the bed collapsed and the two of them suddenly ended up on the floor in a tangle of bedclothes.

Daniel held her until the tremor was over, and then helped her to her feet.

"Quickly. Get dressed," he told her as he pulled on his breeches.

Sounds of terror rose from the city reaching them clearly. The sky was lit by fires that now blazed out of control. They could see a fire at the wharf, and Daniel was desperate to get there. He feared for the safety of the *Kestrel* with her magazine newly full of powder.

The rest of the household was awake, DePaul shouting

instructions over the babble of his family. Soon everyone knew what they were supposed to do and scattered. Morgan and Hana were loaded into the cart along with some baggage. Another cart held DePaul's daughters-in-law and grandchildren. The men on foot accompanied them as they started to the waterfront. DePaul had decided that, until the tremors stopped for good, the women and children would be safer on the main island across the bay. He and his sons, however, would remain behind to look after the shop and the houses, keeping them safe from fire and looters.

Juan accompanied Daniel who went on ahead, anxious to see to the safety of the *Kestrel*.

The ship that caught fire, however, was the *Cumberland*. Her crew had been rousted from their beds and now formed a bucket brigade under the direction of the captain. He, in turn, was harried by Oliver who was appalled at the threat to his transportation back to England. To him, the thought of being marooned in the Indies was horrifying.

Unfortunately the *Cumberland* blazed too fiercely to be stopped, and the sailors were forced farther and farther back. Oliver glared with dismay and anger at the ruin of his plans. There had to be another ship, Oliver thought! His eye fell upon the *Kestrel* as she rose and fell, secure at her moorings.

People were leaving Port Royal. Some went on foot up the spit to the mainland, but most came to the dock, looking for anything that would float. Even as they fled, however, another earthquake struck, and the end of the world couldn't have been more devastating. Panic peaked as people ran screaming in every direction.

On the dock, Oliver saw several people looking to the

Kestrel. She was big enough to carry hundreds of people. But he didn't care. He wasn't about to let anyone threaten what he decided was his only hope of ever reaching England again.

"Sergeant!" he called, and the red coated figure obediently trotted over. "Send you men and the crew from the *Cumberland* to that ship there. She's a valuable piece of property." He nodded toward the crowds that were building on the dock. "I foresee some danger from these mobs."

"Aye," the sergeant agreed. He was off, calling orders, his voice raised against the growing din. His men and the crew streamed onto the *Kestrel's* neat decks. The troopers took up stations, their muskets held at ready, to threaten anyone who sought to cross the gangway without invitation.

Oliver braced himself as a third tremor hit. Behind him a building burst into flames. The sea was rising, waves responding to the earthquakes and growing ever higher until they began to lap at the boards at the top of the wharf.

Dawn came and the sun rose, lighting a scene of complete chaos. Daniel and Juan fought their way through panic-stricken mobs, toward the far end of a small pier where De-Paul's sloop was being defended by yet another of his sons. With swift precision, the women and baggage were loaded on board. Morgan stood by the road, her feet and ankles awash in sea water, holding tight to a piling against the heaving of the ground in the fifth earthquake. She refused to board the sloop until Daniel was there. When she saw him running down the quay, her heart grew lighter.

"Daniel!" she yelled and waved to draw him to her.

Oliver heard her voice. He recognized the slender wom-

297

an and then spotted the captain racing toward her. Then the sky opened up and the rain began to fall, deluging the city.

"Sergeant!" he screamed pointing. "There! There they are!"

His voice was lost in the massed sound of rain and screams as people set up their cries at this new disaster. Unable to stand the repeated shocks, the buildings along the waterfront began to fall, bricks and huge beams crashing down. The sea rose even higher and Oliver suddenly realized his own danger. He knocked people out of his way as he ran to the ship.

"Get her under way," he yelled to the captain, late of the *Cumberland.*

"Sir," the man protested. "We have no authority to take this ship."

But Oliver was beyond caring for anything except his own safety. "I'm giving you authority. If you don't, we'll all be killed! Set sail, man! Sail!"

He could see the small sloop carrying his cousin and her pirate lover raising sail. He watched as it left the small pier at the end of the quay, anger building inside of him until he felt his head would explode. Standing on her deck, was Daniel Harris, his arm around Morgan.

Something grew in Oliver's breast, burning him like a fire. He could feel his heart beating wildly as he glared at the little sloop. Then he remembered where he stood and that he had all of the resources of a well armed brigantine at his command.

Oliver whirled and went to find the captain. Morgan wouldn't escape him this time!

Chapter 32

The torrential rain thinned, dwindled to a weak drizzle and finally quit altogether. The sky disappeared behind thick gray clouds reflecting firelight from the burning buildings in Port Royal.

The sloop wasn't alone as it fled the doomed town. The harbor and waters beyond were thick with small craft. Onboard Hana had settled her grandchildren in the small cabin, and was trying to calm one of her daughters-in-law who was having hysterics. Daniel helped set the mainsail and when this was finished came to join Morgan at the rail.

"We'd be better off on board the *Kestrel*," she commented.

"Aye, that we would," he agreed. "But taking her from the troopers was beyond us without more men."

Morgan sighed. "I know."

"No one wants to be on her more than I do," Daniel told her. "But we'll have her again soon."

Morgan looked at the proud ship, her spars outlined against the burning town. Were her eyes betraying her, or had the vessel moved? It looked as if there were men in the rigging.

"Daniel ..." she pointed.

He clutched the railing as he leaned out and stared. "Hell and blast!" he cursed softly.

"She's moving, isn't she?"

"Aye."

"But how? Who's on her?"

"I don't know -- unless it's the troopers?" Daniel shook his head. "They must be moving her because of the fires."

"But she ..." Morgan began. Then her words were cut off by a gasp of sheer terror.

While Morgan and Daniel watched from the deck of the sloop, another series of violent earthquakes hit Port Royal. From their vantage point on the water, they could see the land actually ripple, rising and falling as if it was shaken by giant hands. To their horror, the quay and all the buildings along the ocean front lifted one last time and then slowly began to slide into the sea.

Dust and smoke rose from the wreckage, and the sea came to meet it, rising in enormous waves. Daniel looked and saw the *Kestrel* moving slowly, but still ahead of disaster. As he watched more canvas dropped and the brigantine began to gain speed. From all the evidence whoever was on board had some knowledge of sailing, and that was a relief. Watching his ship under someone else's command was a vastly uncomfortable experience. The sooner he was back on her quarterdeck, the happier he would be.

"Captin! Captin!" came a call from Dicken, DePaul's middle son who was piloting the sloop.

Daniel turned to see the man pointing to the east.

"Daniel!" Morgan cried, clutching his arm. Her face was suddenly as white as the material of her shift.

Coming in from the east under a full load of canvas was a Spanish ship of the line, the flags of Leon and Castile flying from her top mast and all of her guns showing from the gun ports. Gilt and scarlet paint trimmed the carving that decorated her decks and stern. Keeled over in the wind, with foam streaming along her hull, the ship was a sight to behold, one designed to strike terror into the heart of her enemy.

"No," Daniel breathed.

"Daniel? What? What is it?"

"The *Santa Clara*," he said. "I told you about her."

"The ship that's been hunting you?"

He nodded.

Morgan shivered in fear. "When they found out you escaped from Cartagena ..."

"They sent her to bring me back. Or better yet, to kill me," Daniel finished. "Her captain has been trying for years. This time he's determined enough to come right into the harbor."

"The *Kestrel*," Morgan told him. "They think you're on board!"

Daniel didn't answer right away. He put his arm around her, holding on for his own sake as much as hers. His eyes never left the enormous ship.

The *Santa Clara* neither paused nor turned aside for any of the smaller craft, and they were in some haste to get out of her way. As an arrow she flew, straight to the *Kestrel*.

"Likely you were right, lass, "Daniel breathed, watching the spectacle and helpless to intervene.

The *Kestrel* sailed out of the harbor, coming after the sloop, seemingly unaware of the Spaniard that had her in its sights. Morgan kept looking from one to the other when she thought she saw a familiar figure on the deck of Daniel's ship.

"Daniel," she pointed. "Is that Oliver?"

Daniel looked, his eyes somewhat keener than hers. "Aye. It could be him all right. And it seems he's using my ship to come after you."

Dicken was steering the sloop ever westward. The *Kestrel* veered as well when a shot from the Spanish ship went across her bows. This was the traditional order to stand and surrender. Or fight. There was a commotion on the decks of the *Kestrel* and several of the guns were loaded and run out.

The *Santa Clara* turned southeast, preparing to pass the *Kestrel* broadside.

Daniel drew his breath in with a gasp. "No!" he exclaimed. "She can never stand a direct hit from those guns. Turn her away! Turn her and run!" he urged the substitute captain.

But the *Kestrel's* commander had little skill in naval warfare. Although he realized something was wrong and tried to maneuver out of danger, he was too slow in responding. Flame and smoke belched from the side of the Spanish ship, and the *Kestrel* was engulfed. Seconds later the thundering sound of the guns reached the sloop.

Daniel didn't want to watch, but he couldn't turn away. It was his ship, his *Kestrel*, and she was dying before his eyes while he stood helpless.

They had to have hit the magazine, he realized later, for the deck of the *Kestrel* suddenly went up in a great roar and a flash of light. When the smoke cleared there was nothing left but a blazing hulk and pieces of wood falling to the surface of the water where they burned. There was nothing left of the *Kestrel* or of the men who sailed aboard her.

Daniel stood deathly still, his hand gripping the rail of the sloop, his knuckles white. He couldn't turn away from the place where his ship had once been.

Morgan stood very close to him, neither touching him nor speaking. What could she say that would ease the hurt he had just suffered? All she could do was offer the silent comfort of her presence.

The great Spanish ship ignored all of the smaller craft filling the water around her. Her task finished, she turned in a graceful arc and sailed away toward the south.

Morgan watched her go, a killer ship seeming to come out of nowhere, wreak havoc, and then disappear again. It was the stuff from which legends were made.

A ray from the sun broke through the clouds, touching the sloop with light. They were well away from Port Royal by now, and Dicken turned her to the north. Here it was brighter, the sun shining in a blue sky as if nothing as horrible as earthquakes ever happened.

Morgan looked up at her love and saw that he was looking down at her.

"Daniel, I'm so sorry," she began.

But he shook his head. "It's time for a new beginning," he told her. "The *Kestrel* was part of my old life. Now I can put that behind me."

"But, Daniel, you loved that ship."

"That I did, lass, but now I have something better. Now I have you. And, it seems, I have a plantation. I wonder how I'll like the life of a planter."

"As well as my father did, I'll warrant," she told him with a smile.

His arm went around her, holding her close. "Aye. I know I'll like it that well," he agreed.

"And there will be another ship," she ventured.

"There already is," Daniel responded. "She's called the *Bright Folly*."

"So everything will be all right?"

"We will make it so." Daniel's arms tightened around her and brought her hard against him. "Apparently we're the kind of people who make their own destiny."

"Well, that's a good thing," she began, but her words were stopped by Daniel's kiss.

The End

If you liked this novel, tell your friends.
For more good books, check out these other titles
by JM Bolton

THE CITY OF THREE MOONS – *stranded on a living planet, Mac & Riley have to learn to work together and communicate with this alien mind before all human life is obliterated.* - Science Fiction

THE ALIEN WITHIN – *lost & exiled, Winter and Shaw need to find the answers about their past so they might have a chance to survive long enough to have a future.*
- Science Fiction

HEIRS TO THE EMPIRE – *what do a vampire, a beautiful assassin, and an emperor have in common? Alliances are formed and then betrayed as each of the characters in this drama try to fulfill their own agenda.* - Science Fiction

TANGLED TALES – *Here be dragons, vampires, demons, and samurai warriors in tales likely and unlikely. This collection of short stories will take you on journeys to places as near as next door and s far away as outer space. And in this collection, everyone's a storyteller, even the dog.*
- Short Stories

All these titles are available in both eBooks and TreeBooks from Amazon.com as well as some other online booksellers

IDBPI BOOK

About the Author

As well as novels, award winning author, Johanna M Bolton has also written textbooks including the GED books for Barron's Educational Series, fanzines, and features for newspapers. A musician, she collects and arranges music for the fiddle and the bowed psaltery. At different times Bolton has studied fine art, music, biology, history, tai chi, karate; and has taught classes in pre-school, high school, & college. All of this, she says, is because her father once told her not to tell him what she was going to do, but to show him what she had done. She now lives in the woods in Florida with a couple of spoiled Australian Cattle Dogs. According to Bolton, "Everything in my life is subject to change at any time and without notice."

Reviewers say about the Lady and the Pirate …

"If you are looking for fun, for romance, for an historical setting, for suspense and a female protagonist...then read Lady and the Pirate. Once it gets going the suspense makes you stay with it … 'til late in the night! The author's knowledge of things like the dress and settings of the year 1690 are very impressive. I suggest you try this very well written romance."

For more books, articles, and news,
visit https://johannambolton.com

If you liked this novel, tell your friends.
For more good books, check out these other titles
by JM Bolton

THE CITY OF THREE MOONS – *stranded on a living planet, Mac & Riley have to learn to work together and communicate with this alien mind before all human life is obliterated.* - Science Fiction

THE ALIEN WITHIN – *lost & exiled, Winter and Shaw need to find the answers about their past so they might have a chance to survive long enough to have a future.*
- Science Fiction

HEIRS TO THE EMPIRE – *what do a vampire, a beautiful assassin, and an emperor have in common? Alliances are formed and then betrayed as each of the characters in this drama try to fulfill their own agenda.* - Science Fiction

TANGLED TALES – *Here be dragons, vampires, demons, and samurai warriors in tales likely and unlikely. This collection of short stories will take you on journeys to places as near as next door and s far away as outer space. And in this collection, everyone's a storyteller, even the dog.*
- Short Stories

All these titles are available in both eBooks and TreeBooks from Amazon.com as well as some other online booksellers

IDBPI BOOK